MARVEL-VERSE
MARY JANE

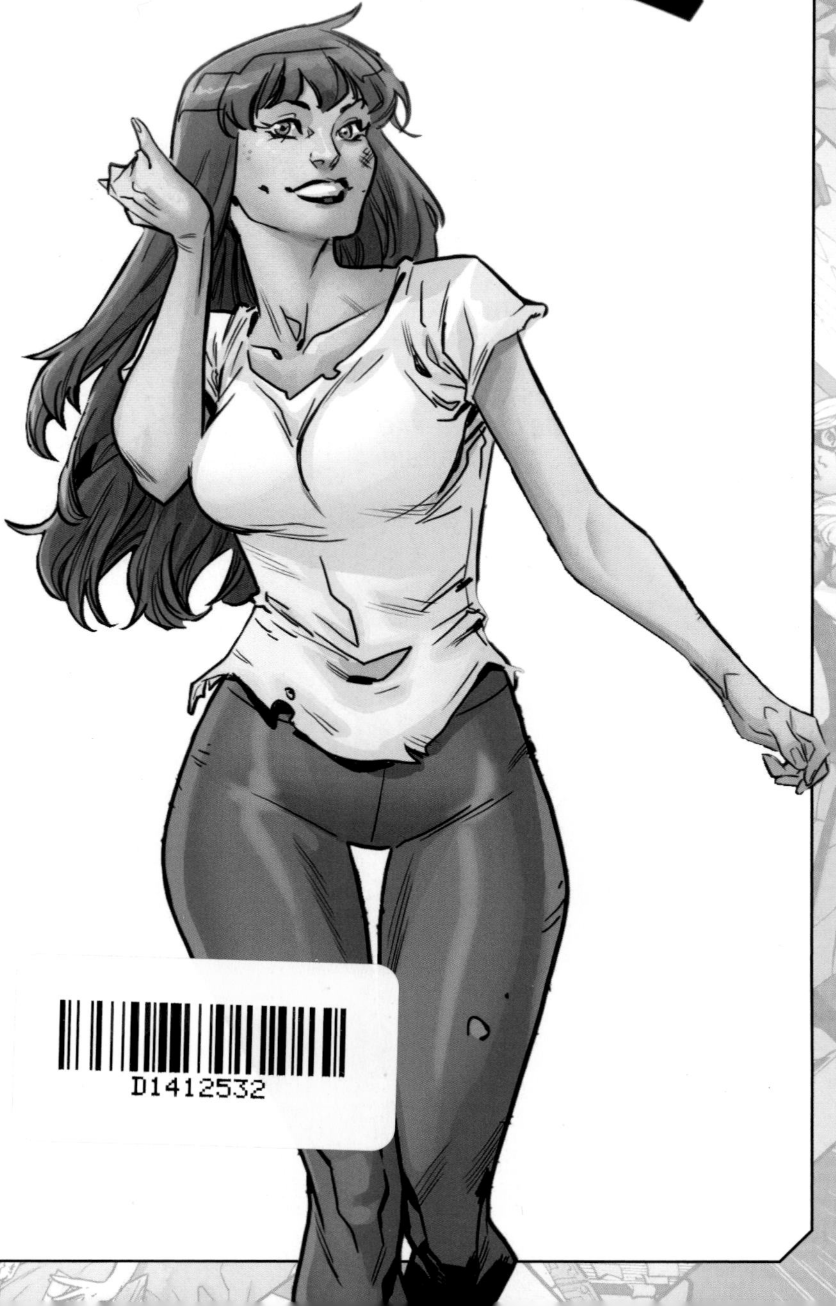

MARVEL-VERSE
MARY JANE

MARY JANE #1

WRITER: **SEAN KELLEY McKEEVER**

PENCILER: **TAKESHI MIYAZAWA**

INKER: **NORMAN LEE**

COLOR ARTIST: **CHRISTINA STRAIN**

LETTERER: **VC's RANDY GENTILE**

COVER ART: **TAKESHI MIYAZAWA** & **CHRISTINA STRAIN**

EDITOR: **MACKENZIE CADENHEAD**

CONSULTING EDITOR: **C.B. CEBULSKI**

SPIDER-MAN LOVES MARY JANE #1

WRITER: **SEAN KELLEY McKEEVER**

ARTIST: **TAKESHI MIYAZAWA**

COLOR ARTIST: **CHRISTINA STRAIN**

LETTERER: **DAVE SHARPE**

COVER ART: **TAKESHI MIYAZAWA, NORMAN LEE** & **CHRISTINA STRAIN**

ASSISTANT EDITOR: **NATHAN COSBY**

EDITOR: **MACKENZIE CADENHEAD**

SPECIAL THANKS TO DAVID GABRIEL

MARVEL-VERSE: MARY JANE. Contains material originally published in magazine form as MARY JANE (2004) #1, SPIDER-MAN LOVES MARY JANE (2005) #1, UNTOLD TALES OF SPIDER-MAN (1995) #16, THE MANY LOVES OF THE AMAZING SPIDER-MAN (2010) #1 and AMAZING MARY JANE (2019) #5. First printing 2023. ISBN 978-1-302-95465-9. Published by MARVEL WORLDWIDE, INC., a subsidiary of MARVEL ENTERTAINMENT, LLC. OFFICE OF PUBLICATION: 1290 Avenue of the Americas, New York, NY 10104. © 2023 MARVEL No similarity between any of the names, characters, persons, and/or institutions in this book with those of any living or dead person or institution is intended, and any such similarity which may exist is purely coincidental. **Printed in Canada.** KEVIN FEIGE, Chief Creative Officer; DAN BUCKLEY, President, Marvel Entertainment; DAVID BOGART, Associate Publisher & SVP of Talent Affairs; TOM BREVOORT, VP, Executive Editor; NICK LOWE, Executive Editor, VP of Content, Digital Publishing; DAVID GABRIEL, VP of Print & Digital Publishing; SVEN LARSEN, VP of Licensed Publishing; MARK ANNUNZIATO, VP of Planning & Forecasting; JEFF YOUNGQUIST, VP of Production & Special Projects; ALEX MORALES, Director of Publishing Operations; DAN EDINGTON, Director of Editorial Operations; RICKEY PURDIN, Director of Talent Relations; JENNIFER GRÜNWALD, Director of Production & Special Projects; SUSAN CRESPI, Production Manager; STAN LEE, Chairman Emeritus. For information regarding advertising in Marvel Comics or on Marvel. com, please contact Vit DeBellis, Custom Solutions & Integrated Advertising Manager, at vdebellis@marvel.com. For Marvel subscription inquiries, please call 888-511-5480. **Manufactured between 12/8/2023 and 1/16/2024 by SOLISCO PRINTERS, SCOTT, QC, CANADA.**

10 9 8 7 6 5 4 3 2 1

UNTOLD TALES OF SPIDER-MAN #16

WRITER: **KURT BUSIEK**

PENCILER: **PAT OLLIFFE**

INKER: **DICK GIORDANO**

COLOR ARTIST: **STEVE MATTSSON**

LETTERERS: **RICHARD STARKINGS** & **COMICRAFT**

COVER ART: **PAT OLLIFFE** & **GEORGE PÉREZ**

ASSISTANT EDITOR: **GLENN GREENBERG**

EDITOR: **TOM BREVOORT**

THE MANY LOVES OF THE AMAZING SPIDER-MAN

WRITER: **ROGER STERN**

PENCILER: **RON FRENZ**

INKER: **VICTOR OLAZABA**

COLOR ARTIST: **ANDREW DALHOUSE**

LETTERER: **DAVE SHARPE**

COVER ART: **JASON LEVESQUE**

EDITORS: **TOM BRENNAN** & **JODY LeHEUP**

SUPERVISING EDITOR: **STEPHEN WACKER**

AMAZING MARY JANE #5

WRITER: **LEAH WILLIAMS**

ARTIST: **CARLOS GÓMEZ**

COLOR ARTIST: **CARLOS LOPEZ**

LETTERER: **VC's JOE CARAMAGNA**

COVER ART: **HUMBERTO RAMOS** & **EDGAR DELGADO**

EDITOR: **KATHLEEN WISNESKI**

EXECUTIVE EDITOR: **NICK LOWE**

COLLECTION EDITOR: **DANIEL KIRCHHOFFER** ASSOCIATE MANAGER, TALENT RELATIONS: **LISA MONTALBANO**

DIRECTOR, PRODUCTION & SPECIAL PROJECTS: **JENNIFER GRÜNWALD** VP PRODUCTION & SPECIAL PROJECTS: **JEFF YOUNGQUIST**

RESEARCH: **JESS HARROLD** PRODUCTION: **DEB WEINSTEIN** BOOK DESIGNER: **YOUSSIF BAYOR**

MANAGER & SENIOR DESIGNER: **ADAM DEL RE** LEAD DESIGNER: **JAY BOWEN**

SVP PRINT, SALES & MARKETING: **DAVID GABRIEL** EDITOR IN CHIEF: **C.B. CEBULSKI**

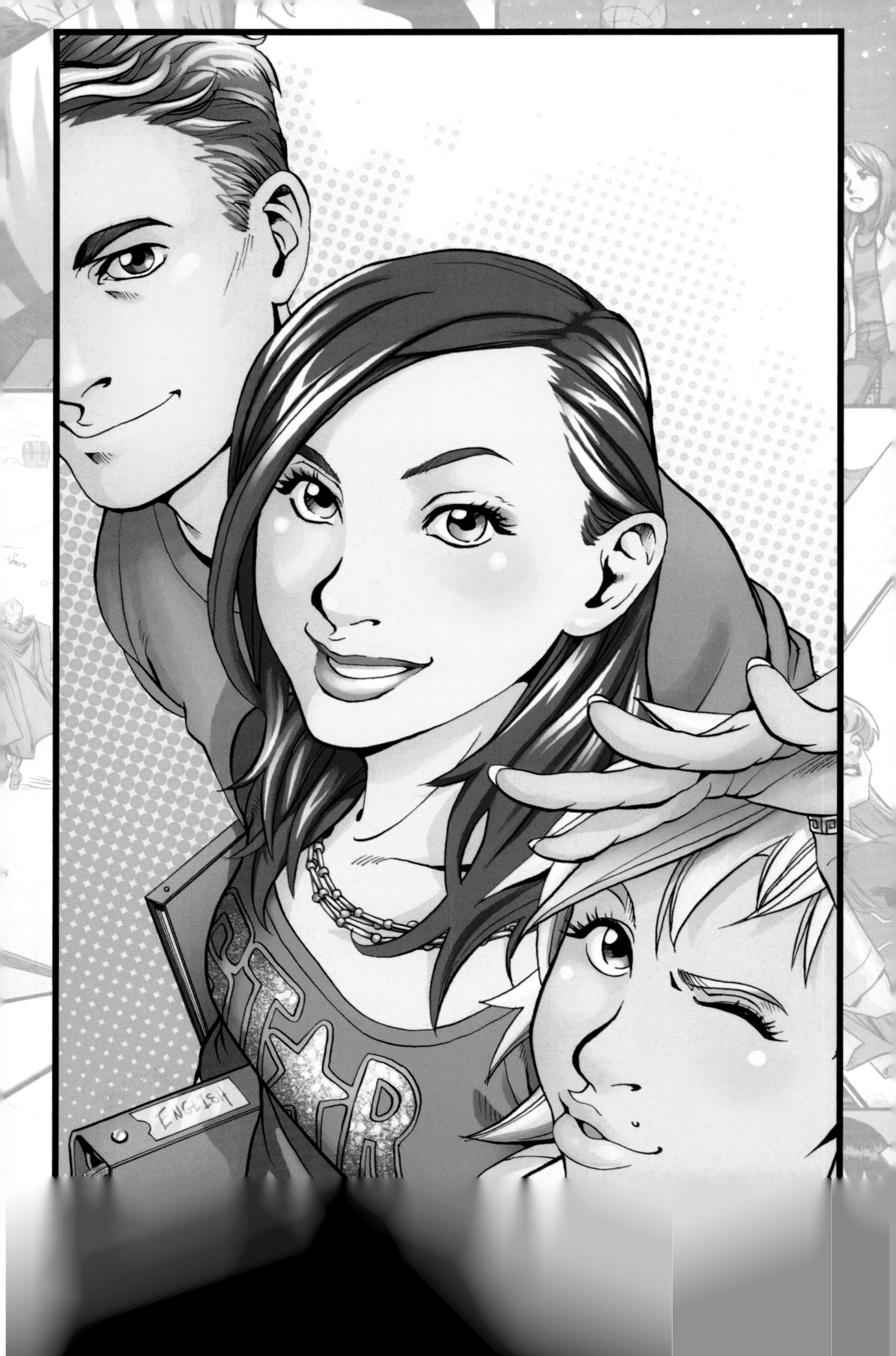
ENGLISH

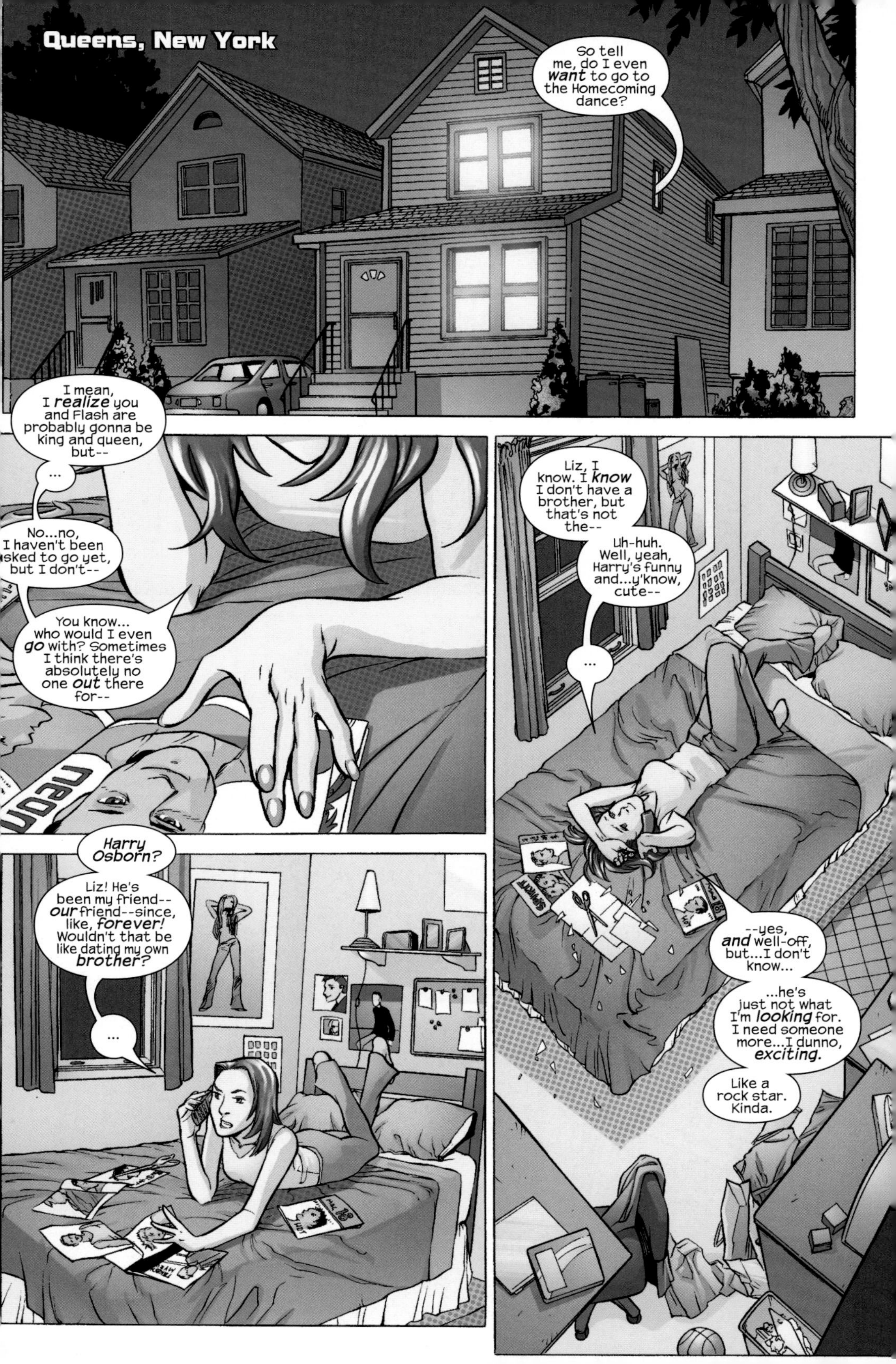

Queens, New York
So tell me, do I even *want* to go to the Homecoming dance?
I mean, I *realize* you and Flash are probably gonna be king and queen, but--
...
No...no, I haven't been sked to go yet, but I don't--
You know... who would I even *go* with? Sometimes I think there's absolutely no one *out* there for--
neon
Harry Osborn?
Liz! He's been my friend-- *our* friend--since, like, *forever!* Wouldn't that be like dating my own *brother?*
...
Liz, I know. I *know* I don't have a brother, but that's not the--
Uh-huh. Well, yeah, Harry's funny and...y'know, cute--
...
--yes, *and* well-off, but...I don't know...
...he's just not what I'm *looking* for. I need someone more...I dunno, *exciting.*
Like a rock star. Kinda.

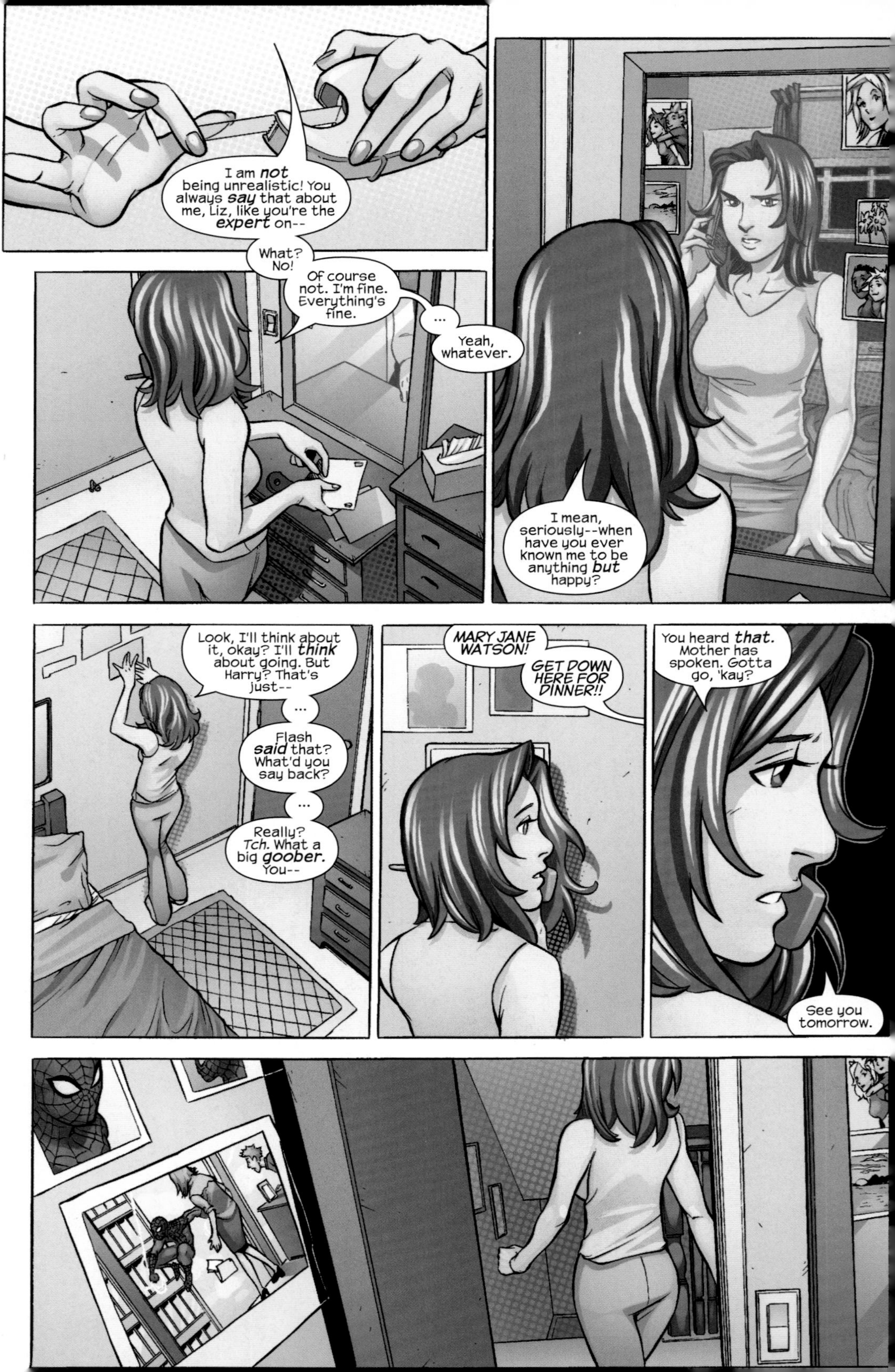
I am not being unrealistic! You always say that about me, Liz, like you're the expert on--
What? No!
Of course not. I'm fine. Everything's fine.
...
Yeah, whatever.
I mean, seriously--when have you ever known me to be anything but happy?
Look, I'll think about it, okay? I'll think about going. But Harry? That's just--
...
Flash said that? What'd you say back?
...
Really? Tch. What a big goober. You--
MARY JANE WATSON!
GET DOWN HERE FOR DINNER!!
You heard that. Mother has spoken. Gotta go, 'kay?
See you tomorrow.

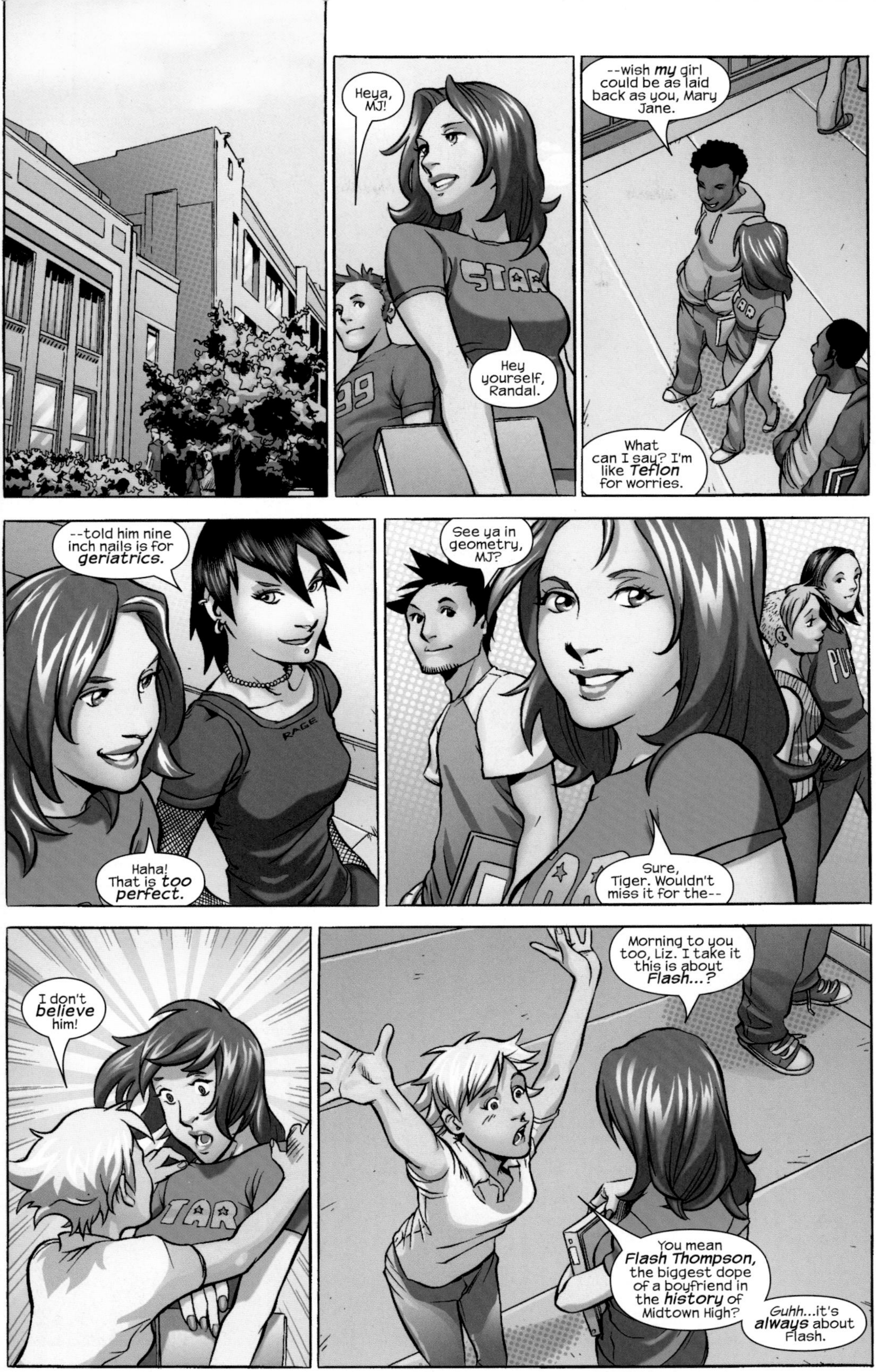
Heya, MJ!
Hey yourself, Randal.
--wish my girl could be as laid back as you, Mary Jane.
What can I say? I'm like Teflon for worries.
--told him nine inch nails is for geriatrics.
Haha! That is too perfect.
See ya in geometry, MJ?
Sure, Tiger. Wouldn't miss it for the--
I don't believe him!
Morning to you too, Liz. I take it this is about Flash...?
You mean Flash Thompson, the biggest dope of a boyfriend in the history of Midtown High?
Guhh...it's always about Flash.

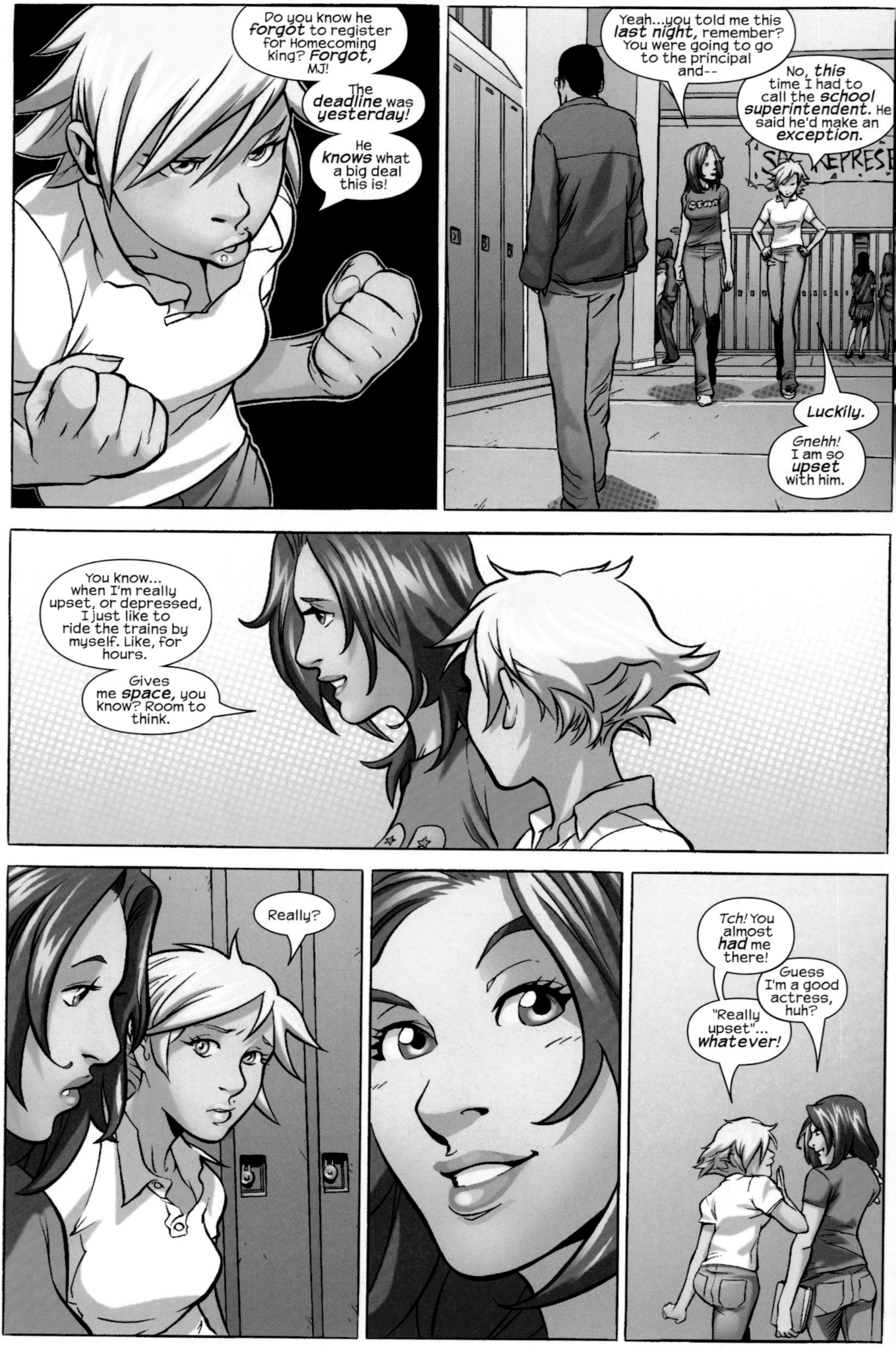
Do you know he *forgot* to register for Homecoming king? *Forgot,* MJ!
The *deadline* was *yesterday!*
He *knows* what a big deal this is!
Yeah...you told me this *last night,* remember? You were going to go to the principal and--
No, *this* time I had to call the *school superintendent.* He said he'd make an *exception.*
Luckily.
Gnehh! I am so *upset* with him.
You know... when I'm really upset, or depressed, I just like to ride the trains by myself. Like, for hours.
Gives me *space,* you know? Room to think.
Really?
Tch! You almost *had* me there!
"Really upset"... *whatever!*
Guess I'm a good actress, huh?

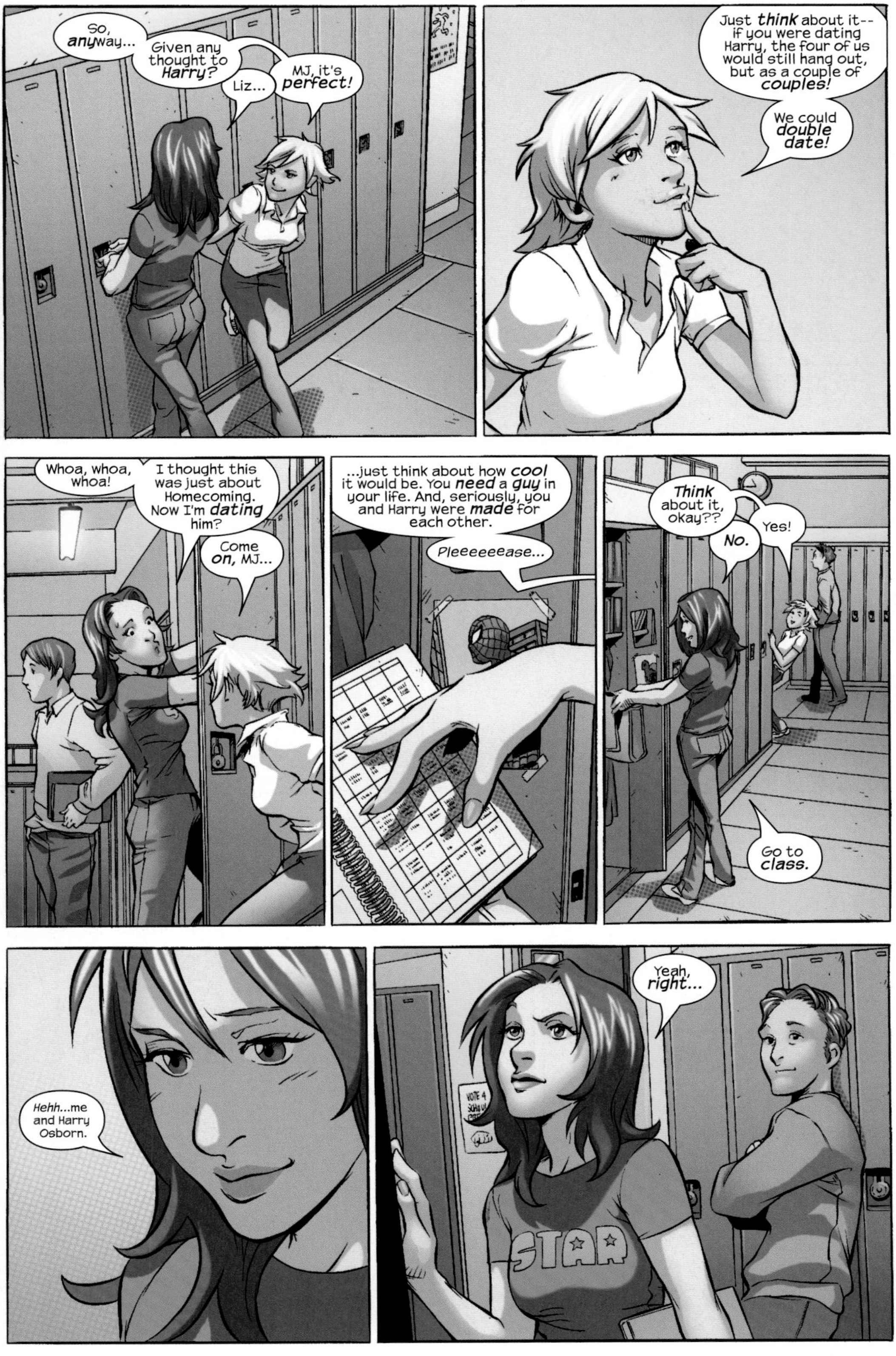
So, *any*way...
Given any thought to *Harry*?
Liz...
MJ, it's *perfect!*
Just *think* about it-- if you were dating Harry, the four of us would still hang out, but as a couple of *couples!*
We could *double date!*
Whoa, whoa, whoa!
I thought this was just about Homecoming. Now I'm *dating* him?
Come *on,* MJ...
...just think about how *cool* it would be. You *need* a *guy* in your life. And, seriously, you and Harry were *made* for each other.
Pleeeeeease...
Think about it, okay??
No.
Yes!
Go to *class.*
Hehh...me and Harry Osborn.
Yeah, *right*...
STAR

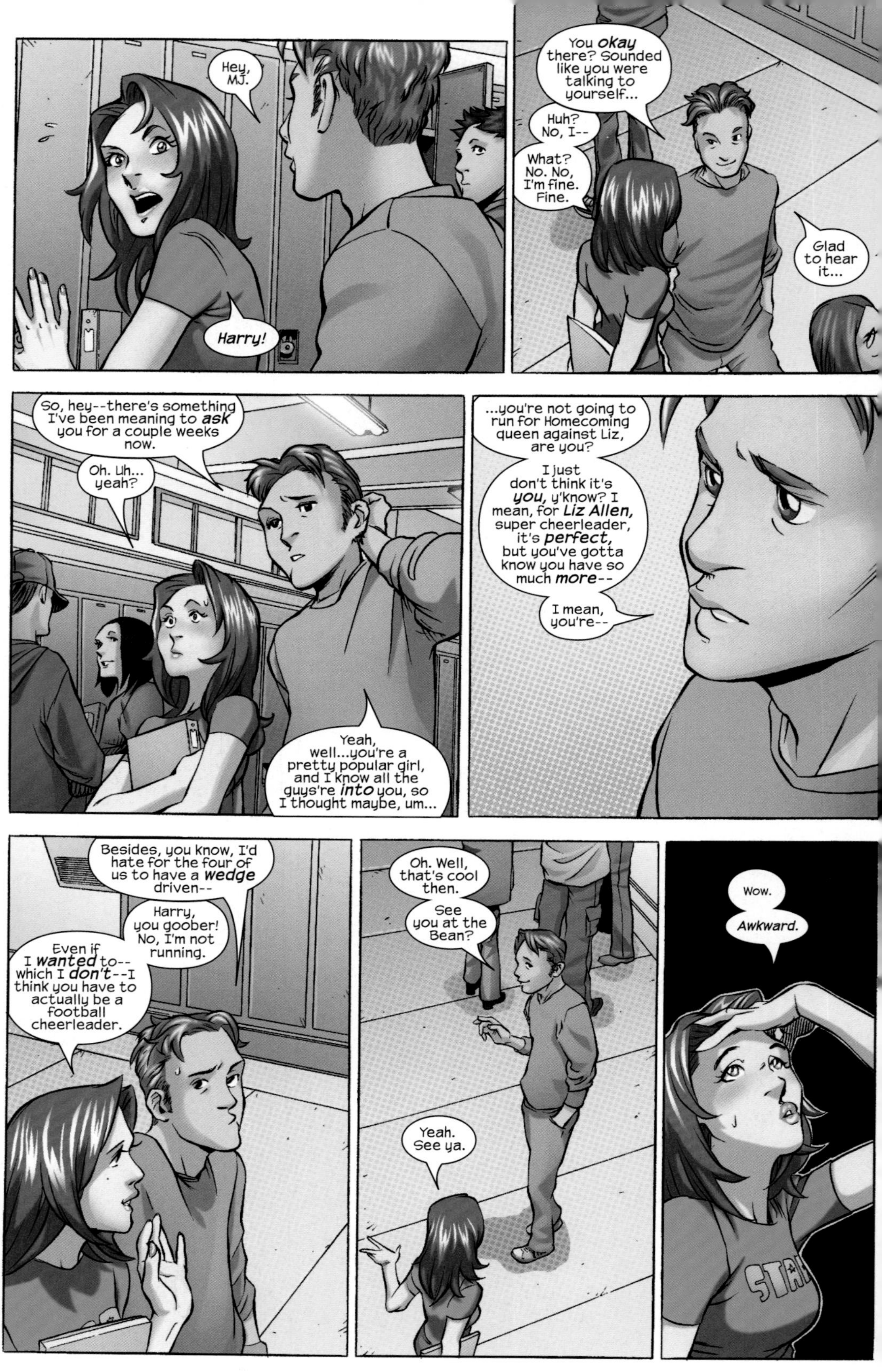
Hey, MJ.
Harry!
You okay there? Sounded like you were talking to yourself...
Huh? No, I--
What? No. No, I'm fine. Fine.
Glad to hear it...
So, hey--there's something I've been meaning to ask you for a couple weeks now.
Oh. Uh... yeah?
Yeah, well...you're a pretty popular girl, and I know all the guys're into you, so I thought maybe, um...
...you're not going to run for Homecoming queen against Liz, are you?
I just don't think it's you, y'know? I mean, for Liz Allen, super cheerleader, it's perfect, but you've gotta know you have so much more--
I mean, you're--
Besides, you know, I'd hate for the four of us to have a wedge driven--
Harry, you goober! No, I'm not running.
Even if I wanted to--which I don't--I think you have to actually be a football cheerleader.
Oh. Well, that's cool then.
See you at the Bean?
Yeah. See ya.
Wow.
Awkward.

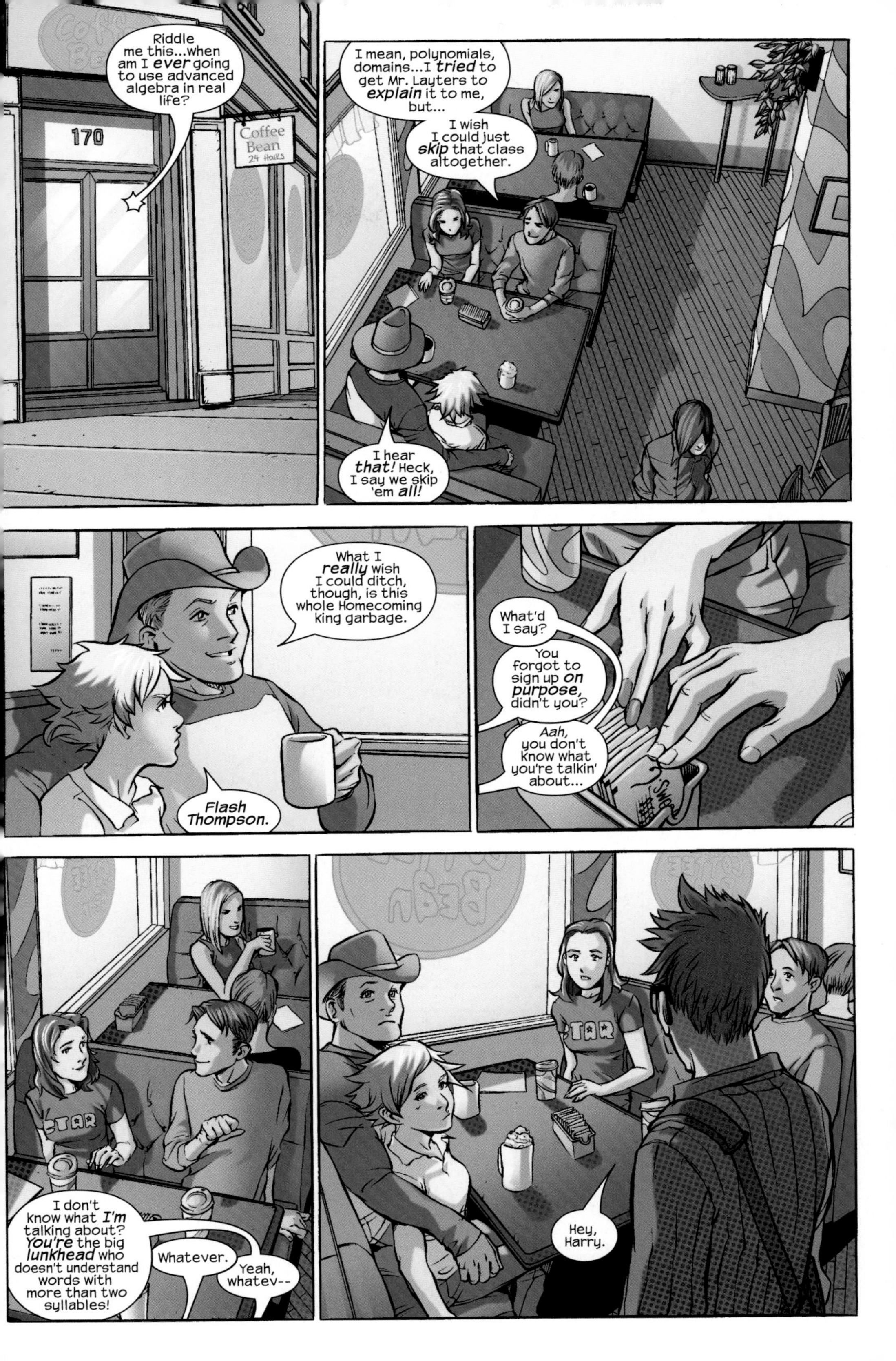
170
Coffee Bean 24 HOURS
Riddle me this...when am I *ever* going to use advanced algebra in real life?
I mean, polynomials, domains...I *tried* to get Mr. Layters to *explain* it to me, but...
I wish I could just *skip* that class altogether.
I hear *that!* Heck, I say we skip 'em *all!*
What I *really* wish I could ditch, though, is this whole Homecoming king garbage.
Flash Thompson.
What'd I say?
You forgot to sign up *on purpose,* didn't you?
Aah, you don't know what you're talkin' about...
I don't know what *I'm* talking about? *You're* the big *lunkhead* who doesn't understand words with more than two syllables!
Whatever.
Yeah, whatev--
Hey, Harry.

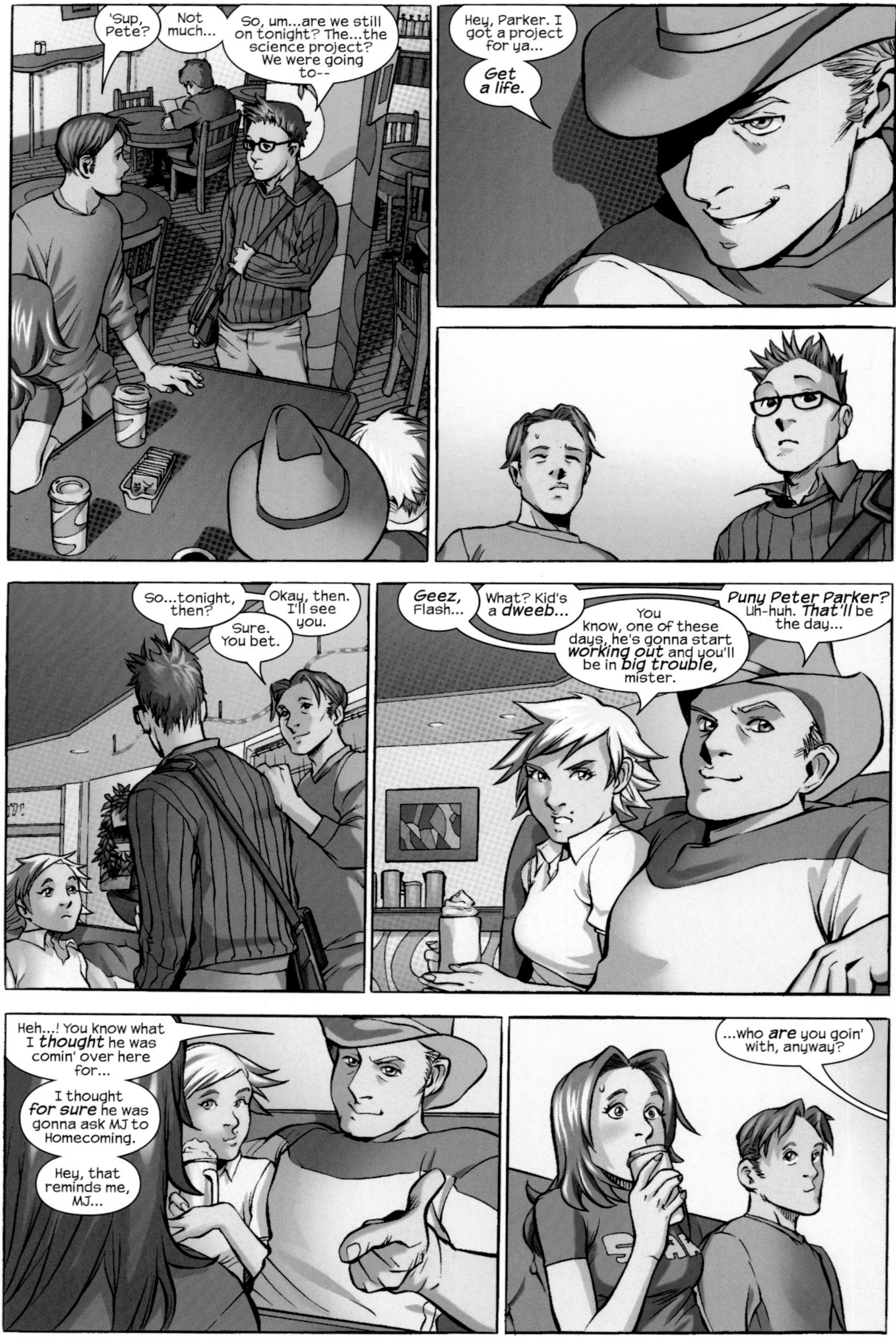
'Sup, Pete?
Not much...
So, um...are we still on tonight? The...the science project? We were going to--
Hey, Parker. I got a project for ya...
Get a life.
So...tonight, then?
Sure. You bet.
Okay, then. I'll see you.
Geez, Flash...
What? Kid's a dweeb...
You know, one of these days, he's gonna start working out and you'll be in big trouble, mister.
Puny Peter Parker? Uh-huh. That'll be the day...
Heh...! You know what I thought he was comin' over here for...
I thought for sure he was gonna ask MJ to Homecoming.
Hey, that reminds me, MJ...
...who are you goin' with, anyway?

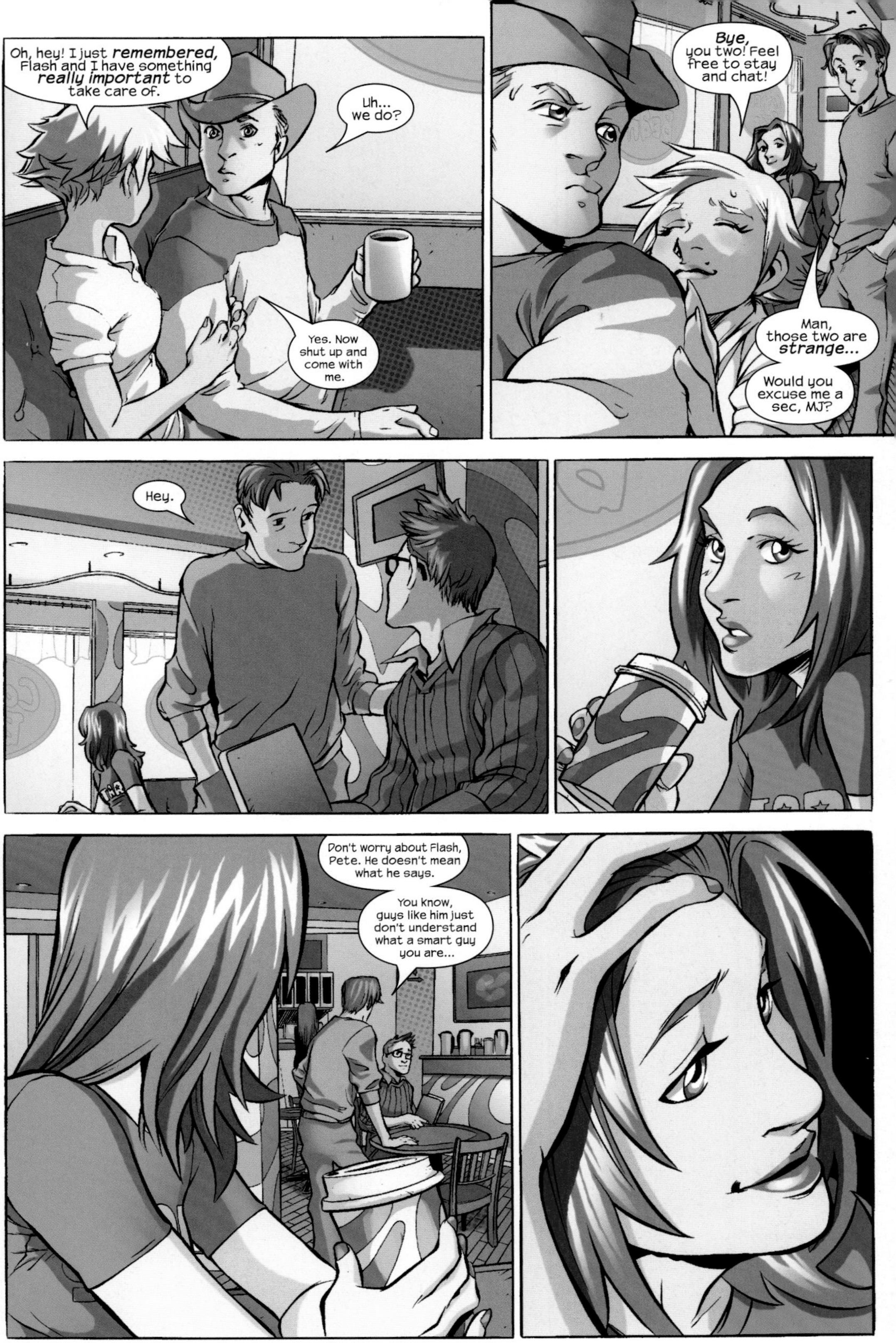
Oh, hey! I just **remembered,** Flash and I have something ***really important*** to take care of.
Uh... we do?
Yes. Now shut up and come with me.
Bye, you two! Feel free to stay and chat!
Man, those two are ***strange...***
Would you excuse me a sec, MJ?
Hey.
Don't worry about Flash, Pete. He doesn't mean what he says.
You know, guys like him just don't understand what a smart guy you are...

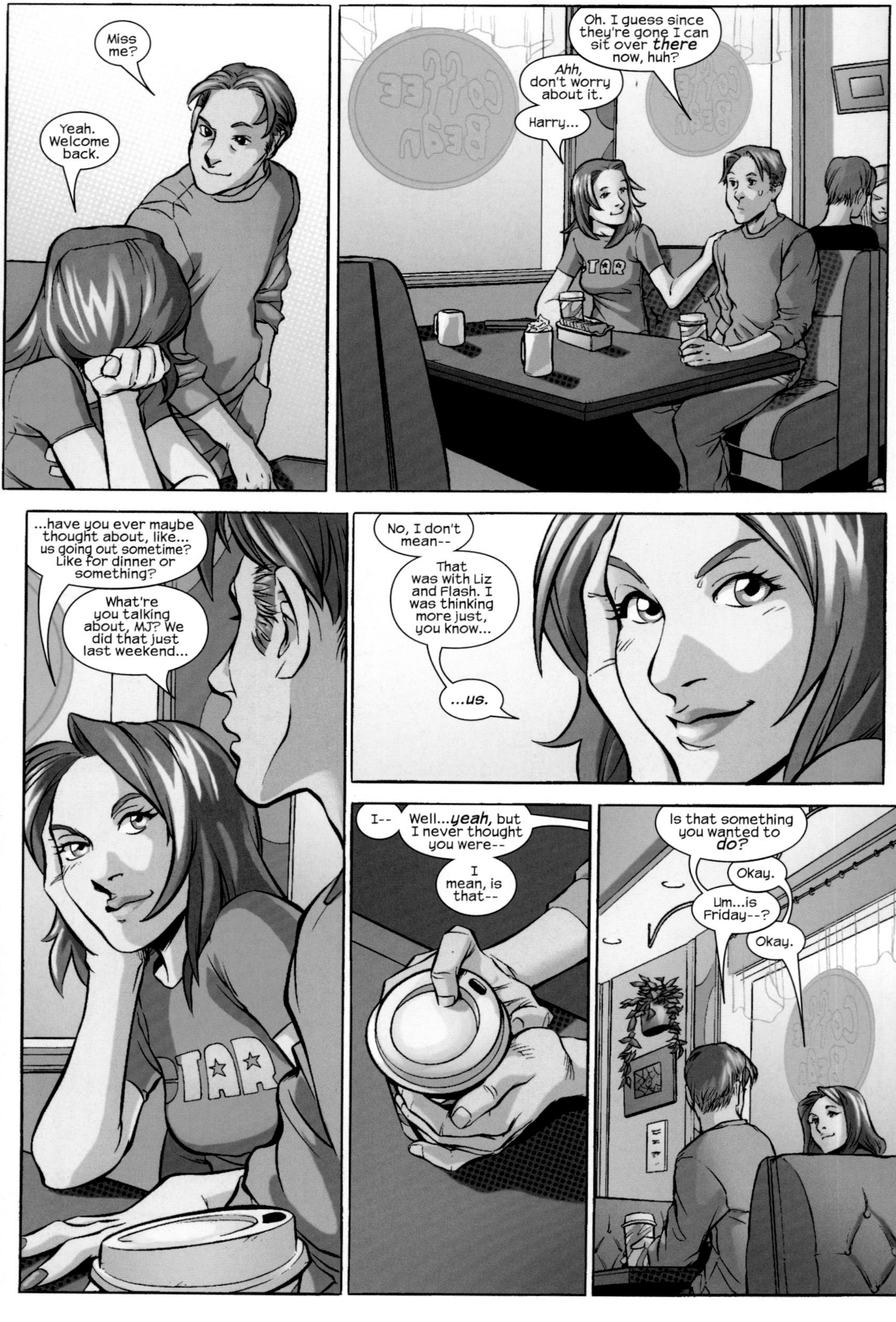
Miss me?
Yeah. Welcome back.
Oh. I guess since they're gone I can sit over *there* now, huh?
Ahh, don't worry about it.
Harry...
...have you ever maybe thought about, like... us going out sometime? Like for dinner or something?
What're you talking about, MJ? We did that just last weekend...
No, I don't mean--
That was with Liz and Flash. I was thinking more just, you know...
...us.
I--
Well...*yeah,* but I never thought you were--
I mean, is that--
Is that something you wanted to *do?*
Okay.
Um...is Friday--?
Okay.

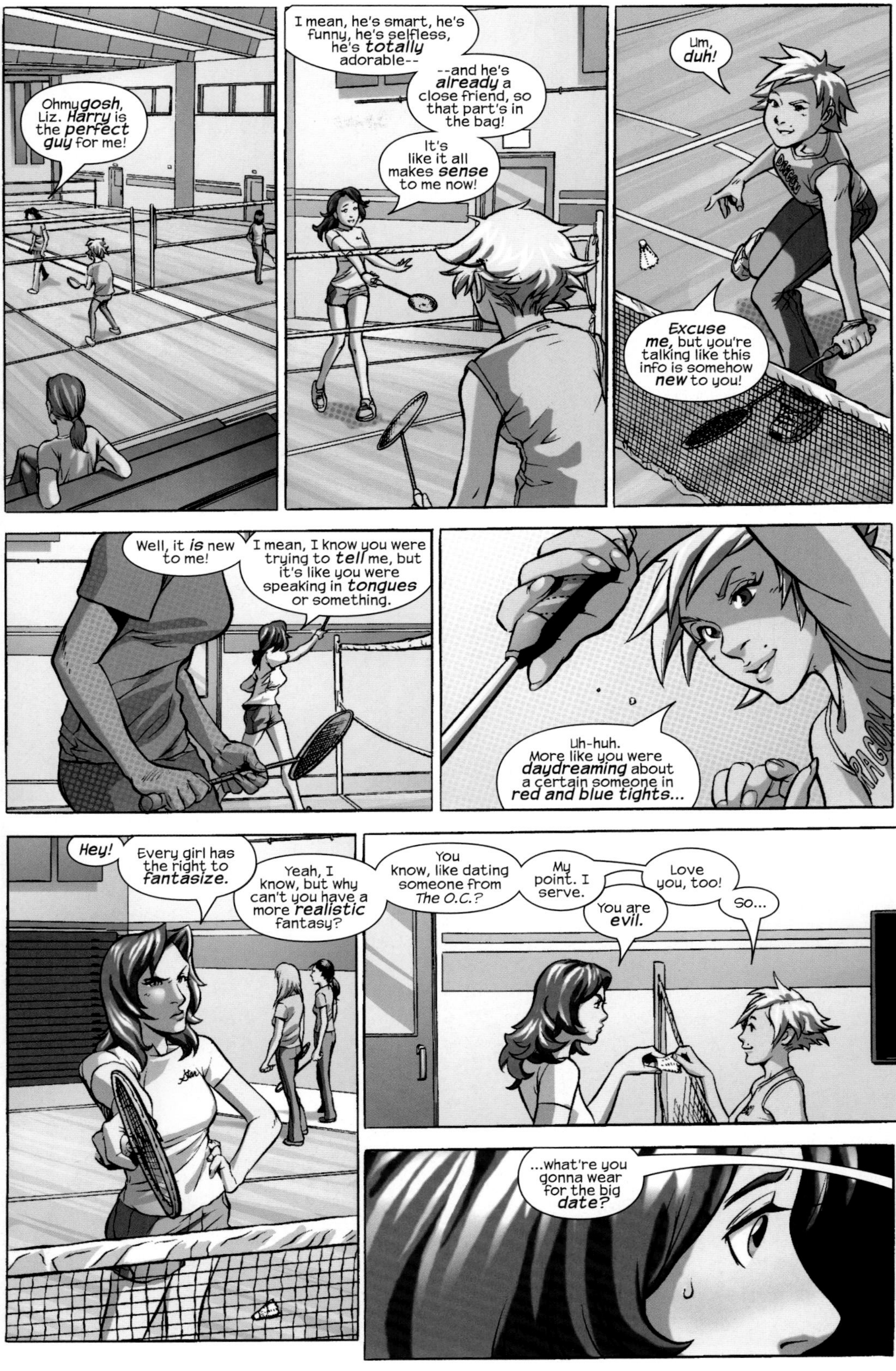
Ohmy gosh, Liz. Harry is the perfect guy for me!
I mean, he's smart, he's funny, he's selfless, he's totally adorable--
--and he's already a close friend, so that part's in the bag!
It's like it all makes sense to me now!
Um, duh!
Excuse me, but you're talking like this info is somehow new to you!
Well, it is new to me!
I mean, I know you were trying to tell me, but it's like you were speaking in tongues or something.
Uh-huh. More like you were daydreaming about a certain someone in red and blue tights...
Hey!
Every girl has the right to fantasize.
Yeah, I know, but why can't you have a more realistic fantasy?
You know, like dating someone from The O.C.?
My point. I serve.
You are evil.
Love you, too!
So...
...what're you gonna wear for the big date?

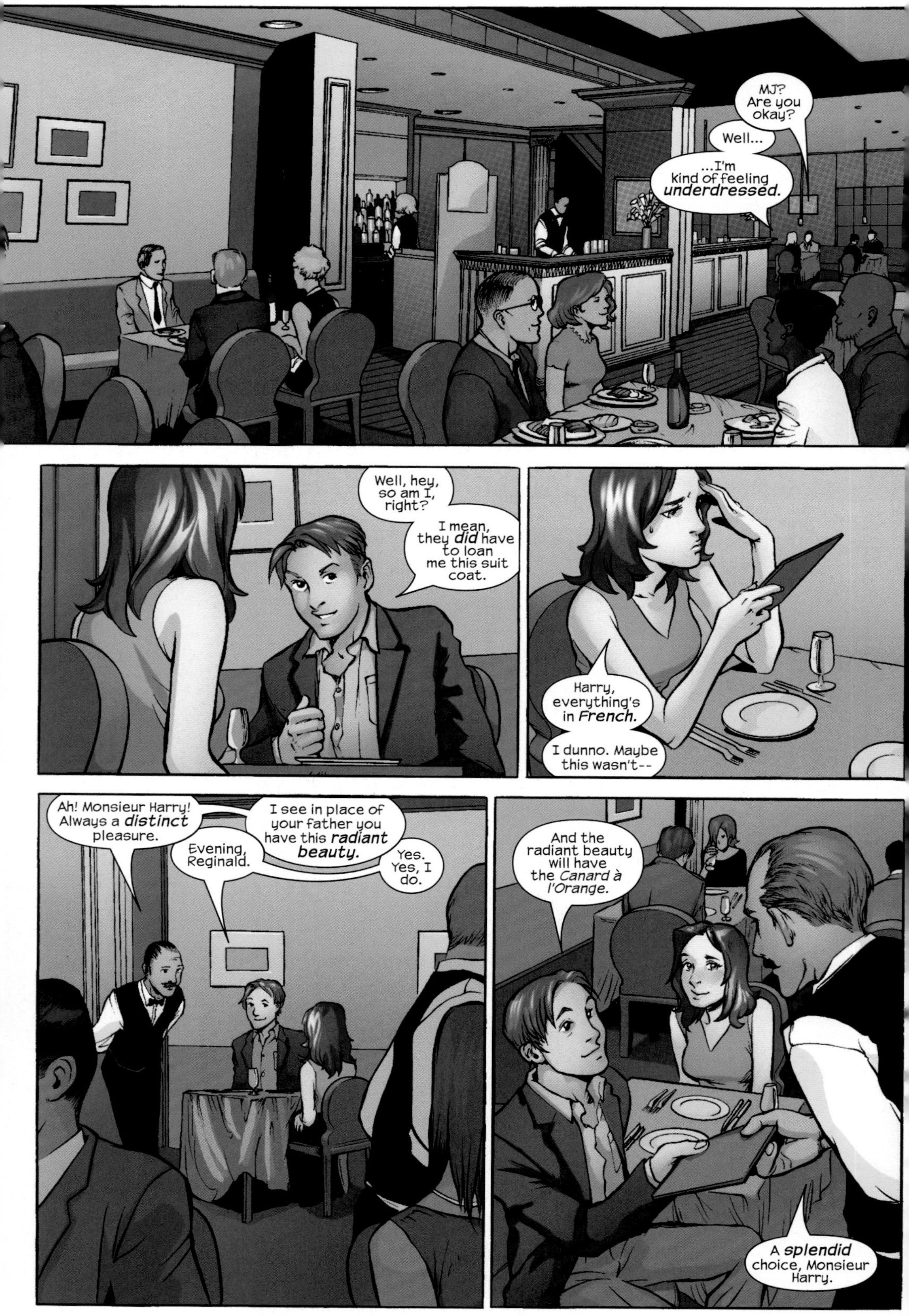
MJ? Are you okay?
Well...
...I'm kind of feeling *underdressed.*
Well, hey, so am I, right?
I mean, they *did* have to loan me this suit coat.
Harry, everything's in *French.*
I dunno. Maybe this wasn't--
Ah! Monsieur Harry! Always a *distinct* pleasure.
Evening, Reginald.
I see in place of your father you have this *radiant beauty.*
Yes. Yes, I do.
And the radiant beauty will have the *Canard à l'Orange.*
A *splendid* choice, Monsieur Harry.

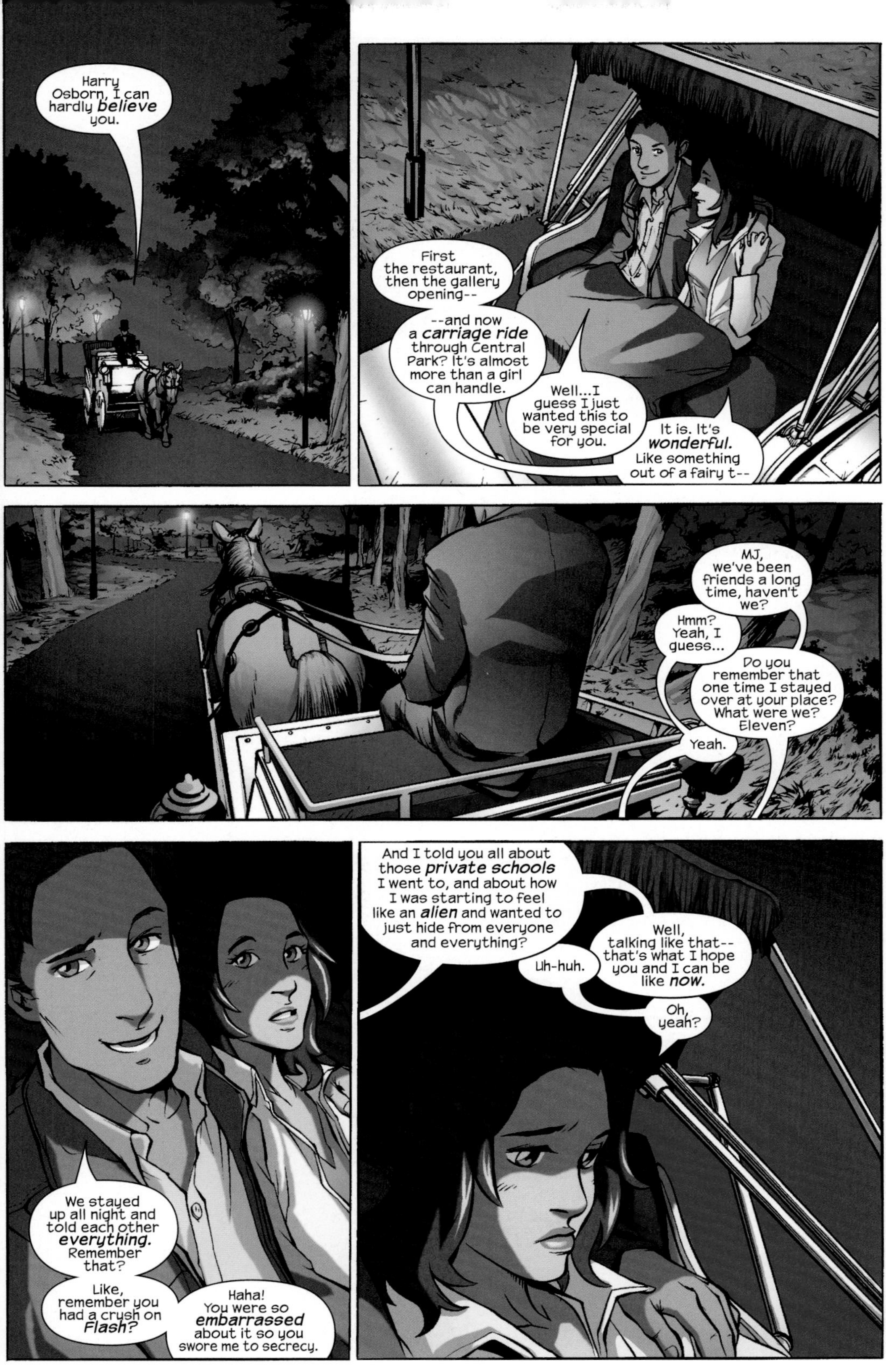

Harry Osborn, I can hardly *believe* you.
First the restaurant, then the gallery opening--
--and now a *carriage ride* through Central Park? It's almost more than a girl can handle.
Well...I guess I just wanted this to be very special for you.
It is. It's *wonderful.* Like something out of a fairy t--
MJ, we've been friends a long time, haven't we?
Hmm? Yeah, I guess...
Do you remember that one time I stayed over at your place? What were we? Eleven?
Yeah.
We stayed up all night and told each other *everything.* Remember that?
Like, remember you had a crush on *Flash?*
Haha! You were so *embarrassed* about it so you swore me to secrecy.
And I told you all about those *private schools* I went to, and about how I was starting to feel like an *alien* and wanted to just hide from everyone and everything?
Uh-huh.
Well, talking like that--that's what I hope you and I can be like *now.*
Oh, yeah?

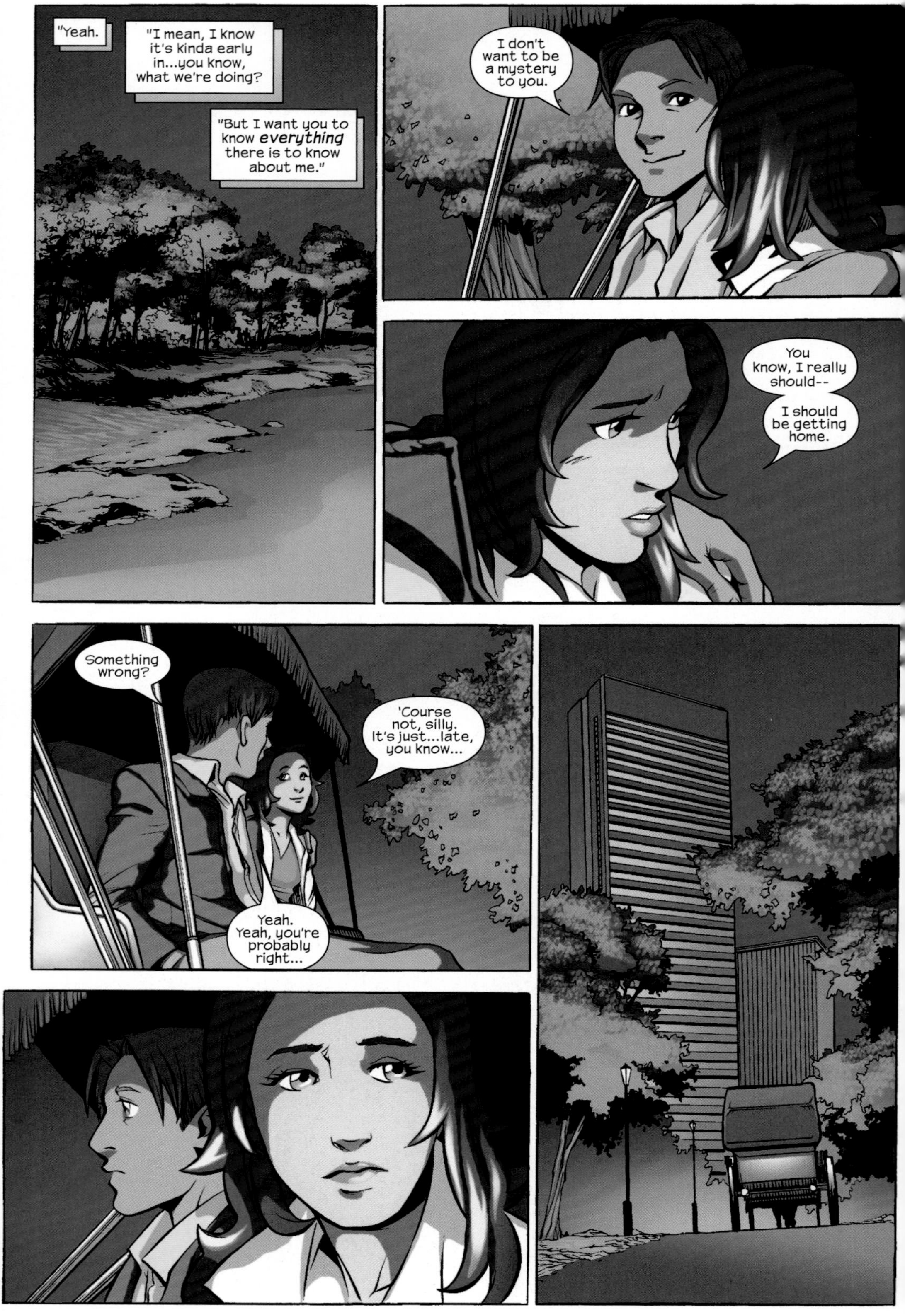
"Yeah.
"I mean, I know it's kinda early in...you know, what we're doing?
"But I want you to know *everything* there is to know about me."
I don't want to be a mystery to you.
You know, I really should--
I should be getting home.
Something wrong?
'Course not, silly. It's just...late, you know...
Yeah. Yeah, you're probably right...

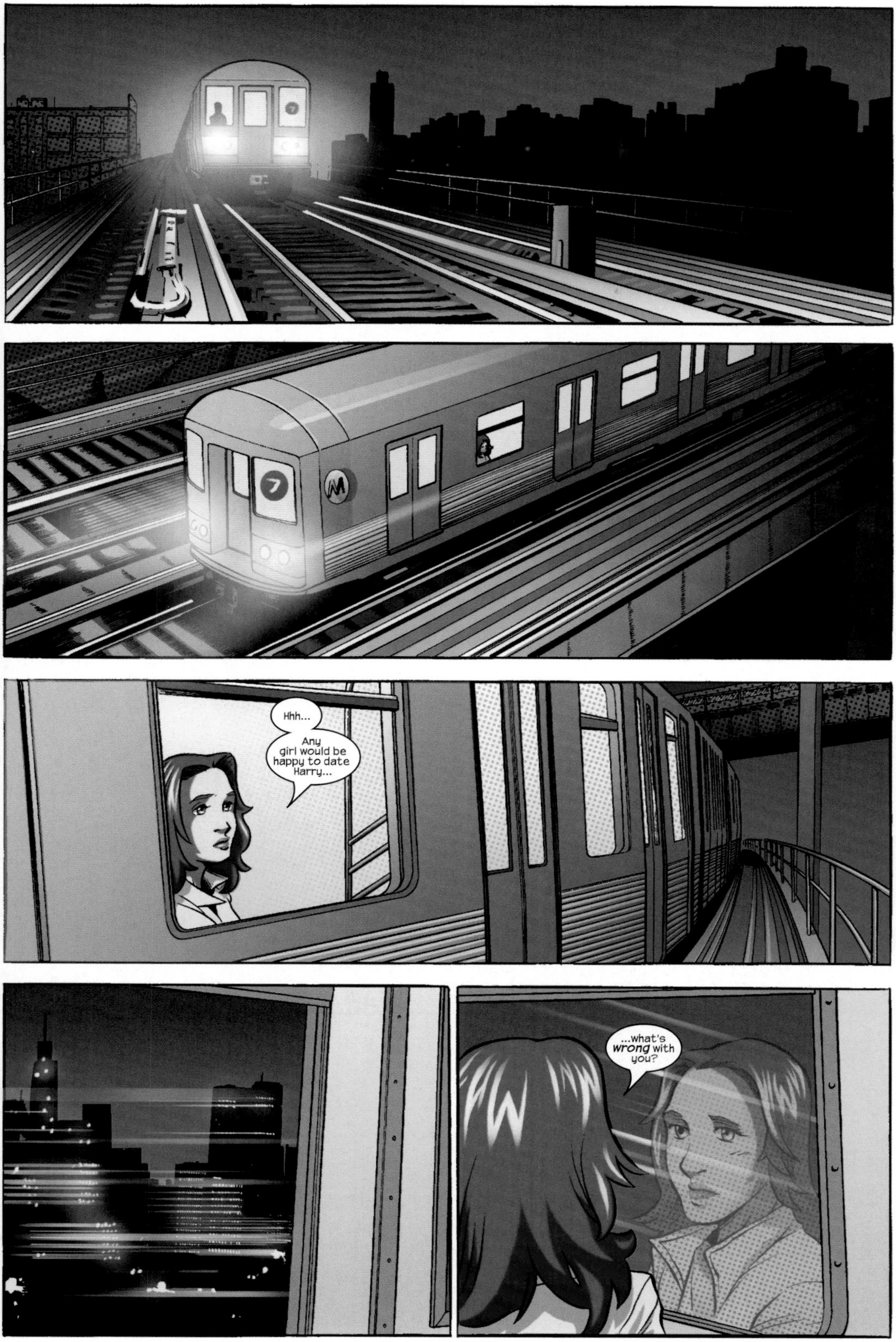
Hhh...
Any girl would be happy to date Harry...
...what's wrong with you?

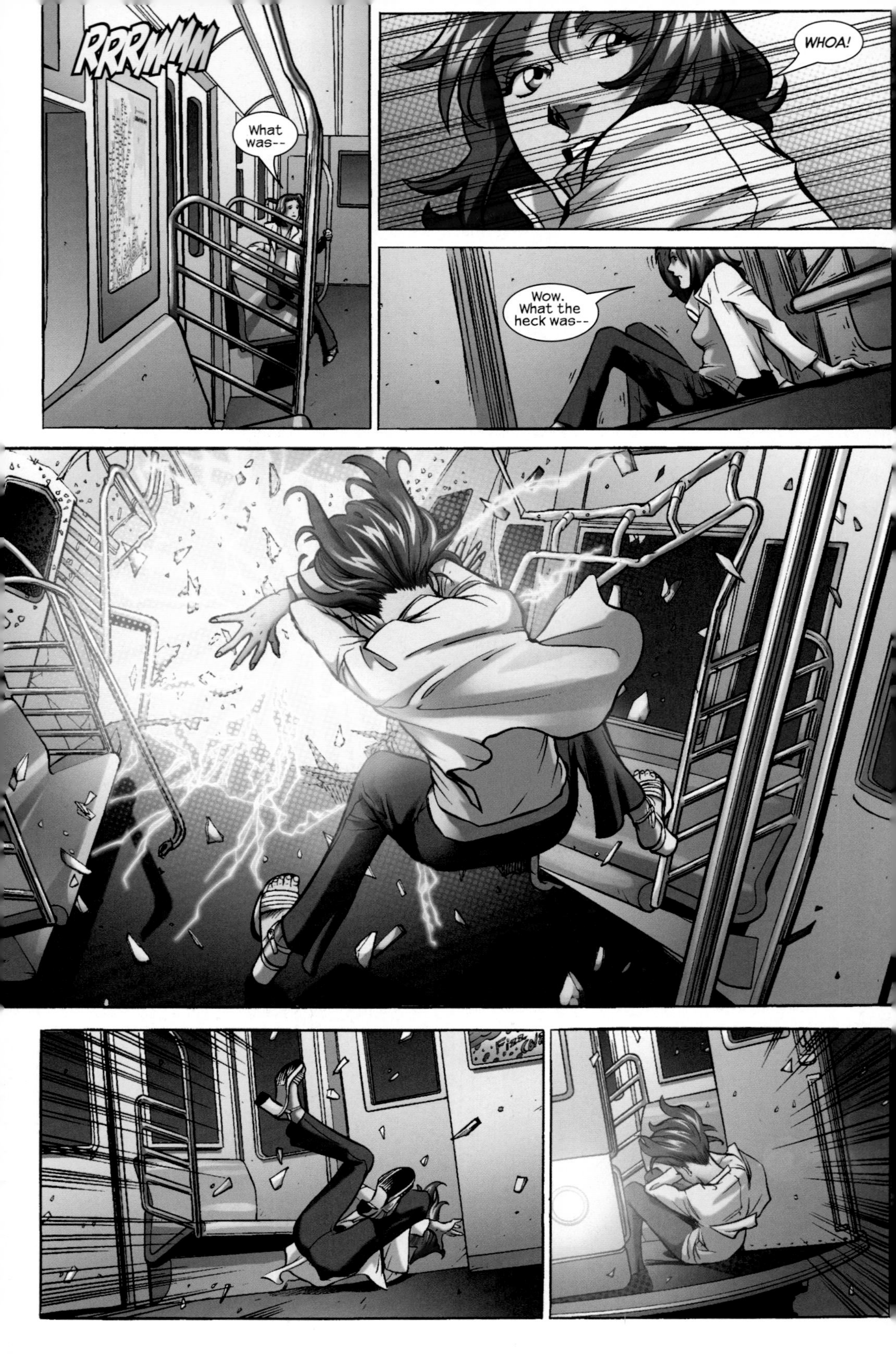
RRRMMM
What was--
WHOA!
Wow. What the heck was--

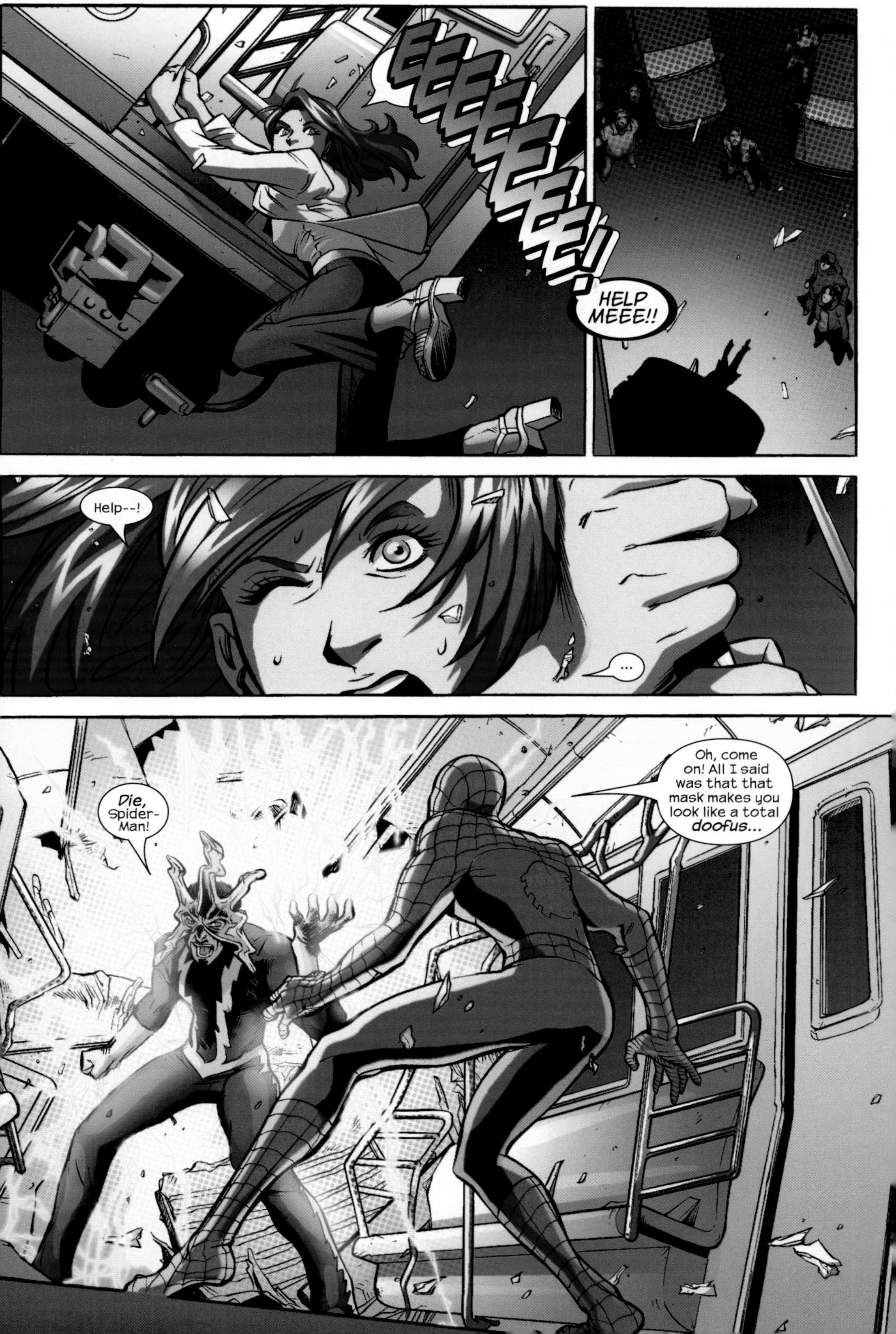
EEEEEEEEEEE!!
HELP MEEE!!
Help--!
...
Die, Spider-Man!
Oh, come on! All I said was that that mask makes you look like a total doofus...

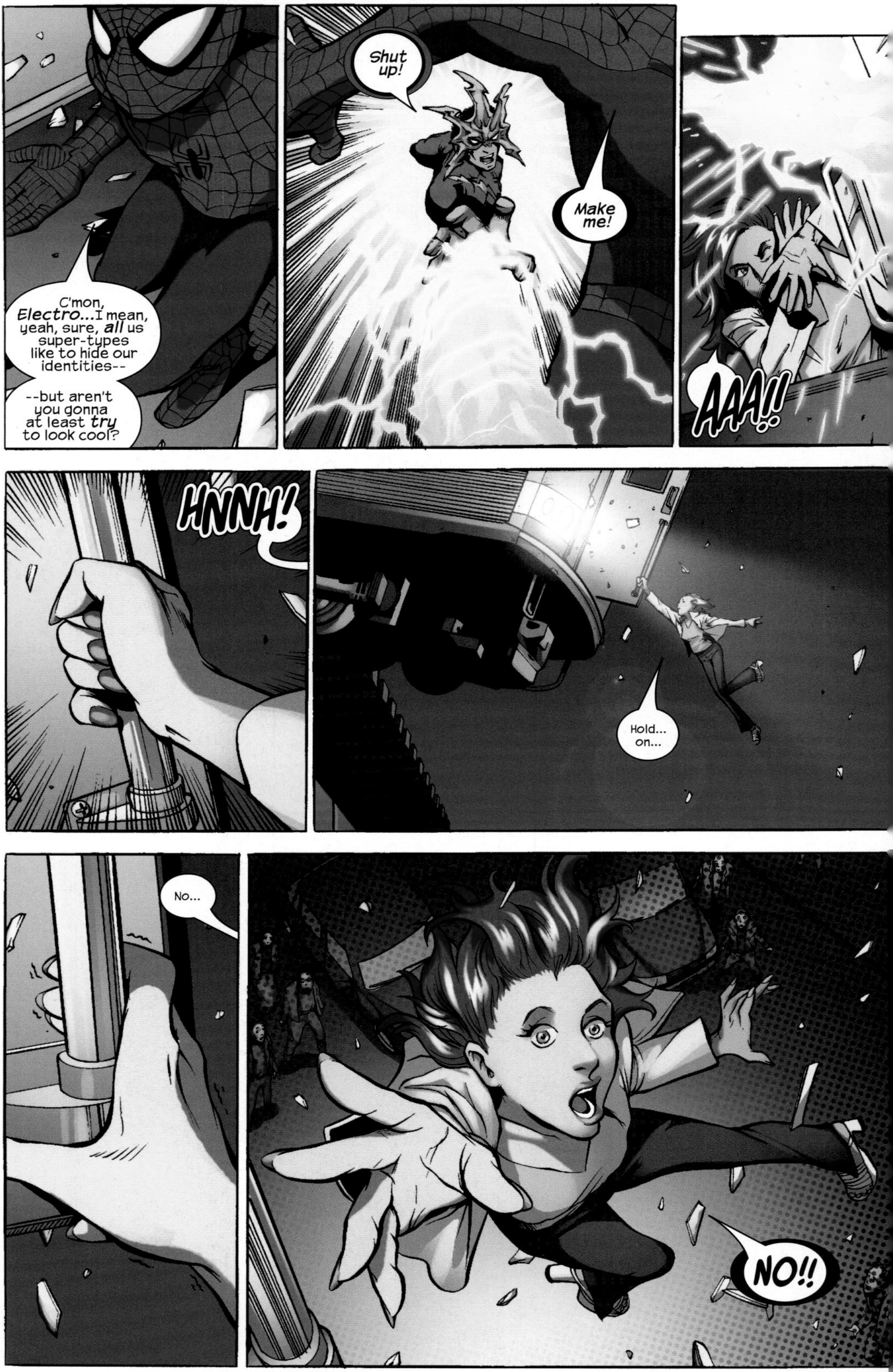

C'mon, Electro...I mean, yeah, sure, all us super-types like to hide our identities--
--but aren't you gonna at least try to look cool?
Shut up!
Make me!
AAA!!
HNNH!
Hold... on...
No...
NO!!

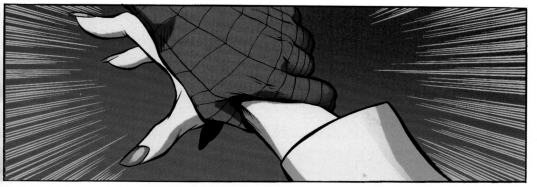

Uh...

...falling would be *bad.*

Now, don't worry, miss, everything's gonna be just--

Spider-Man! *Behind* you!

GMMF!

THWIP

Oh, yeah.

Almost *forgot* about ol' sparky.

Heh... I do that sometimes...

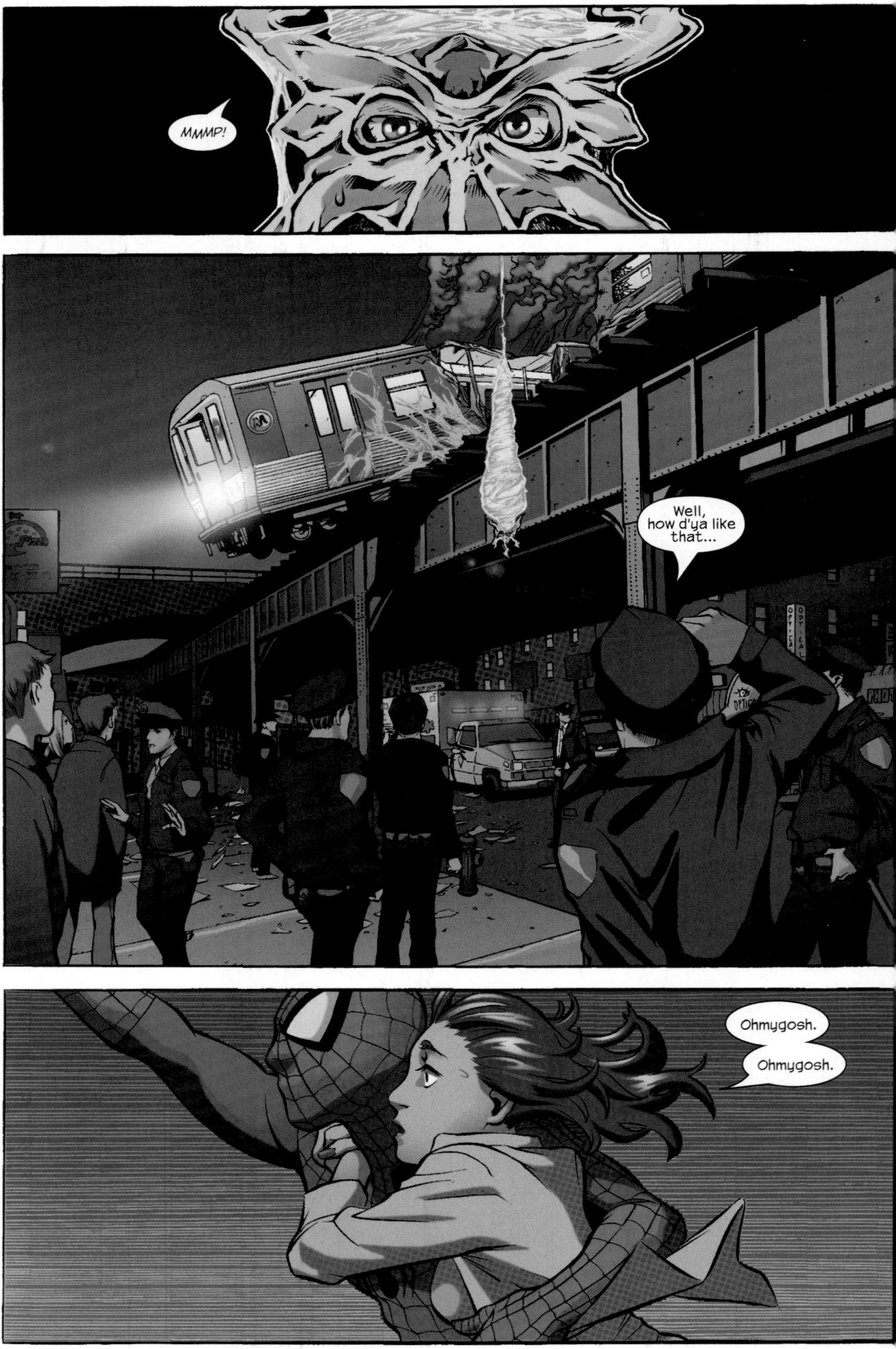
MMMP!
Well, how d'ya like that...
Ohmygosh.
Ohmygosh.

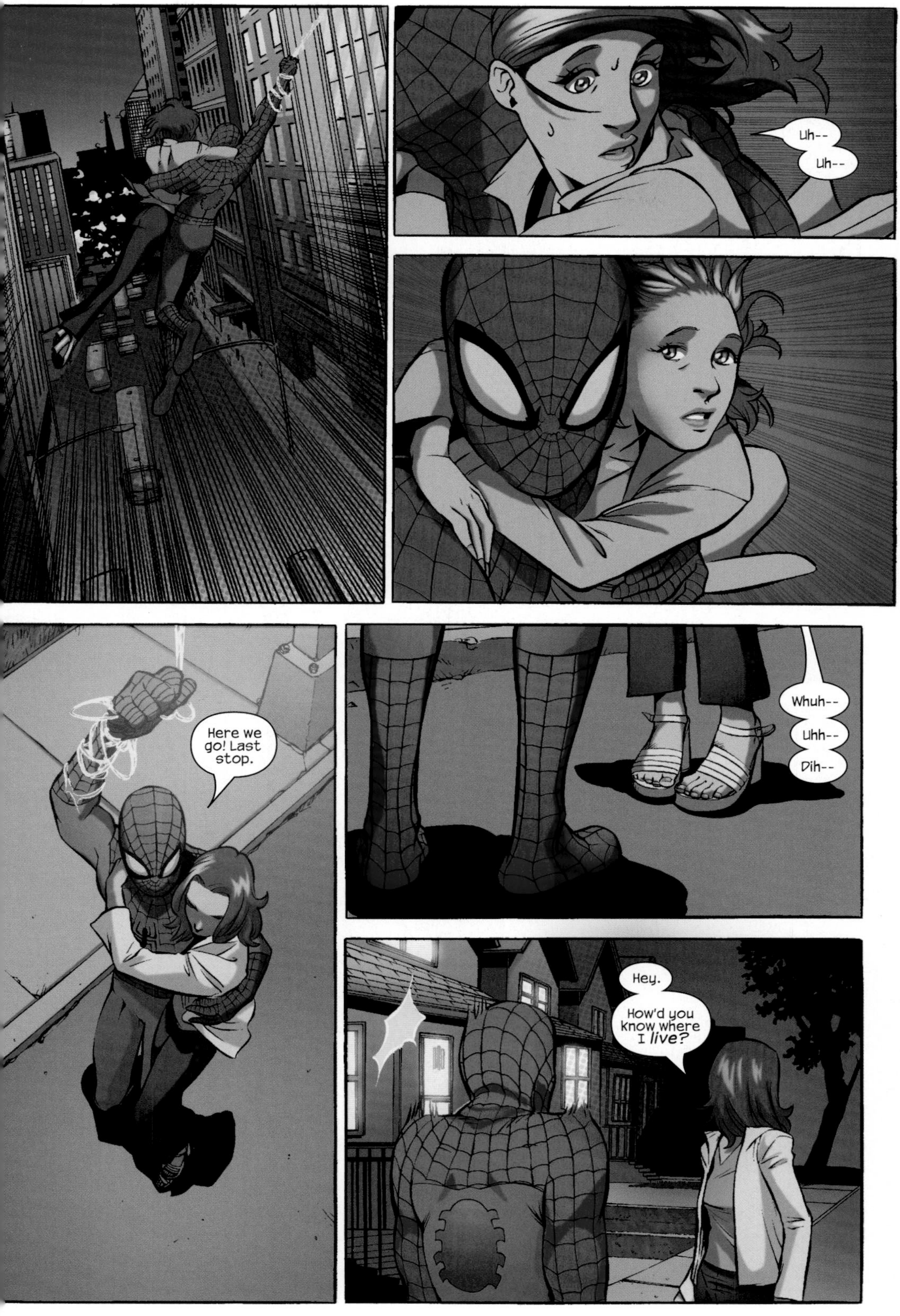
Uh--
Uh--
Here we go! Last stop.
Whuh--
Uhh--
Dih--
Hey.
How'd you know where I *live*?

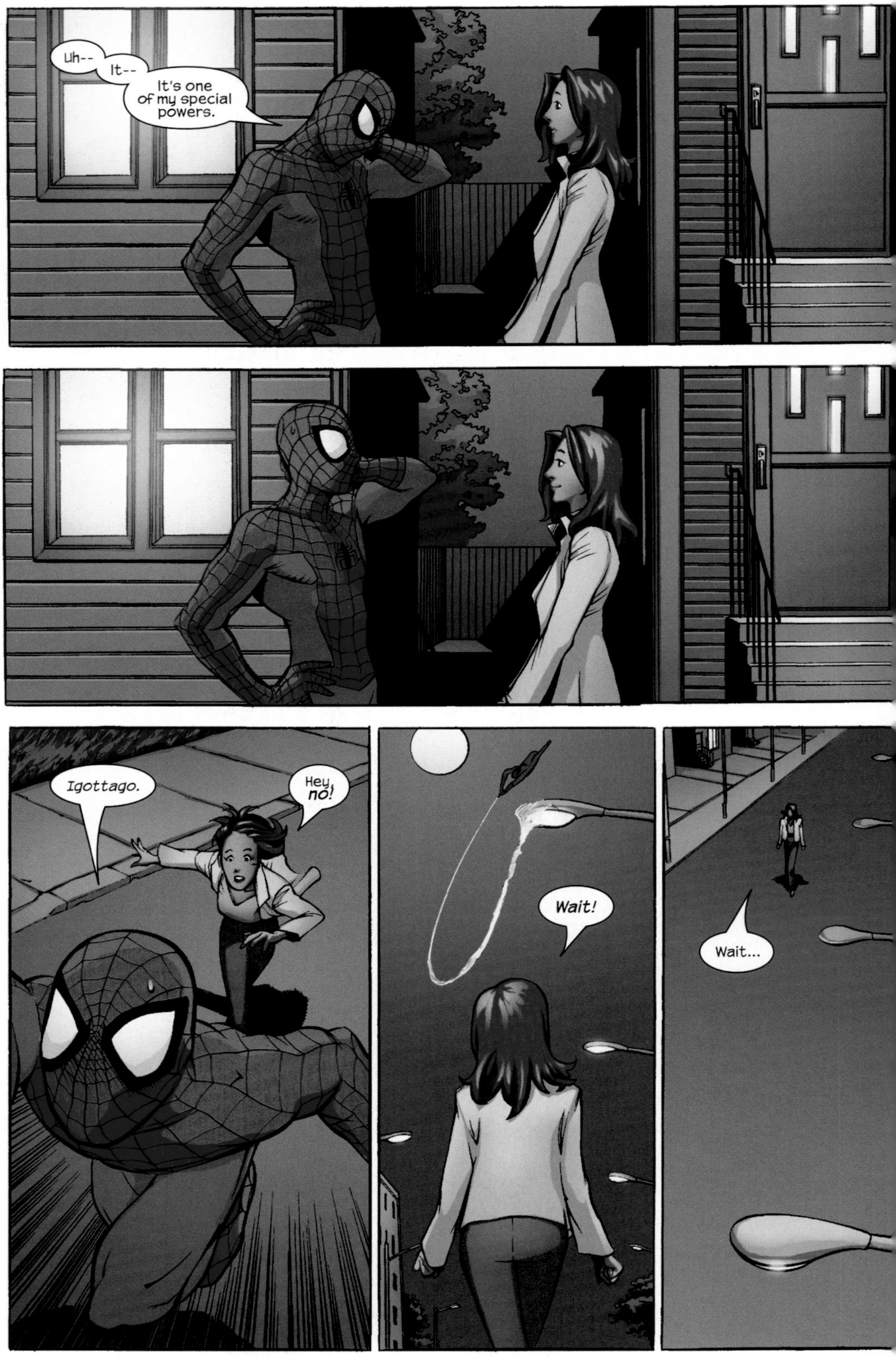

Uh--
It--
It's one of my special powers.
Igottago.
Hey, no!
Wait!
Wait...

--and then he just **took off** into the air, like, like--

ZOOM!

Oh. My **gosh.**

I know. I know!

He **totally** saved my life.

I mean, if it wasn't for **Spider-Man**, I--

Hmm?

Hey, Mary Jane.

Oh. Hi.

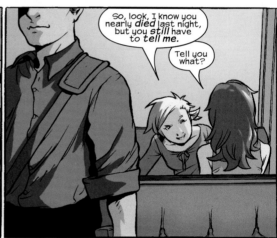

So, look, I know you nearly **died** last night, but you **still** have to **tell me.**

Tell you what?

Harry! The **date,** you big dork!

So, is he your **Prince Charming,** or what?

Well...

I mean, it was **such** a great night, but then--

I dunno.

I just don't think Harry's the **right guy** for me, you know?

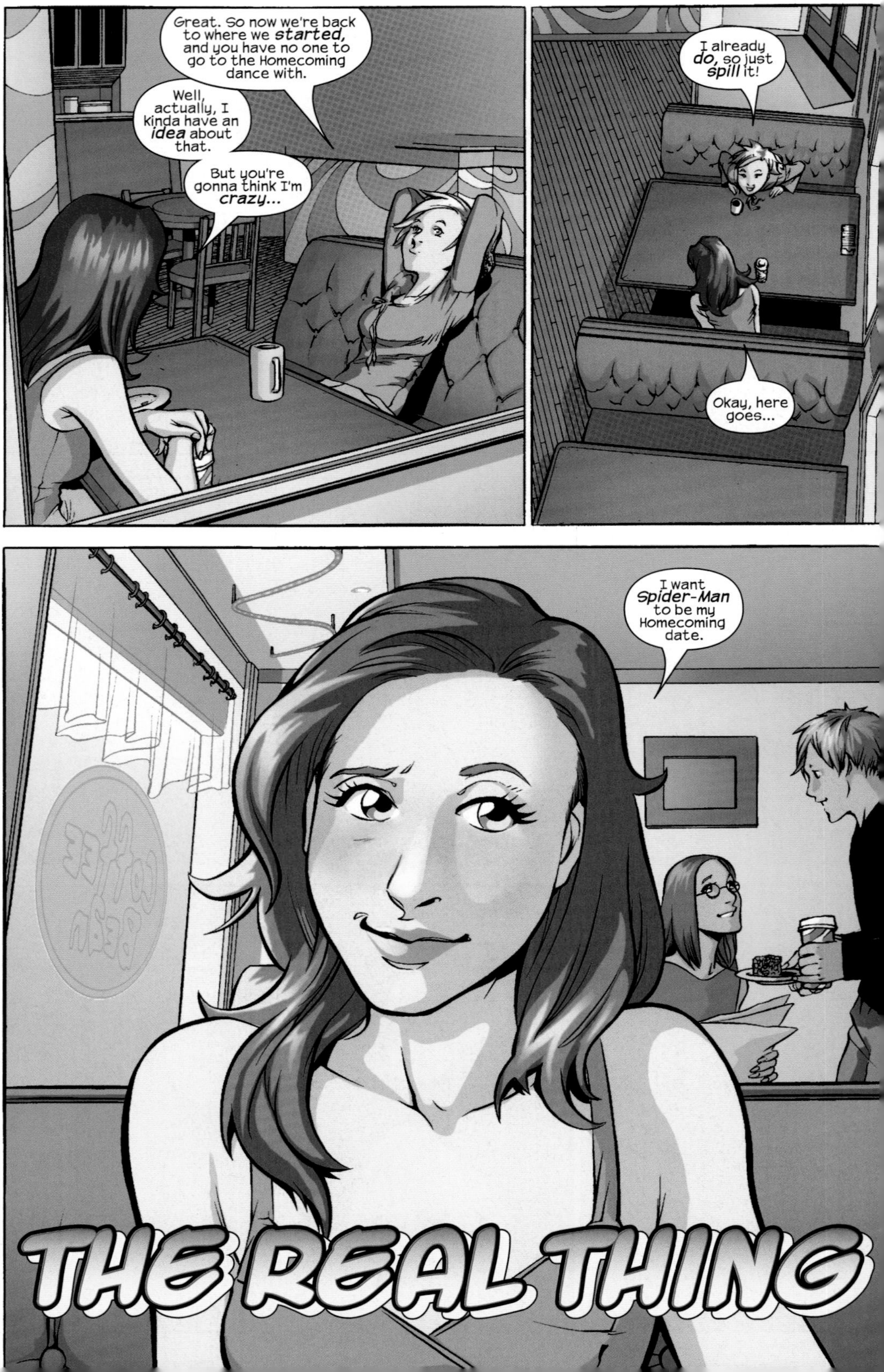

Great. So now we're back to where we started, and you have no one to go to the Homecoming dance with.
Well, actually, I kinda have an idea about that.
But you're gonna think I'm crazy...
I already do, so just spill it!
Okay, here goes...
I want Spider-Man to be my Homecoming date.
COFFEE BEAN
THE REAL THING

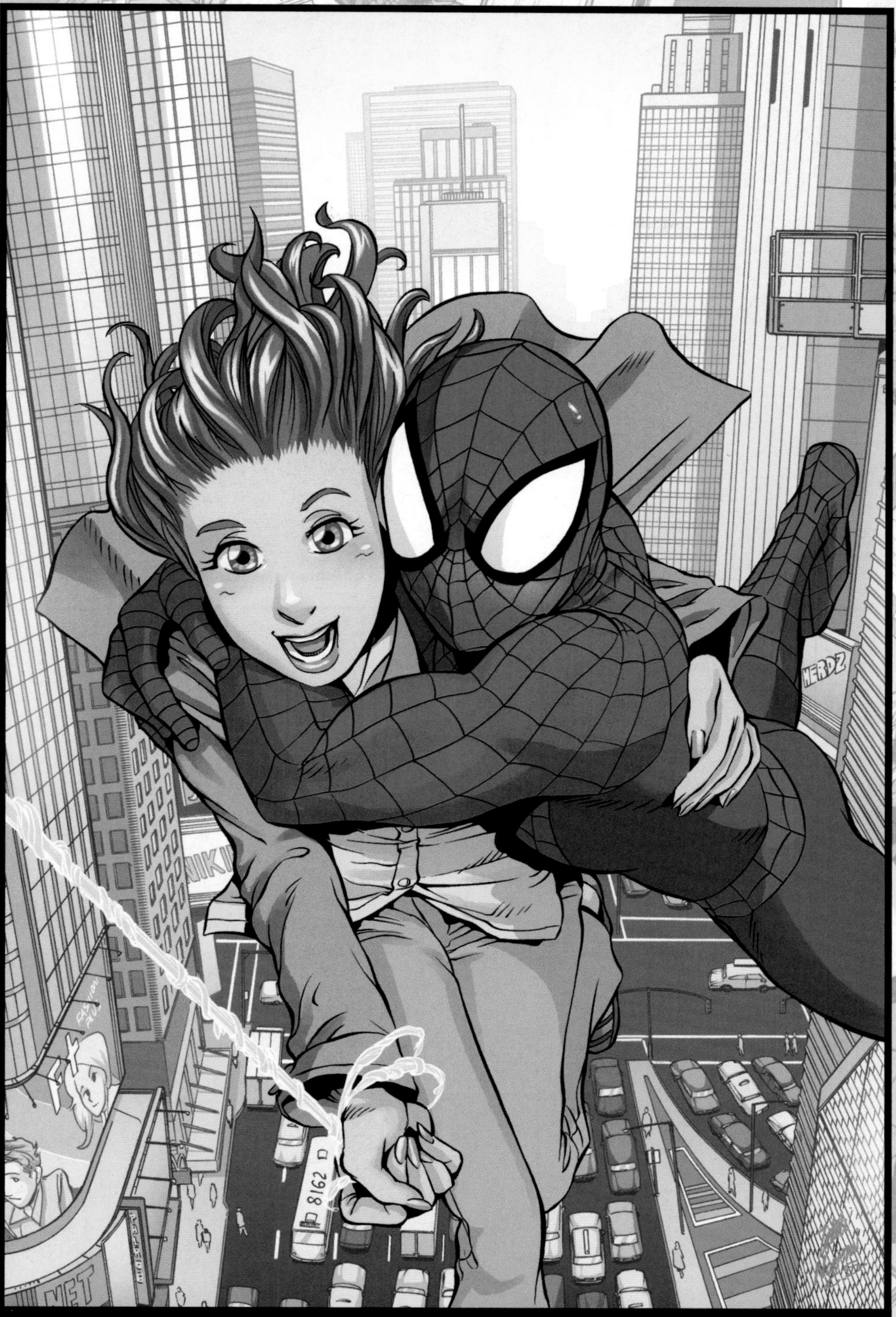

SPIDER-MAN LOVES MARY JANE #1

MJ HAS A CRUSH ON A CERTAIN WALL-CRAWLING SUPER HERO — AND SHE'S DETERMINED TO LET HIM KNOW, NO MATTER WHAT IT TAKES!

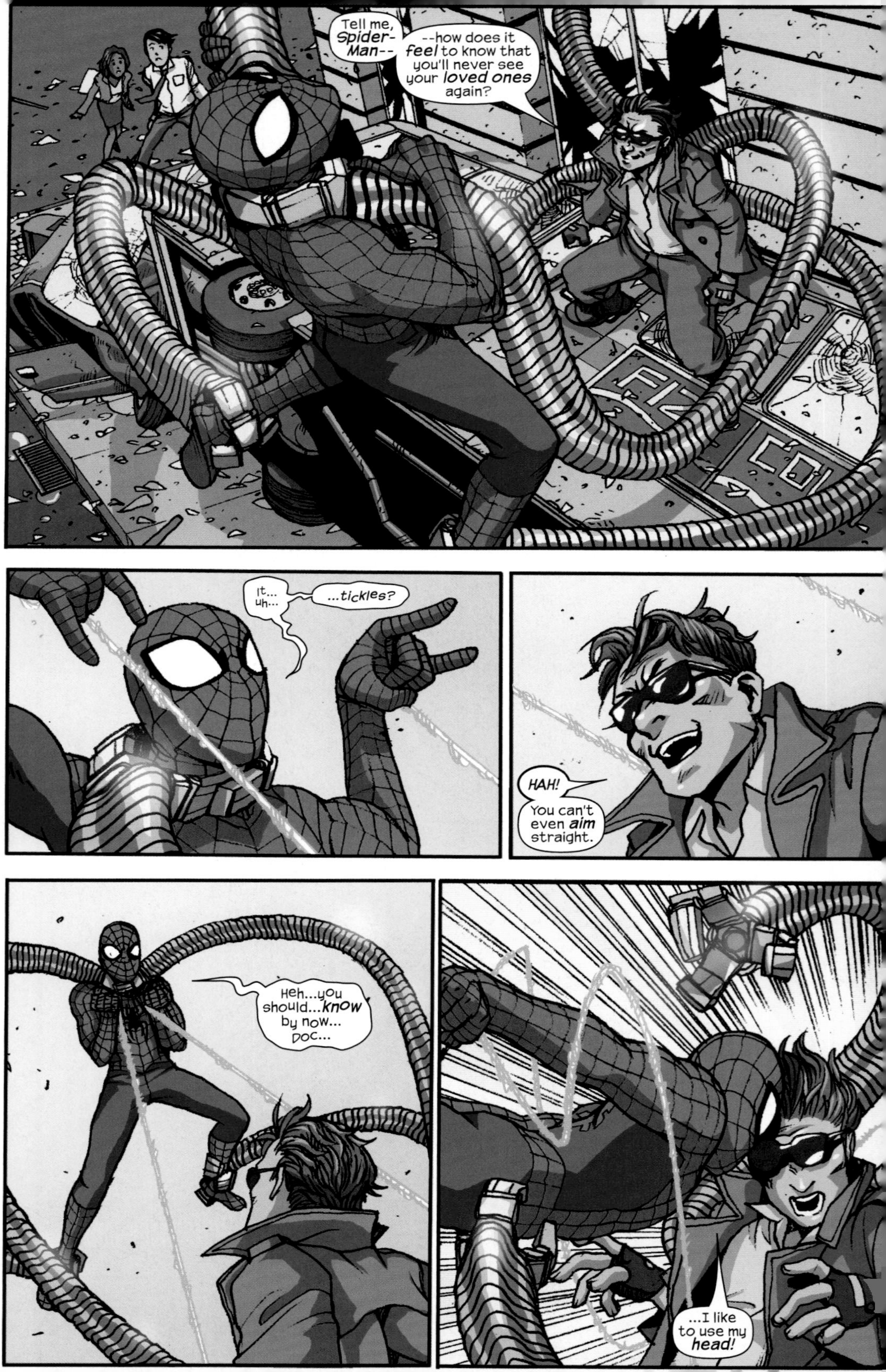
Tell me, Spider-Man--
--how does it feel to know that you'll never see your loved ones again?
It... uh...
...tickles?
HAH!
You can't even aim straight.
Heh...you should...know by now... Doc...
...I like to use my head!

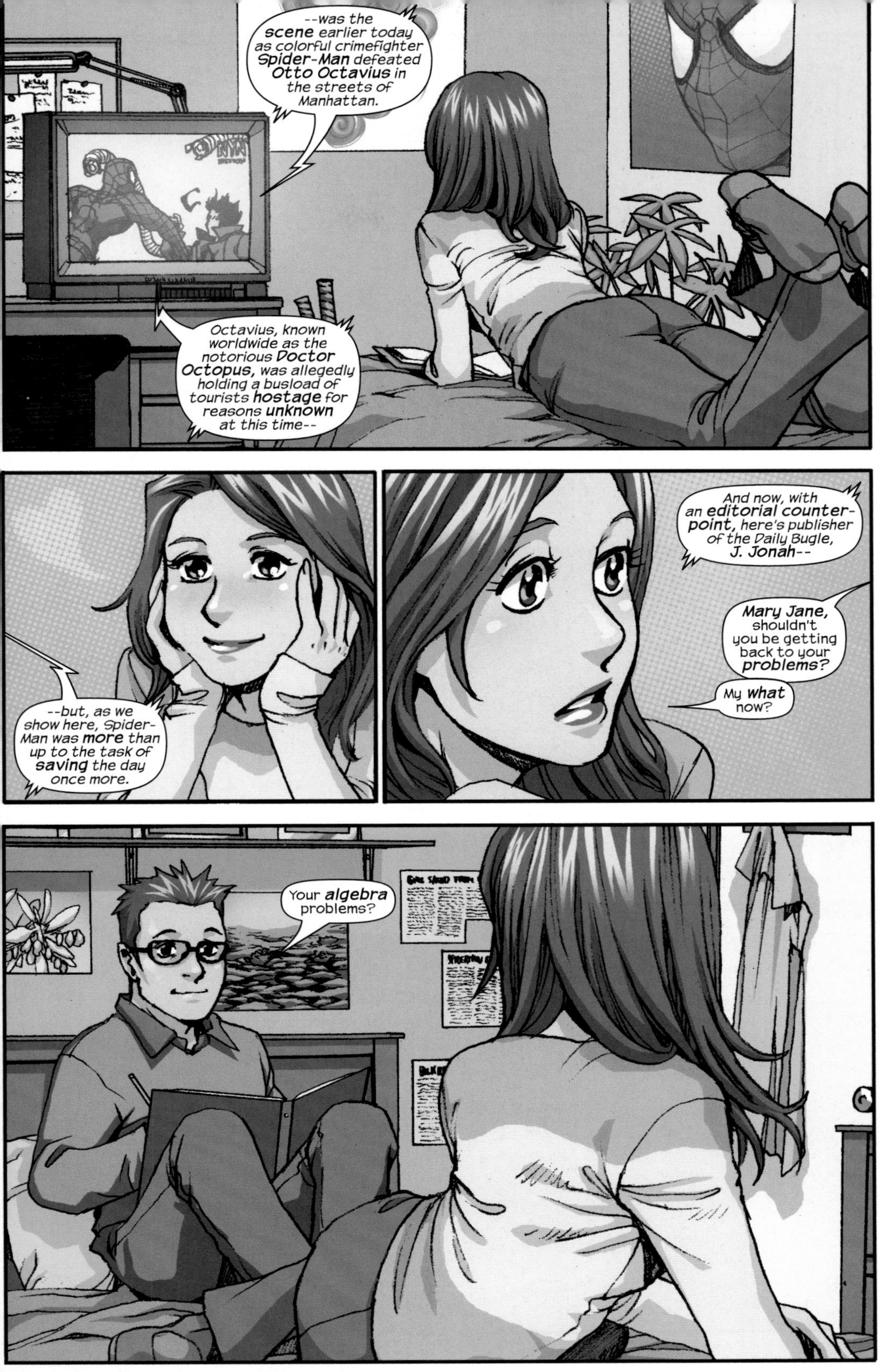
--was the scene earlier today as colorful crimefighter Spider-Man defeated Otto Octavius in the streets of Manhattan.
Octavius, known worldwide as the notorious Doctor Octopus, was allegedly holding a busload of tourists hostage for reasons unknown at this time--
--but, as we show here, Spider-Man was more than up to the task of saving the day once more.
And now, with an editorial counter-point, here's publisher of the Daily Bugle, J. Jonah--
Mary Jane, shouldn't you be getting back to your problems?
My what now?
Your algebra problems?

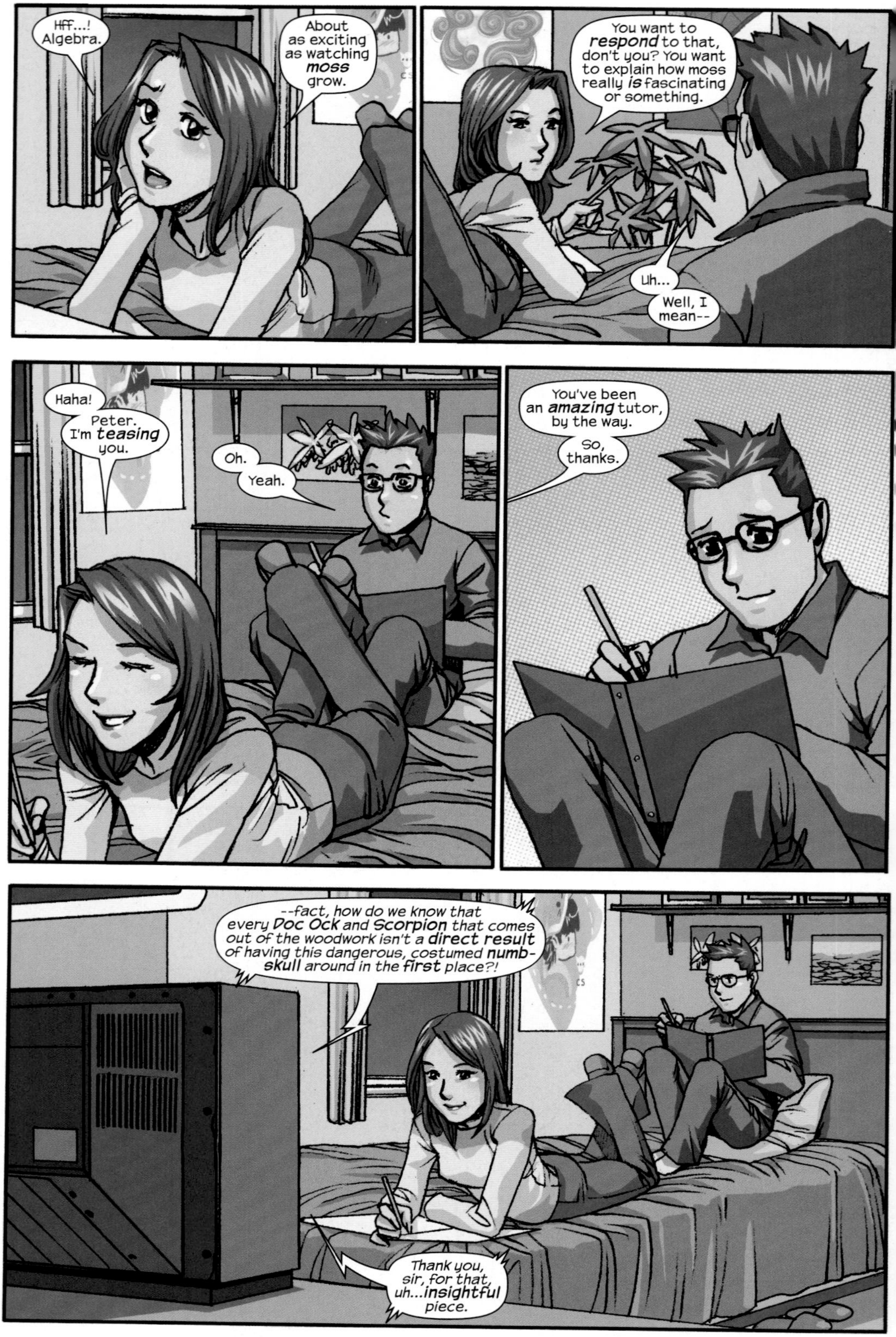
Hff...! Algebra.
About as exciting as watching moss grow.
You want to respond to that, don't you? You want to explain how moss really is fascinating or something.
Uh...
Well, I mean--
Haha!
Peter. I'm teasing you.
Oh.
Yeah.
You've been an amazing tutor, by the way.
So, thanks.
--fact, how do we know that every Doc Ock and Scorpion that comes out of the woodwork isn't a direct result of having this dangerous, costumed numb-skull around in the first place?!
Thank you, sir, for that, uh...insightful piece.

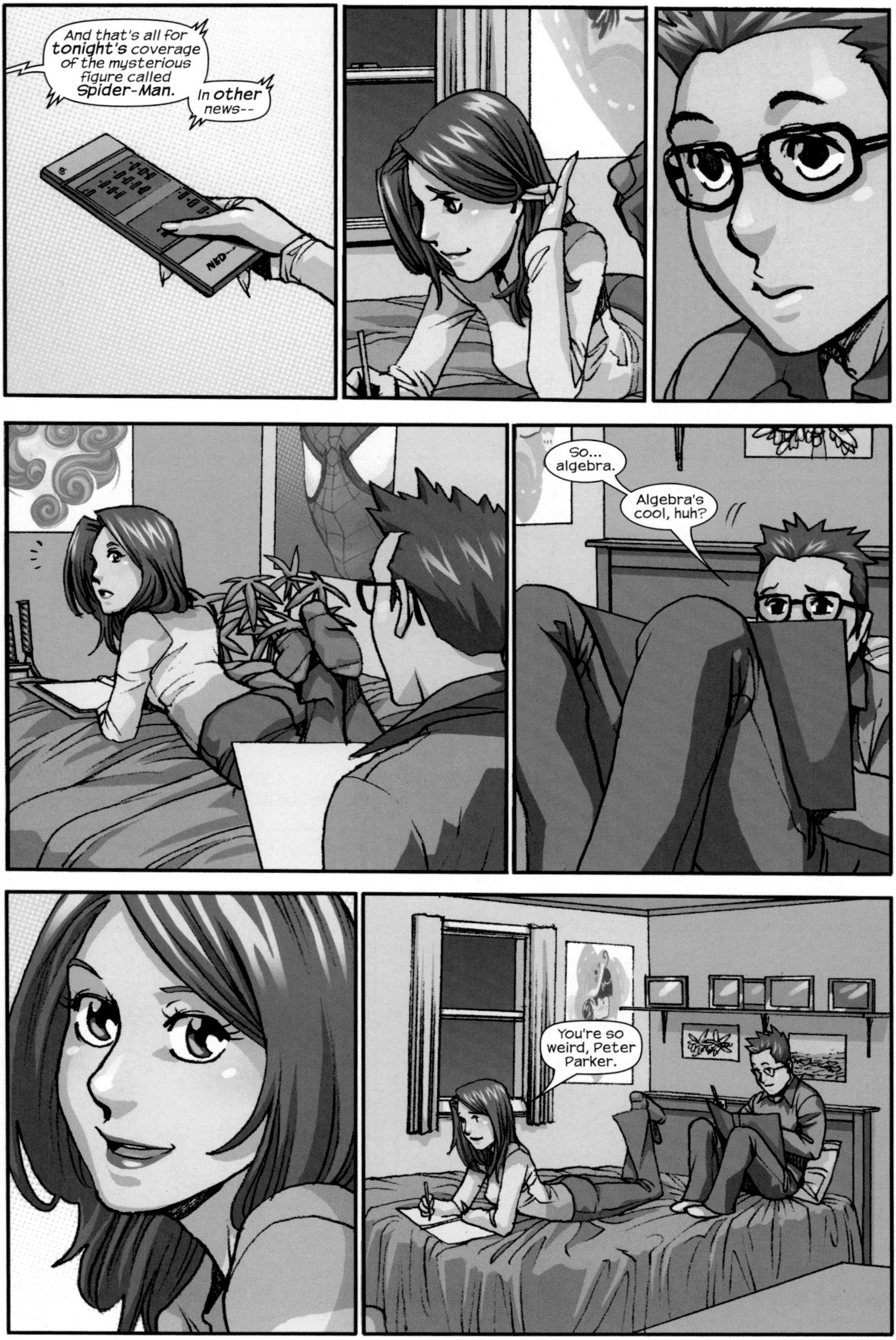
And that's all for tonight's coverage of the mysterious figure called Spider-Man.
In other news--
NED
So... algebra.
Algebra's cool, huh?
You're so weird, Peter Parker.

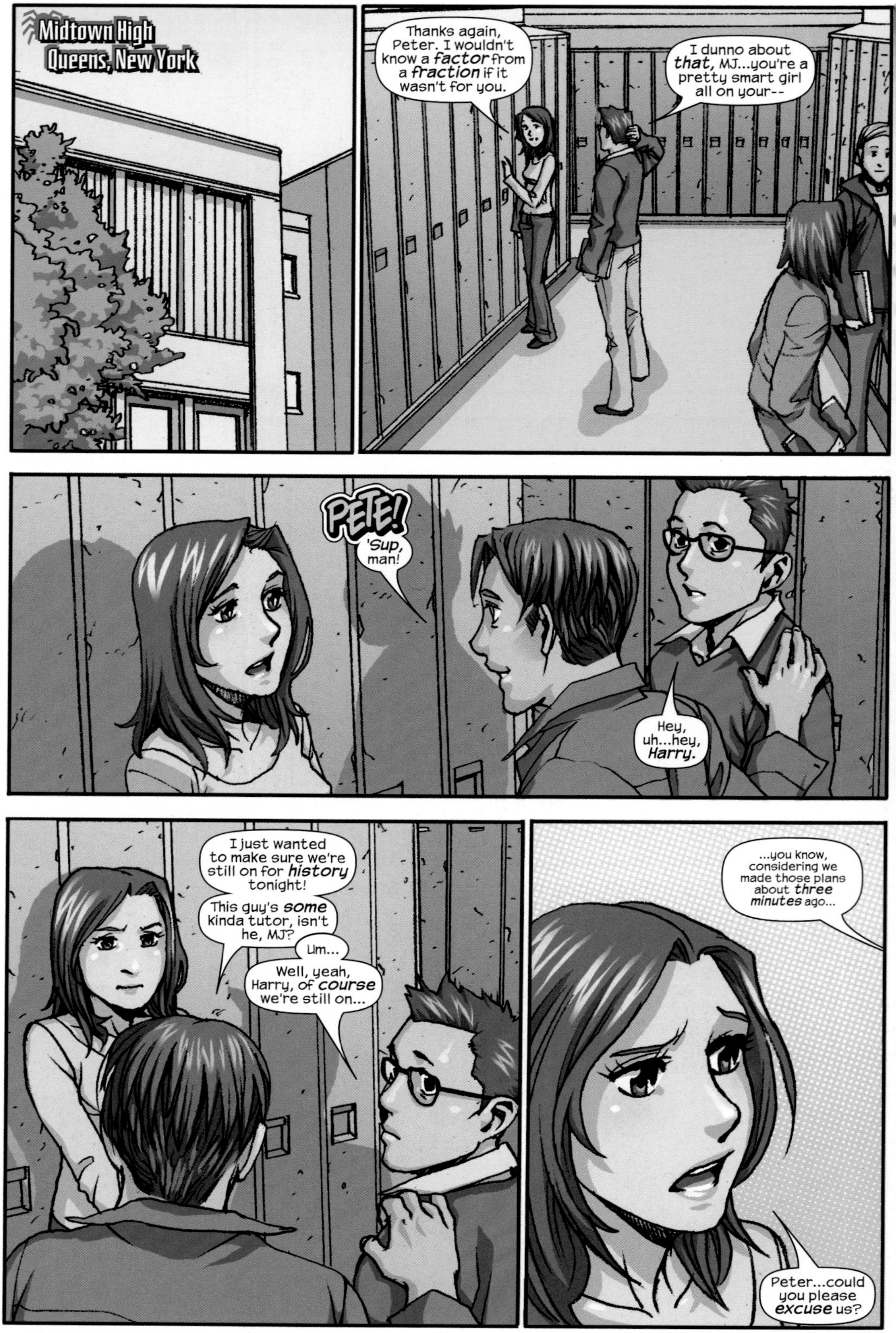

Midtown High
Queens, New York
Thanks again, Peter. I wouldn't know a factor from a fraction if it wasn't for you.
I dunno about that, MJ...you're a pretty smart girl all on your--
PETE!
'Sup, man!
Hey, uh...hey, Harry.
I just wanted to make sure we're still on for history tonight!
This guy's some kinda tutor, isn't he, MJ?
Um...
Well, yeah, Harry, of course we're still on...
...you know, considering we made those plans about three minutes ago...
Peter...could you please excuse us?

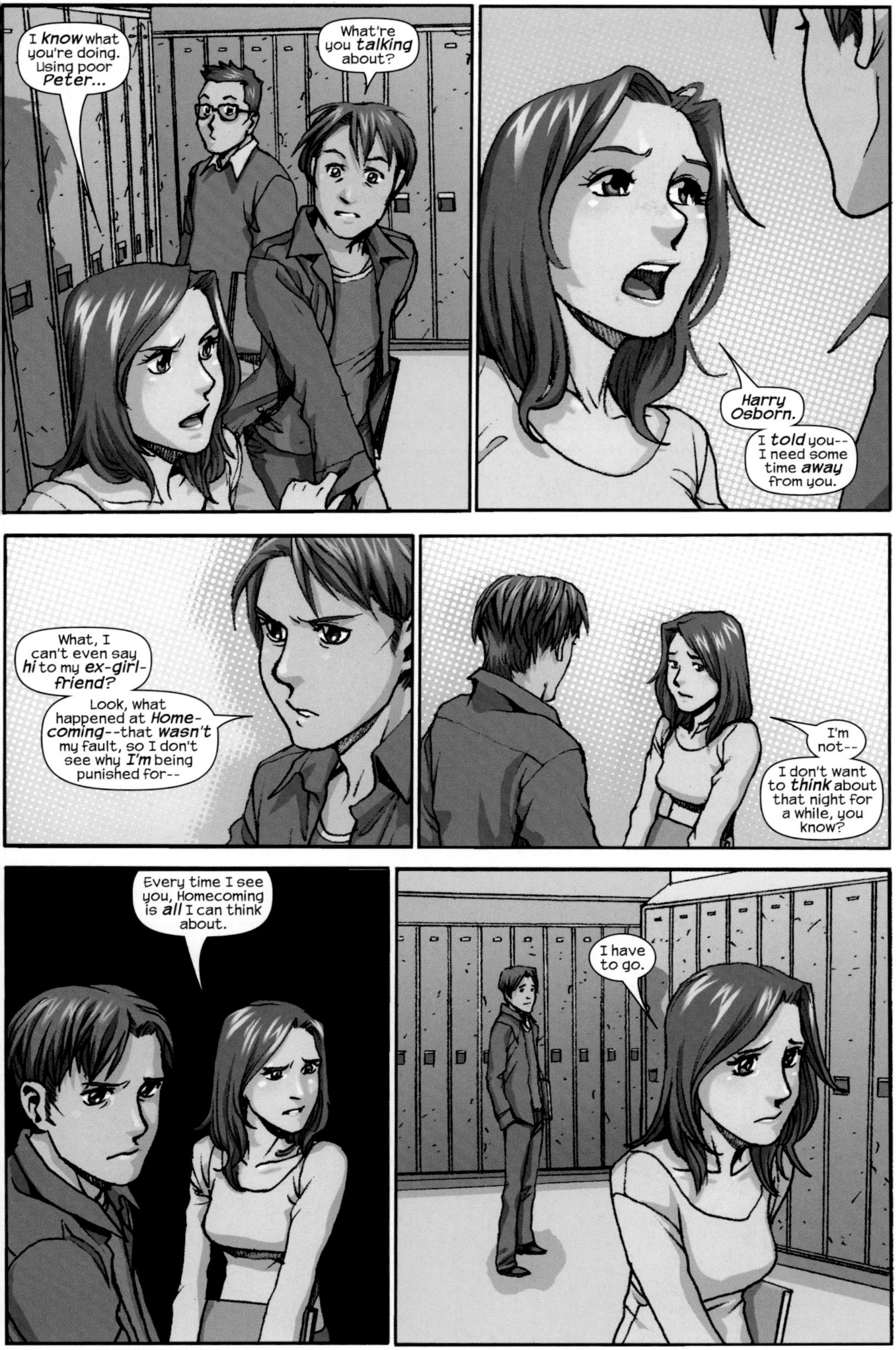

I know what you're doing. Using poor Peter...
What're you talking about?
Harry Osborn.
I told you-- I need some time away from you.
What, I can't even say hi to my ex-girlfriend?
Look, what happened at Homecoming--that wasn't my fault, so I don't see why I'm being punished for--
I'm not--
I don't want to think about that night for a while, you know?
Every time I see you, Homecoming is all I can think about.
I have to go.

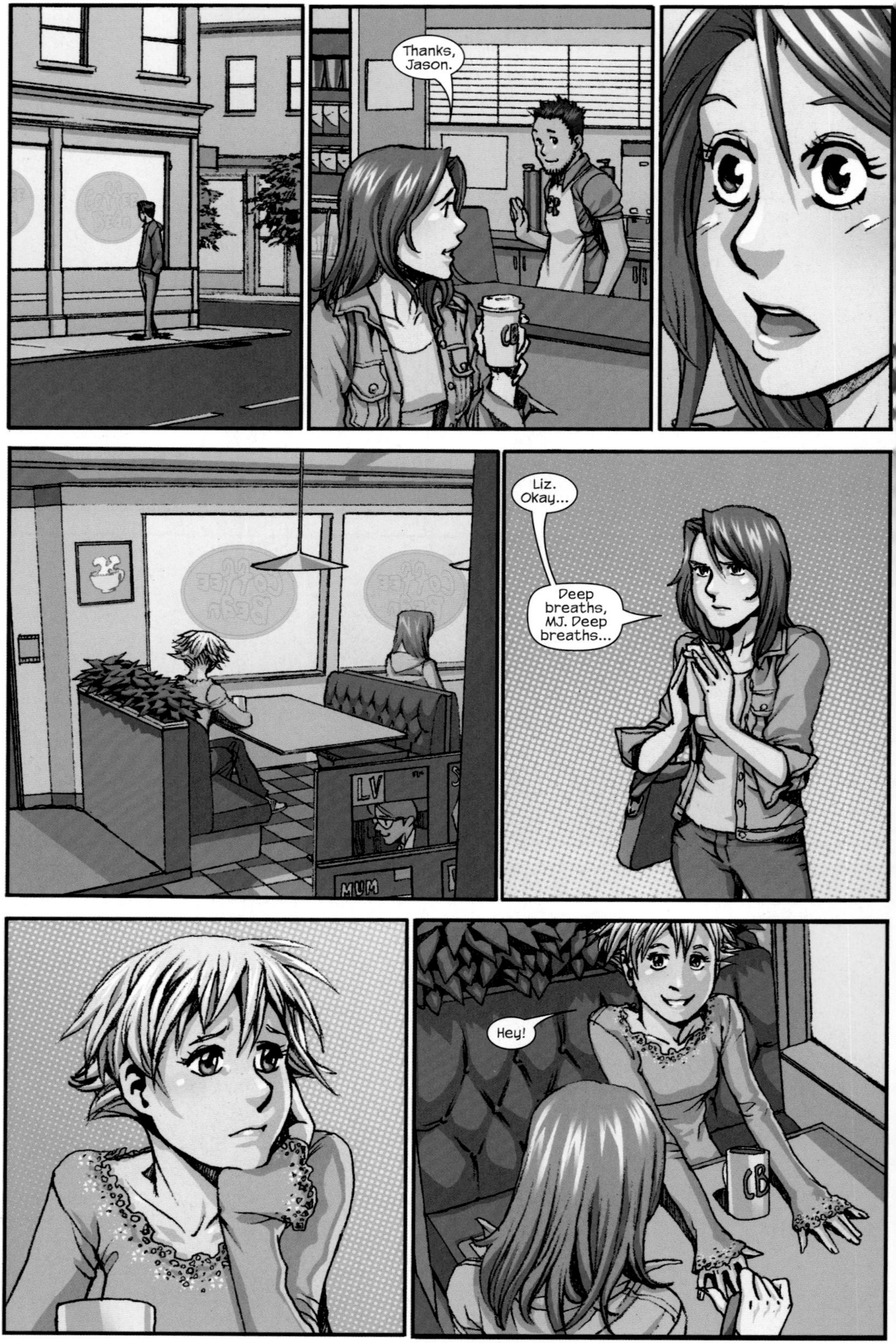

Thanks, Jason.
Liz. Okay...
Deep breaths, MJ. Deep breaths...
LV
MUM
Hey!

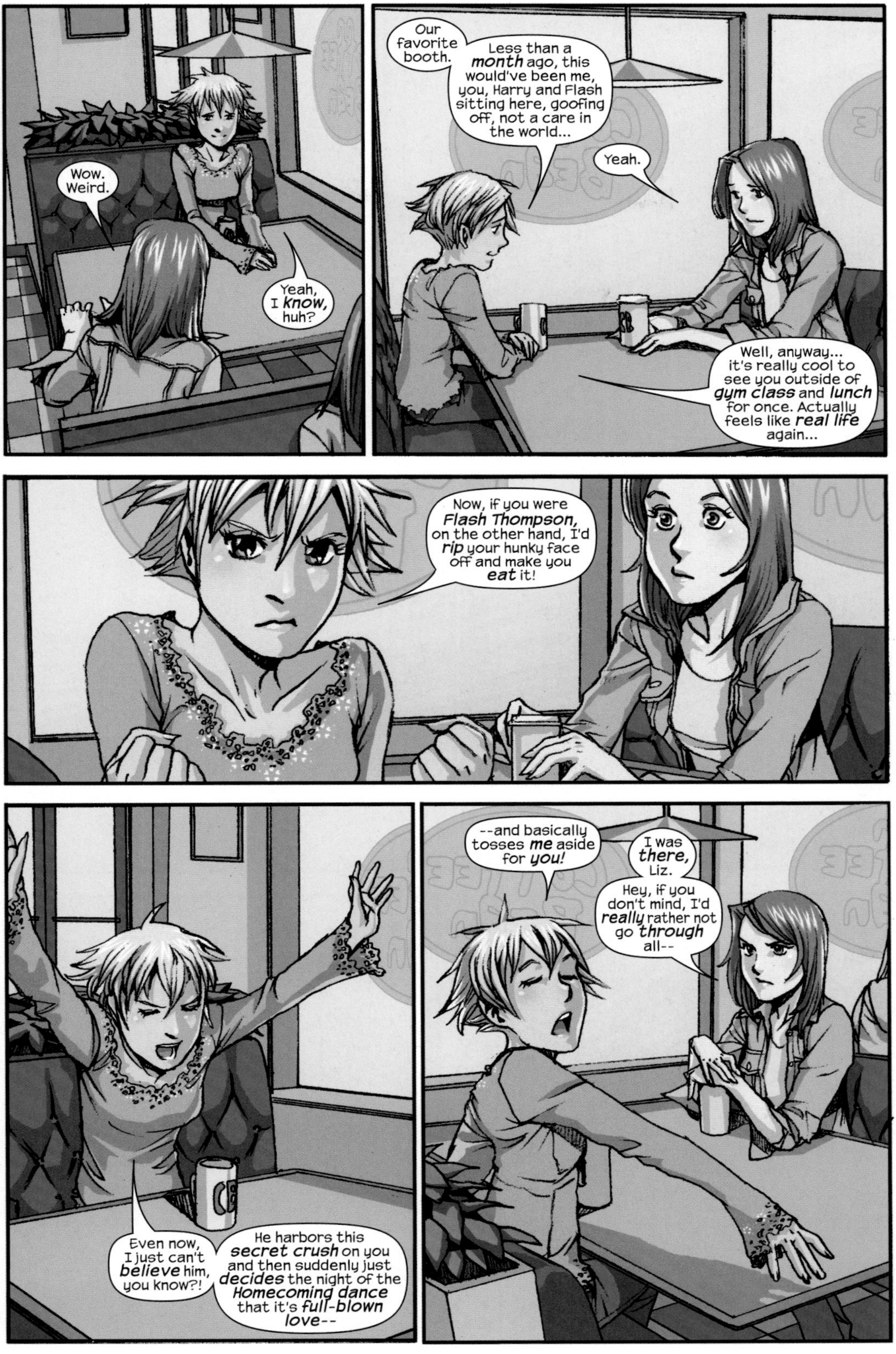
Wow. Weird.
Yeah, I know, huh?
Our favorite booth.
Less than a month ago, this would've been me, you, Harry and Flash sitting here, goofing off, not a care in the world...
Yeah.
Well, anyway... it's really cool to see you outside of gym class and lunch for once. Actually feels like real life again...
Now, if you were Flash Thompson, on the other hand, I'd rip your hunky face off and make you eat it!
Even now, I just can't believe him, you know?!
He harbors this secret crush on you and then suddenly just decides the night of the Homecoming dance that it's full-blown love--
--and basically tosses me aside for you!
I was there, Liz.
Hey, if you don't mind, I'd really rather not go through all--

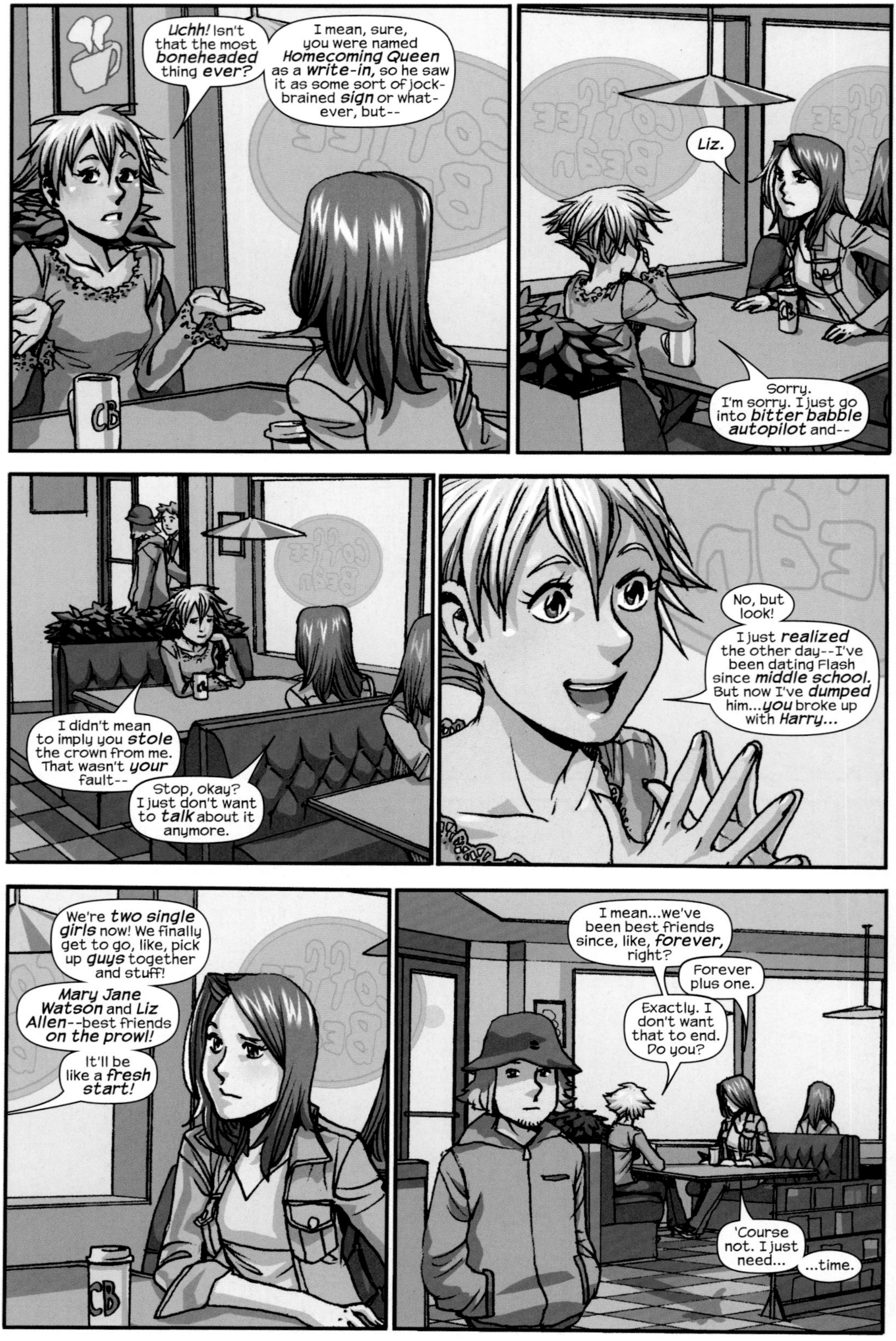

Uchh! Isn't that the most boneheaded thing ever?
I mean, sure, you were named Homecoming Queen as a write-in, so he saw it as some sort of jock-brained sign or what-ever, but--
Liz.
Sorry. I'm sorry. I just go into bitter babble autopilot and--
I didn't mean to imply you stole the crown from me. That wasn't your fault--
Stop, okay? I just don't want to talk about it anymore.
No, but look!
I just realized the other day--I've been dating Flash since middle school. But now I've dumped him...you broke up with Harry...
We're two single girls now! We finally get to go, like, pick up guys together and stuff!
Mary Jane Watson and Liz Allen--best friends on the prowl!
It'll be like a fresh start!
I mean...we've been best friends since, like, forever, right?
Forever plus one.
Exactly. I don't want that to end. Do you?
'Course not. I just need...
...time.

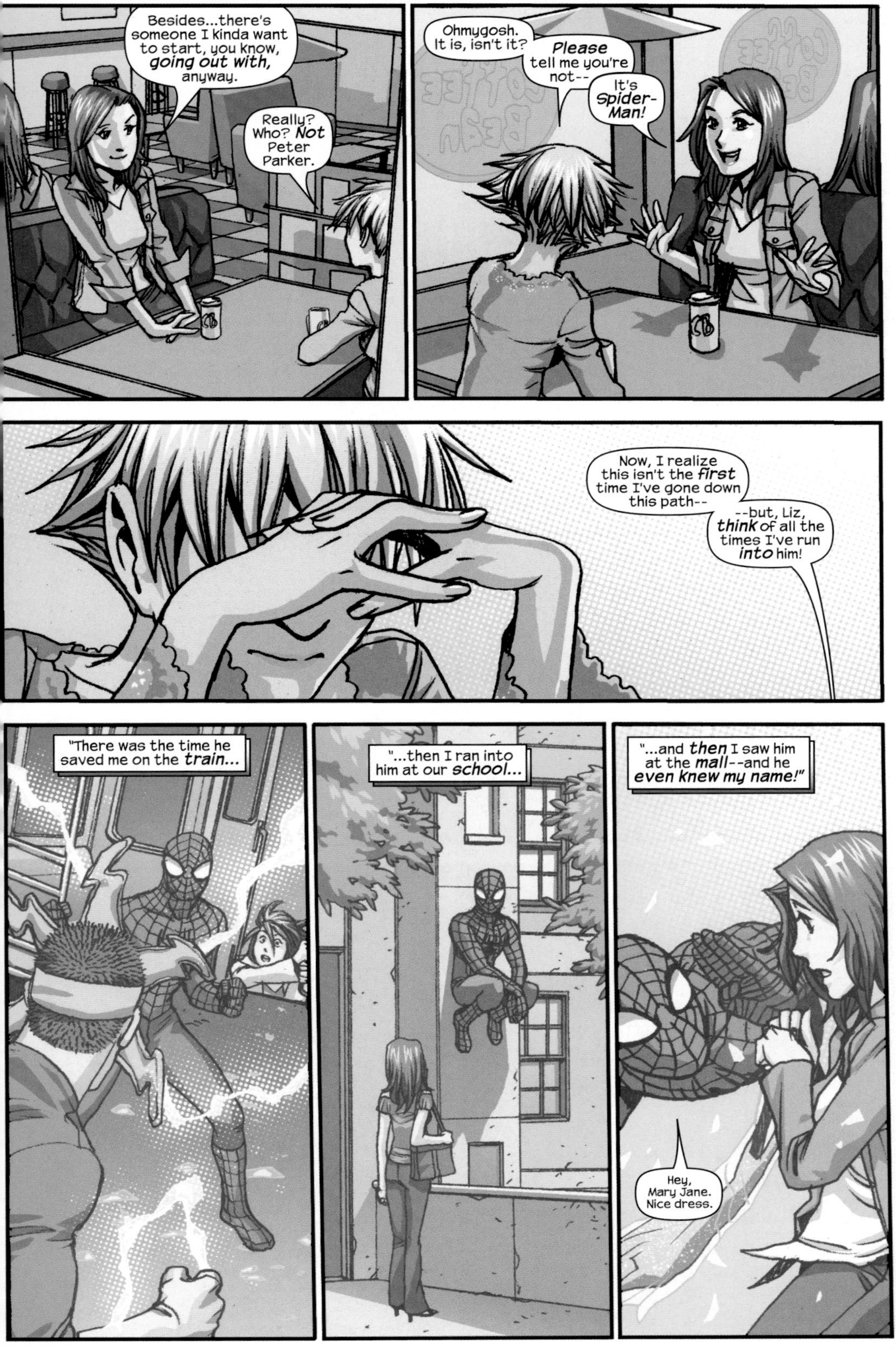

Besides...there's someone I kinda want to start, you know, going out with, anyway.
Really? Who? Not Peter Parker.
Ohmygosh. It is, isn't it?
Please tell me you're not--
It's Spider-Man!
Now, I realize this isn't the first time I've gone down this path--
--but, Liz, think of all the times I've run into him!
"There was the time he saved me on the train...
"...then I ran into him at our school...
"...and then I saw him at the mall--and he even knew my name!"
Hey, Mary Jane. Nice dress.

I mean, that's just too much of a *coincidence* for it to not *mean* something, right?

MJ...you have to *know* that what you're talking about isn't the *least bit realistic*, right? It would *never* happen.

Besides which, you don't know the *first thing* about him as a *person*. What if he's a *lunatic* or looks like that freaky *Gollum* guy under there?

Look, even if you *could* be Spider-Man's girlfriend, Mary Jane--

--the *last* thing you need right now is *another* boyfriend!

Oh, whatever. You're just being a *doofus*. That doesn't make the least bit of sense.

Yeah, whatever!

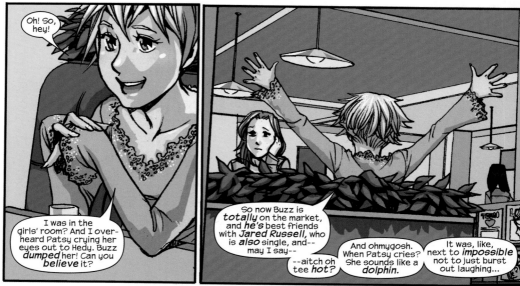

Oh! So, hey!

I was in the girls' room? And I over-heard Patsy crying her eyes out to Hedy. Buzz *dumped* her! Can you *believe* it?

So now Buzz is *totally* on the market, and *he's* best friends with *Jared Russell*, who is *also* single, and-- may I say-- --aitch oh tee *hot*?

And ohmygosh. When Patsy *cries*? She sounds like a *dolphin*.

It was, like, next to *impossible* not to just burst out laughing...

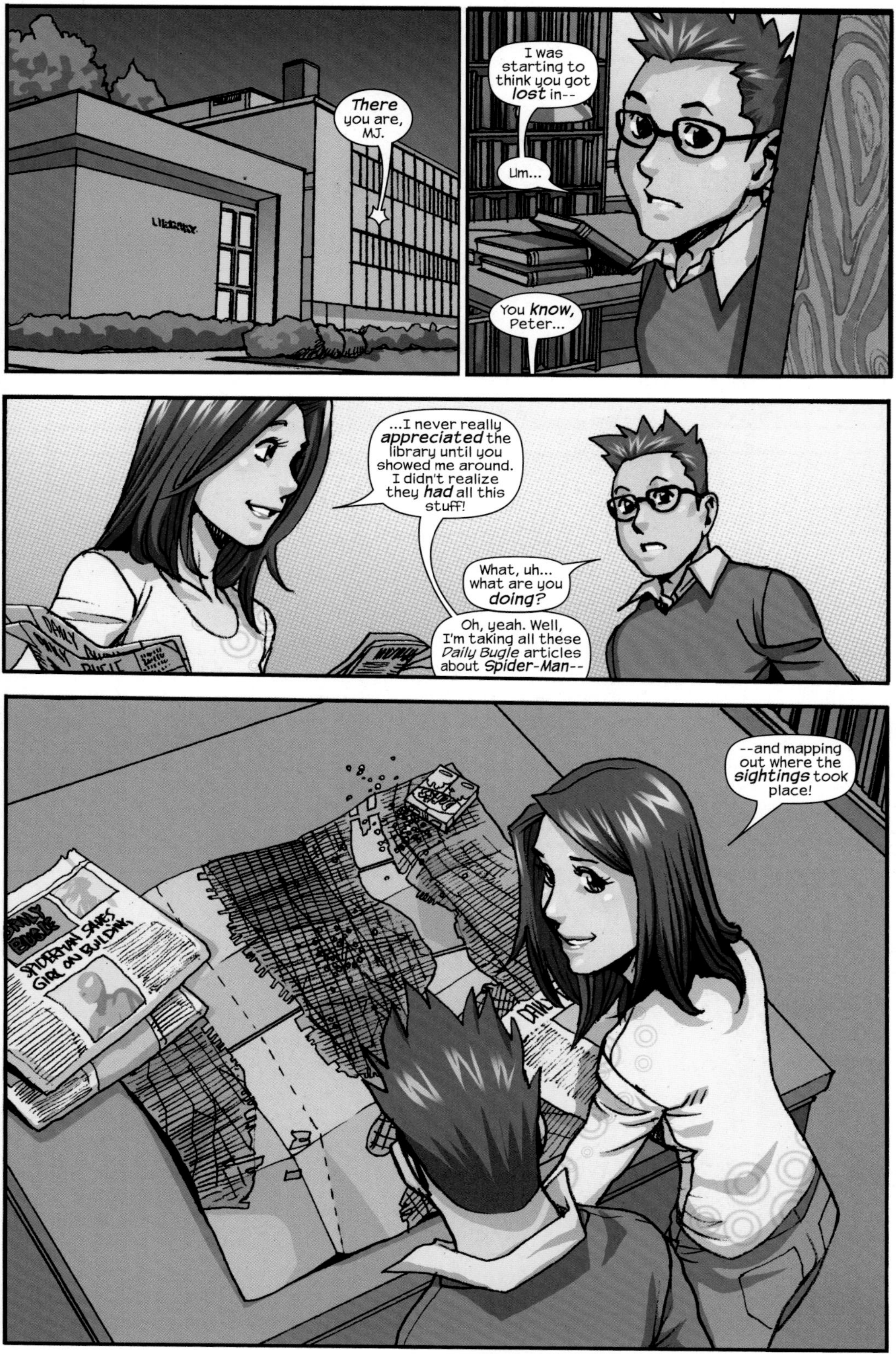
There you are, MJ.
I was starting to think you got *lost* in--
Um...
You *know,* Peter...
...I never really *appreciated* the library until you showed me around. I didn't realize they *had* all this stuff!
What, uh... what are you *doing?*
Oh, yeah. Well, I'm taking all these *Daily Bugle* articles about *Spider-Man*--
--and mapping out where the *sightings* took place!
DAILY BUGLE
SPIDERMAN SAVES GIRL ON BUILDING

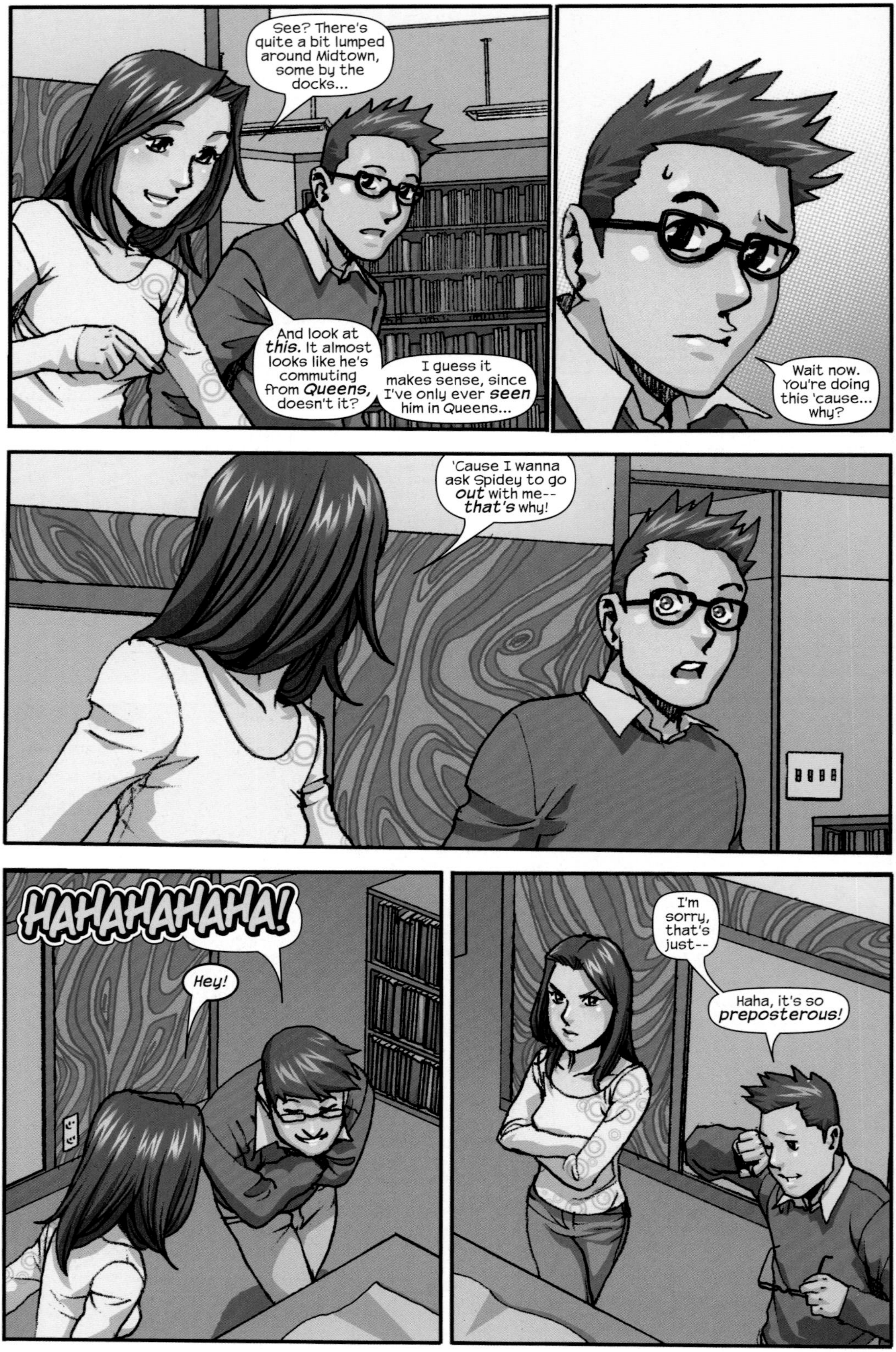
See? There's quite a bit lumped around Midtown, some by the docks...
And look at *this.* It almost looks like he's commuting from *Queens,* doesn't it?
I guess it makes sense, since I've only ever *seen* him in Queens...
Wait now. You're doing this 'cause... why?
'Cause I wanna ask Spidey to go *out* with me-- *that's* why!
HAHAHAHAHA!
Hey!
I'm sorry, that's just--
Haha, it's so *preposterous!*

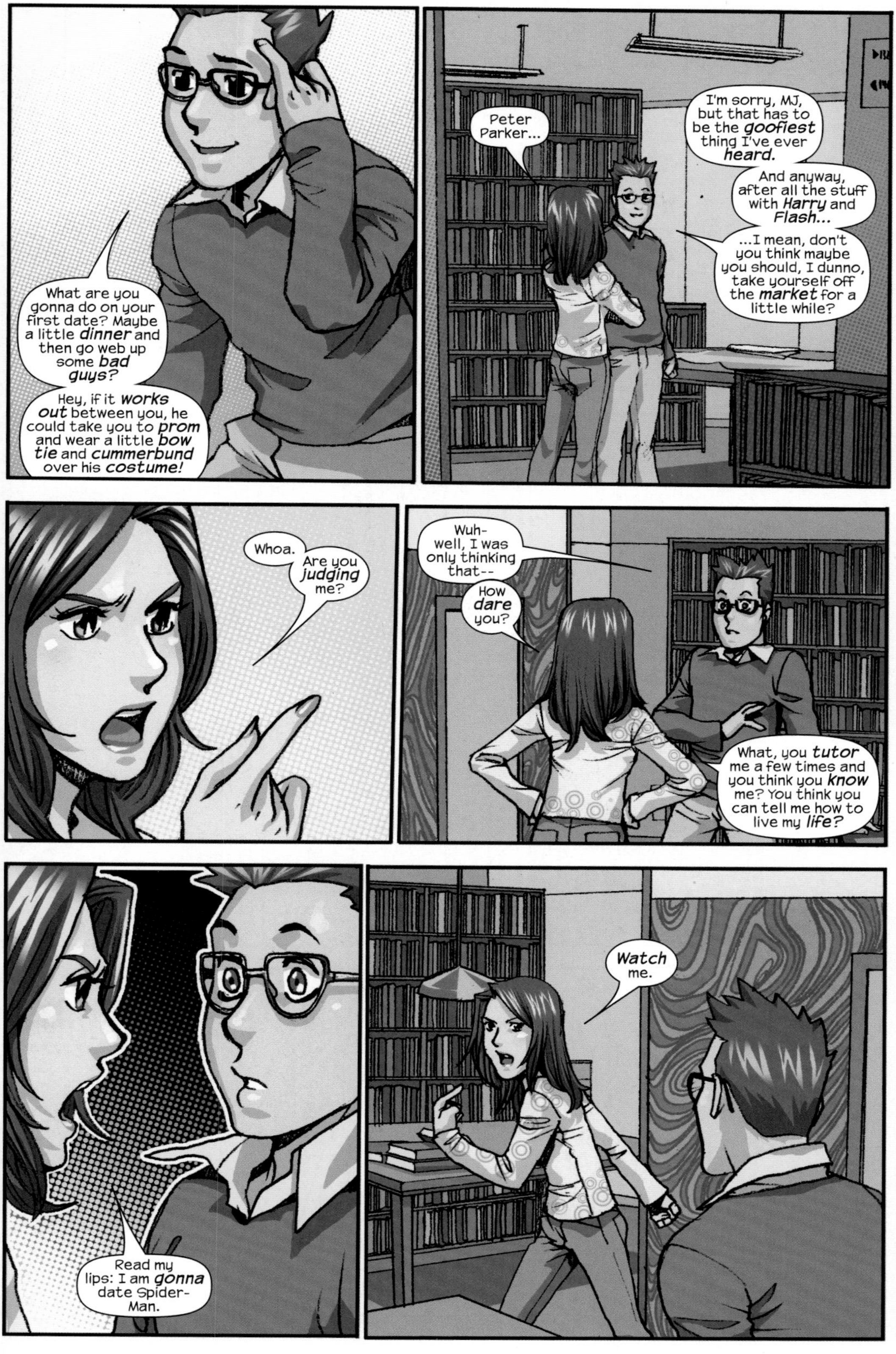
What are you gonna do on your first date? Maybe a little dinner and then go web up some bad guys?
Hey, if it works out between you, he could take you to prom and wear a little bow tie and cummerbund over his costume!
Peter Parker...
I'm sorry, MJ, but that has to be the goofiest thing I've ever heard.
And anyway, after all the stuff with Harry and Flash...
...I mean, don't you think maybe you should, I dunno, take yourself off the market for a little while?
Whoa. Are you judging me?
Wuh-well, I was only thinking that--
How dare you?
What, you tutor me a few times and you think you know me? You think you can tell me how to live my life?
Read my lips: I am gonna date Spider-Man.
Watch me.

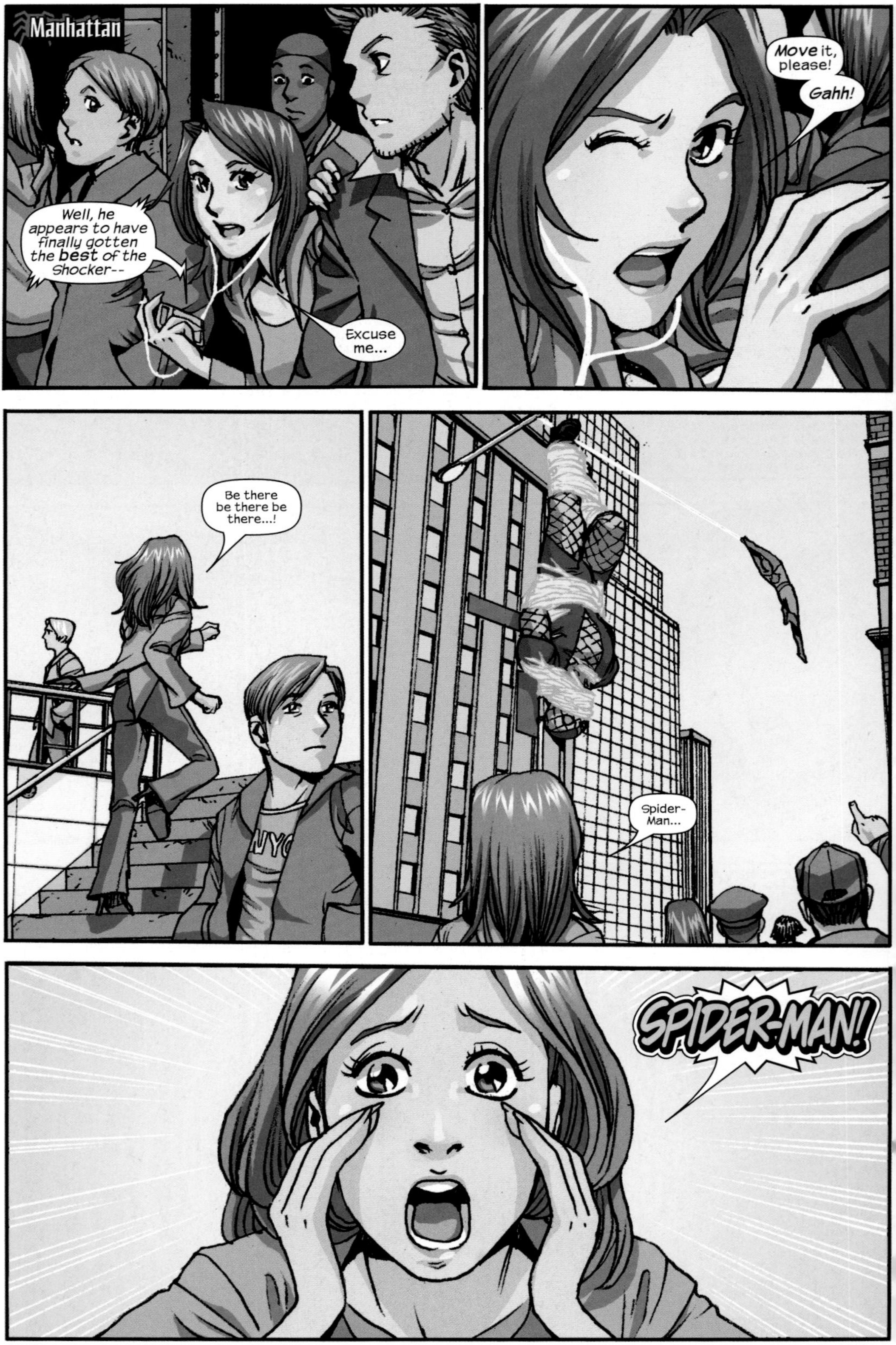
Manhattan
Well, he appears to have finally gotten the best of the Shocker--
Excuse me...
Move it, please!
Gahh!
Be there be there be there...!
Spider-Man...
SPIDER-MAN!

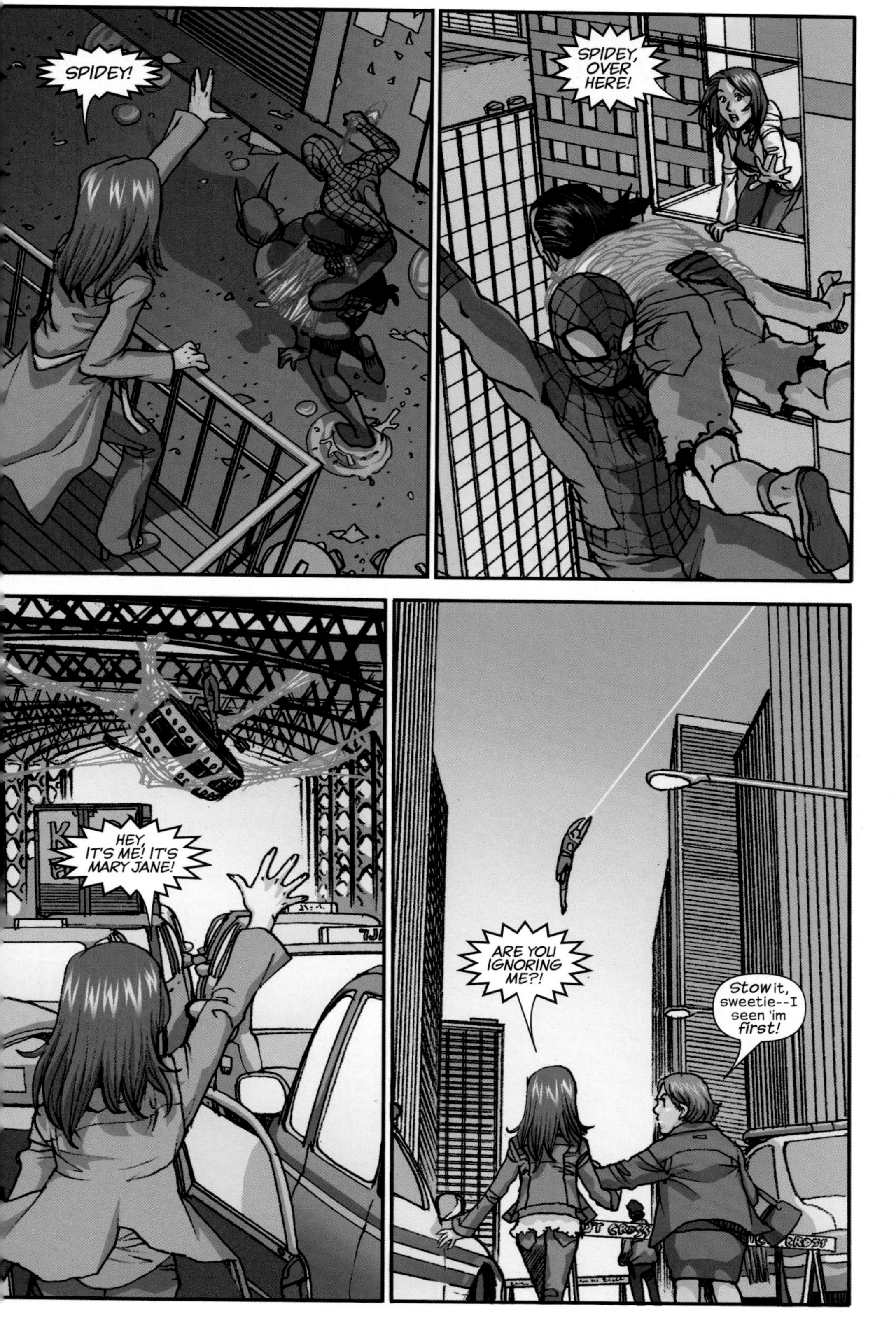
SPIDEY!
SPIDEY, OVER HERE!
HEY, IT'S ME! IT'S MARY JANE!
ARE YOU IGNORING ME?!
Stow it, sweetie--I seen 'im first!

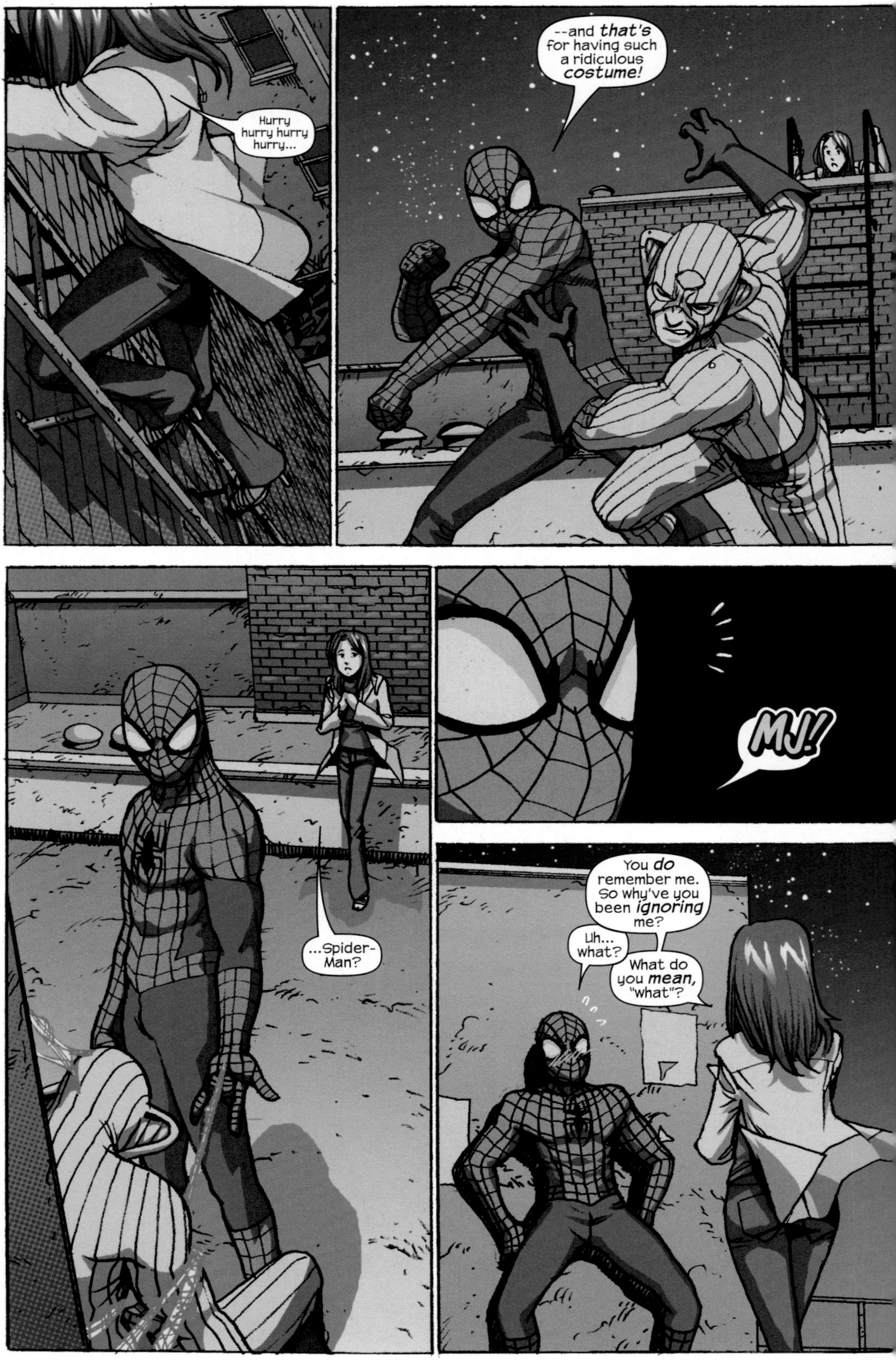
Hurry hurry hurry hurry...
--and that's for having such a ridiculous costume!
MJ!
...Spider-Man?
You do remember me. So why've you been ignoring me?
Uh... what?
What do you mean, "what"?

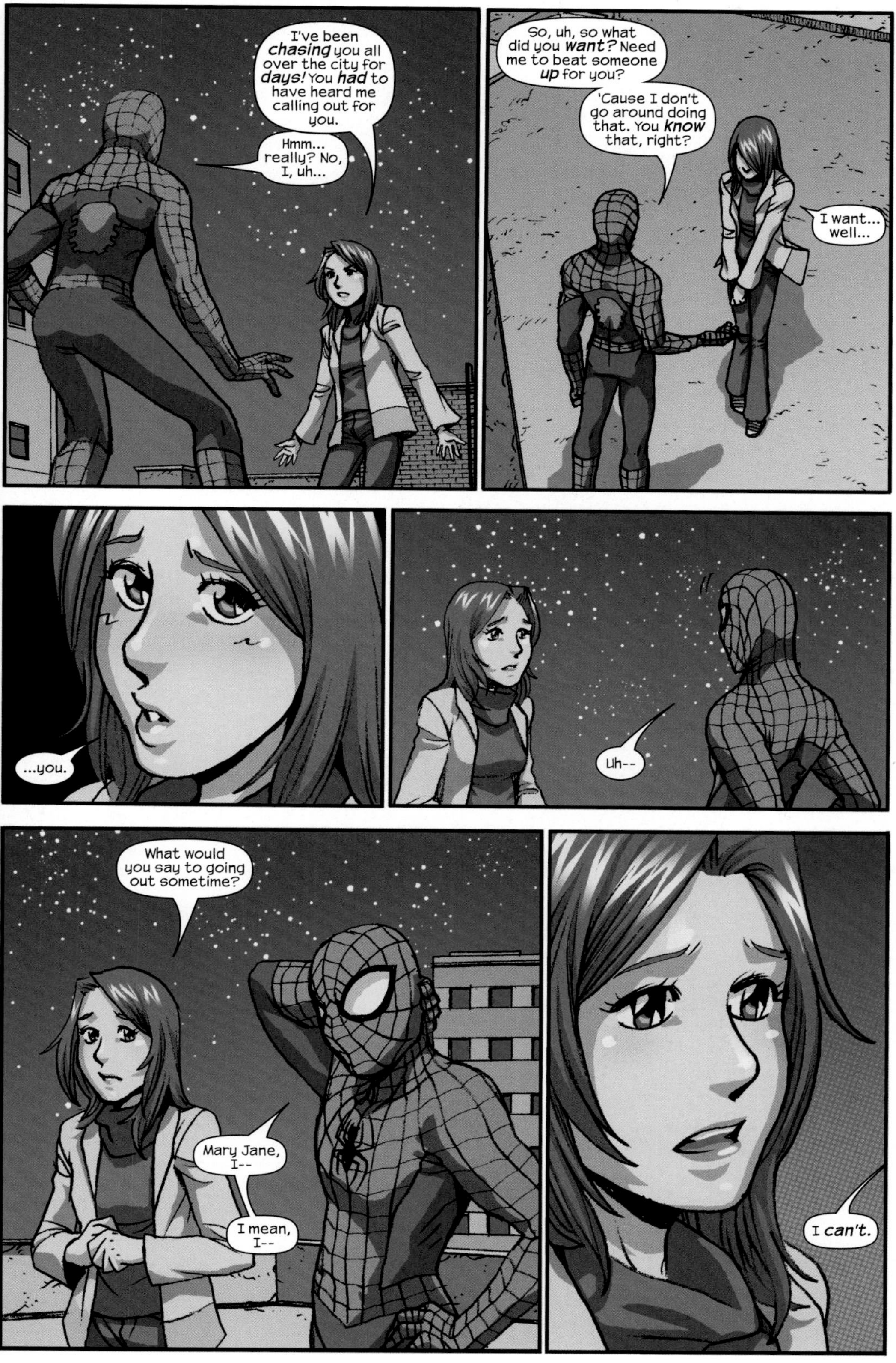
I've been chasing you all over the city for days! You had to have heard me calling out for you.
Hmm... really? No, I, uh...
So, uh, so what did you want? Need me to beat someone up for you?
'Cause I don't go around doing that. You know that, right?
I want... well...
...you.
Uh--
What would you say to going out sometime?
Mary Jane, I--
I mean, I--
I can't.

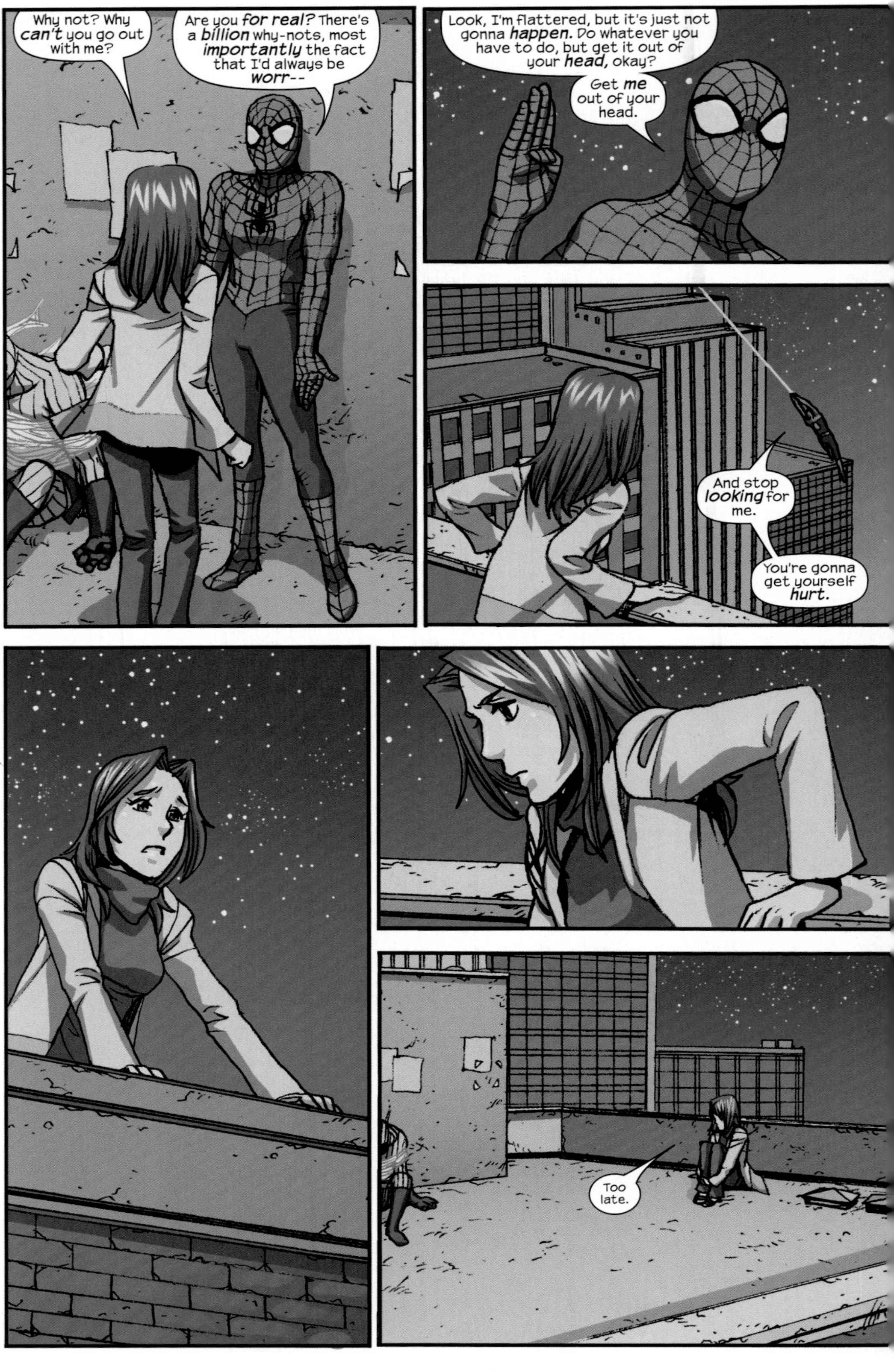
Why not? Why *can't* you go out with me?
Are you ***for real?*** There's a ***billion*** why-nots, most ***importantly*** the fact that I'd always be ***worr--***
Look, I'm flattered, but it's just not gonna ***happen.*** Do whatever you have to do, but get it out of your ***head,*** okay?
Get ***me*** out of your head.
And stop ***looking*** for me.
You're gonna get yourself ***hurt.***
Too late.

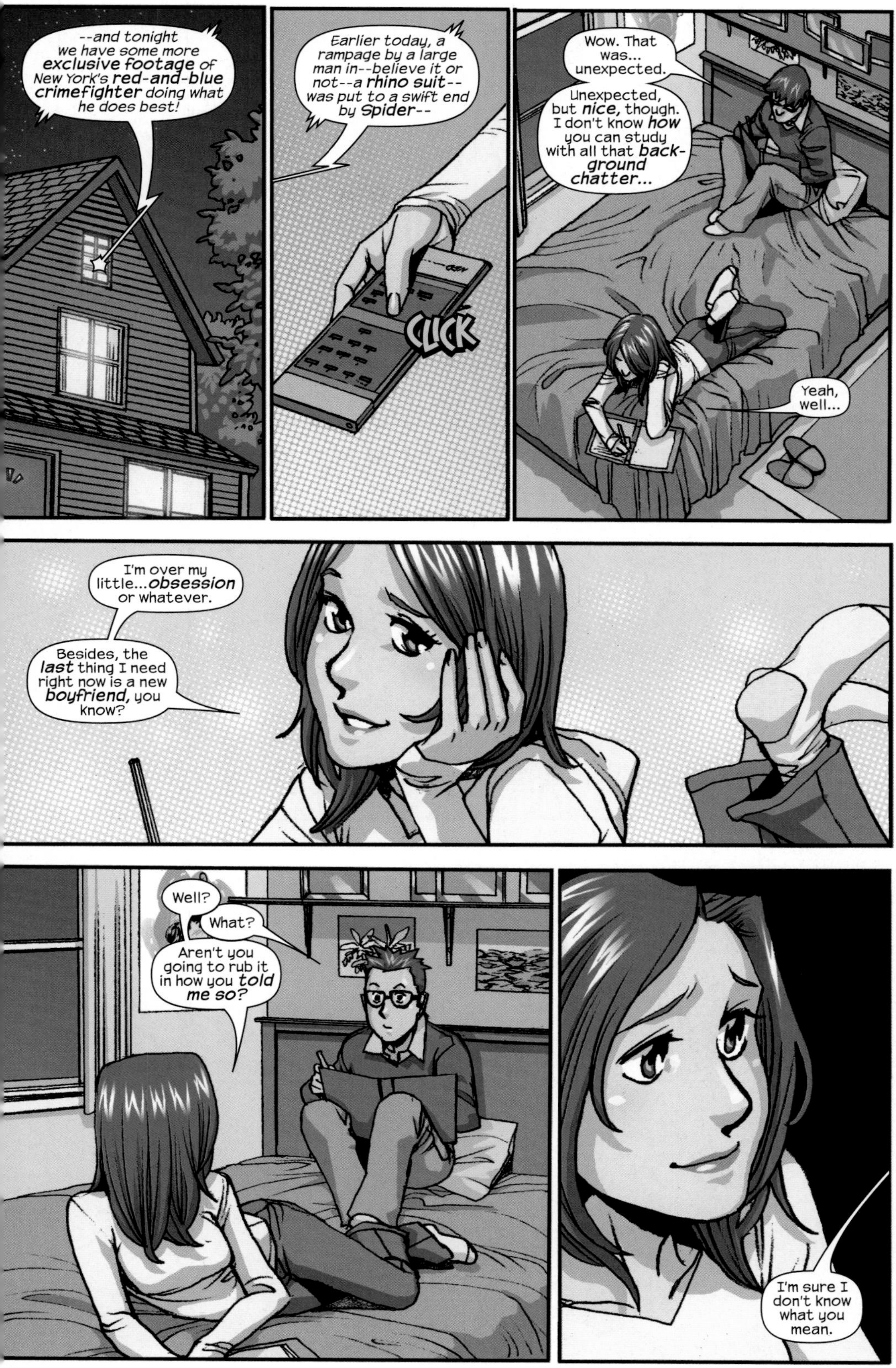
--and tonight we have some more exclusive footage of New York's red-and-blue crimefighter doing what he does best!
Earlier today, a rampage by a large man in--believe it or not--a rhino suit--was put to a swift end by Spider--
CLICK
Wow. That was... unexpected.
Unexpected, but nice, though. I don't know how you can study with all that back-ground chatter...
Yeah, well...
I'm over my little...obsession or whatever.
Besides, the last thing I need right now is a new boyfriend, you know?
Well?
What?
Aren't you going to rub it in how you told me so?
I'm sure I don't know what you mean.

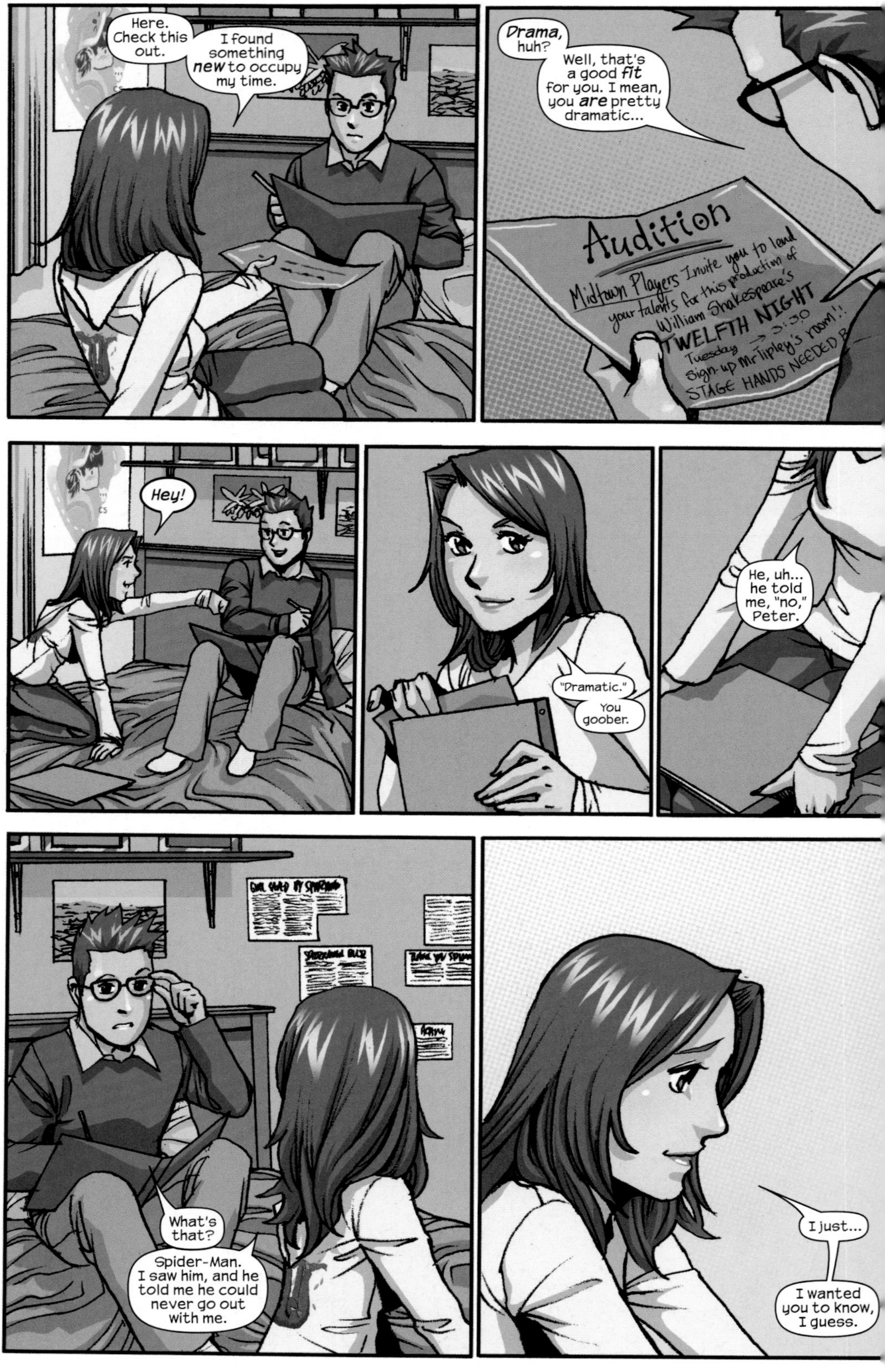
Here. Check this out.
I found something *new* to occupy my time.
Drama, huh?
Well, that's a good *fit* for you. I mean, you *are* pretty dramatic...
Audition
Midtown Players Invite you to lend your talents for this production of William Shakespeare's
TWELFTH NIGHT
Tuesday → 3:30
Sign-up Mr Tipley's room!!
STAGE HANDS NEEDED
Hey!
"Dramatic." You goober.
He, uh... he told me, "no," Peter.
What's that?
Spider-Man. I saw him, and he told me he could never go out with me.
I just...
I wanted you to know, I guess.

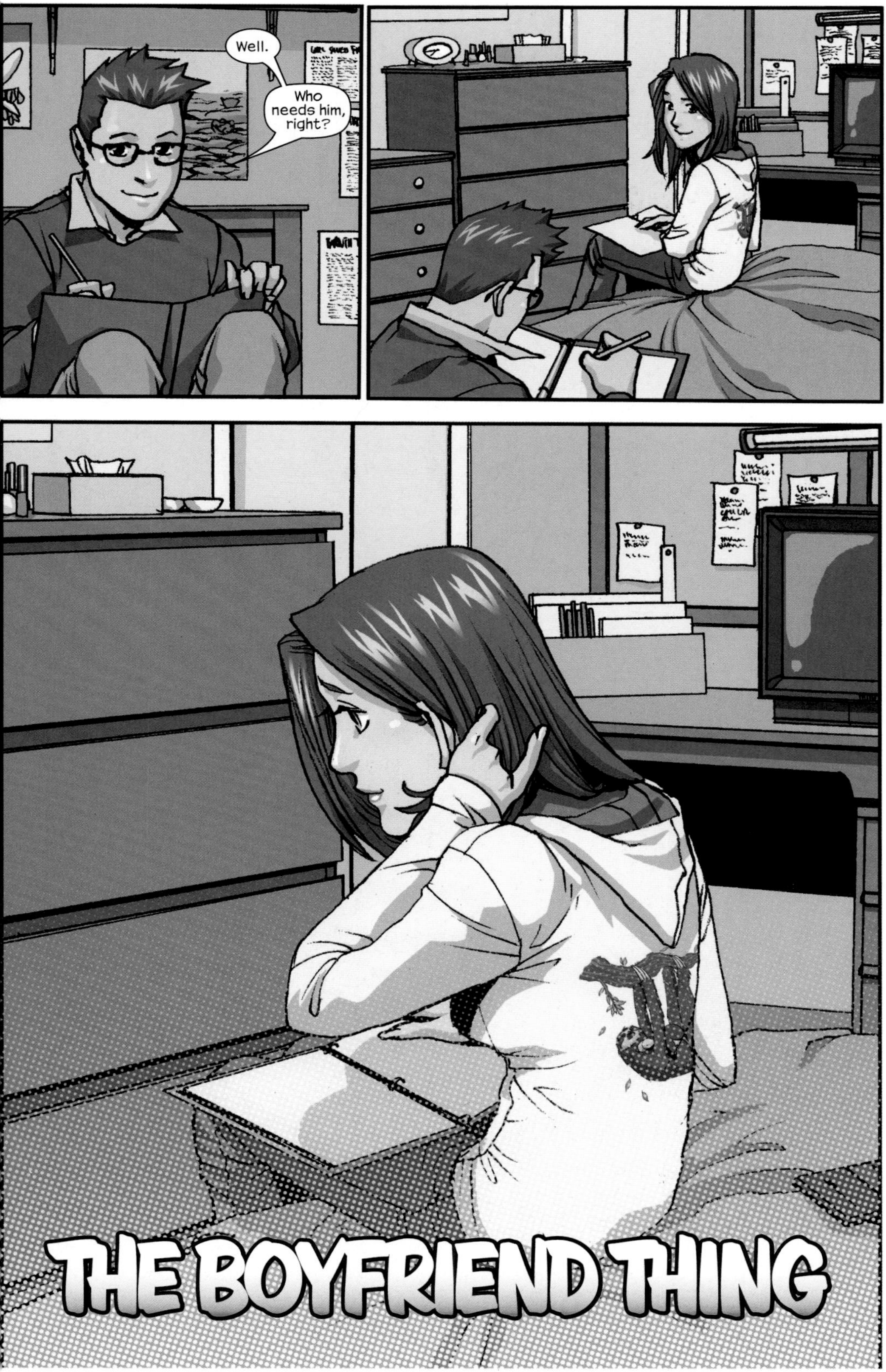
Well.
Who needs him, right?
THE BOYFRIEND THING

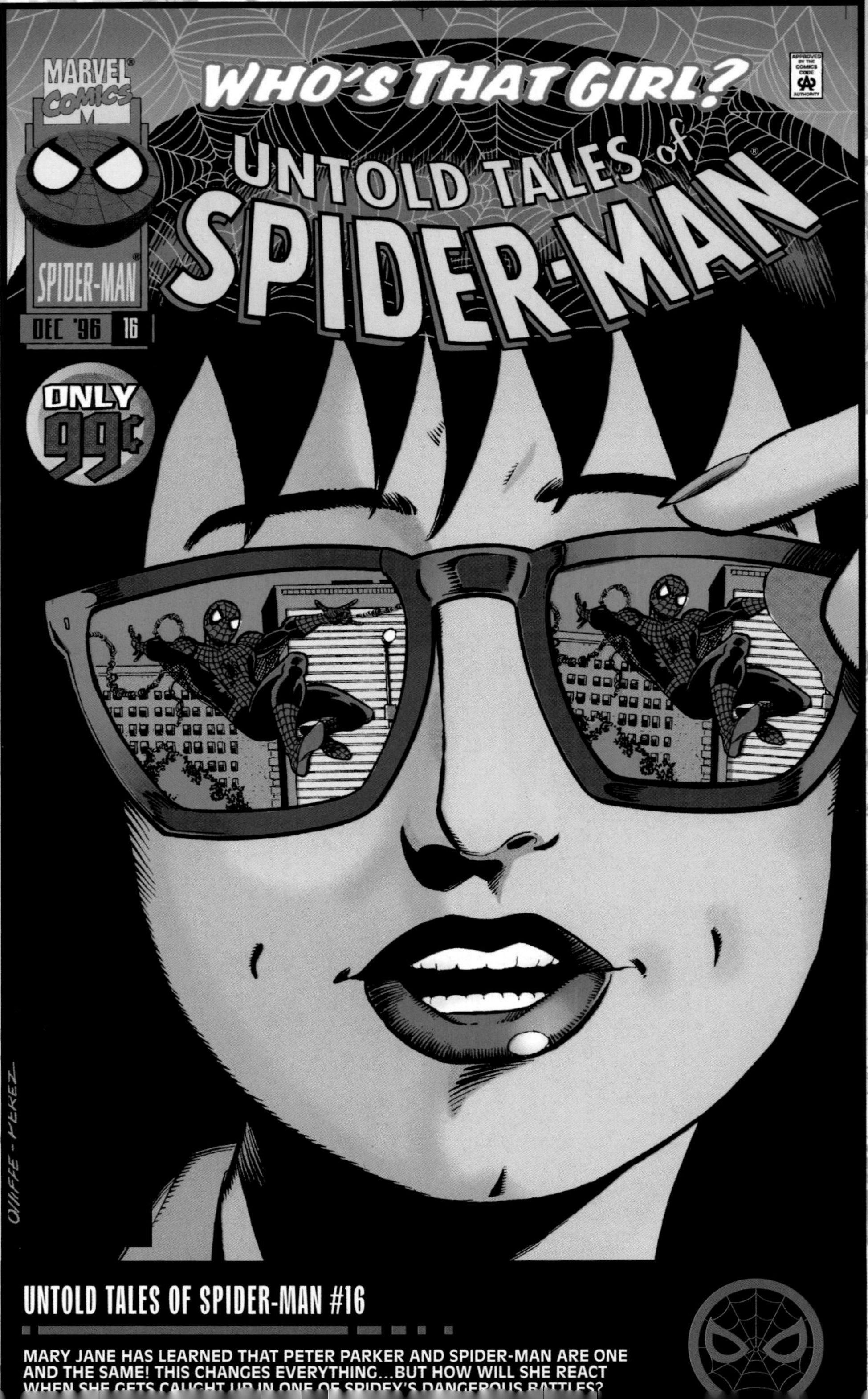
MARVEL COMICS
WHO'S THAT GIRL?
UNTOLD TALES of SPIDER-MAN
SPIDER-MAN
DEC '96 16
ONLY 99¢
APPROVED BY THE COMICS CODE AUTHORITY

UNTOLD TALES OF SPIDER-MAN #16

MARY JANE HAS LEARNED THAT PETER PARKER AND SPIDER-MAN ARE ONE AND THE SAME! THIS CHANGES EVERYTHING...BUT HOW WILL SHE REACT WHEN SHE GETS CAUGHT UP IN ONE OF SPIDEY'S DANGEROUS BATTLES?

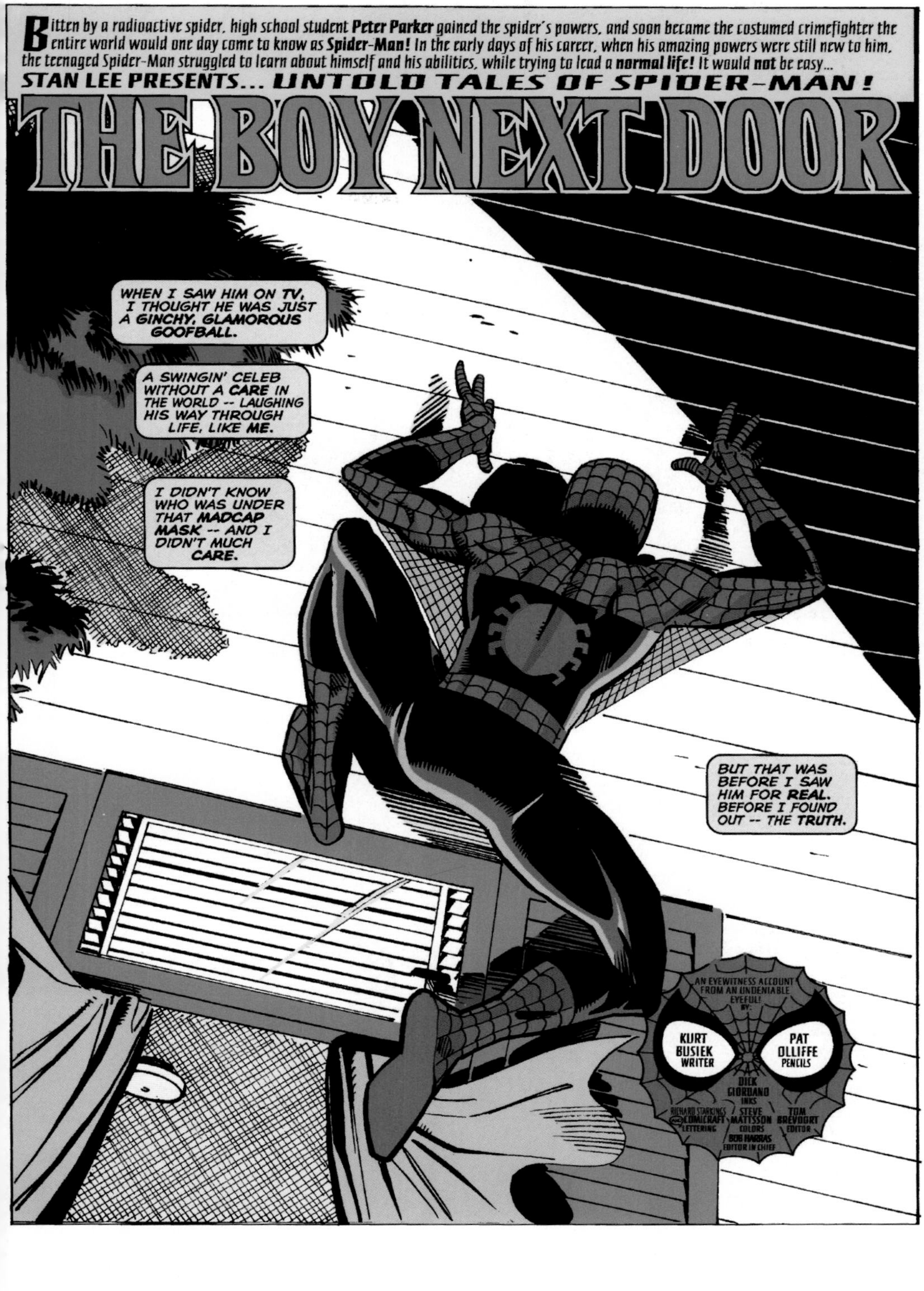
Bitten by a radioactive spider, high school student Peter Parker gained the spider's powers, and soon became the costumed crimefighter the entire world would one day come to know as Spider-Man! In the early days of his career, when his amazing powers were still new to him, the teenaged Spider-Man struggled to learn about himself and his abilities, while trying to lead a normal life! It would not be easy...
STAN LEE PRESENTS... UNTOLD TALES OF SPIDER-MAN!
THE BOY NEXT DOOR
WHEN I SAW HIM ON TV, I THOUGHT HE WAS JUST A GINCHY, GLAMOROUS GOOFBALL.
A SWINGIN' CELEB WITHOUT A CARE IN THE WORLD -- LAUGHING HIS WAY THROUGH LIFE, LIKE ME.
I DIDN'T KNOW WHO WAS UNDER THAT MADCAP MASK -- AND I DIDN'T MUCH CARE.
BUT THAT WAS BEFORE I SAW HIM FOR REAL. BEFORE I FOUND OUT -- THE TRUTH.
AN EYEWITNESS ACCOUNT FROM AN UNDENIABLE EYEFUL! BY:
KURT BUSIEK WRITER
PAT OLLIFFE PENCILS
DICK GIORDANO INKS
RICHARD STARKINGS AND COMICRAFT LETTERING
STEVE MATTSSON COLORS
TOM BREVOORT EDITOR
BOB HARRAS EDITOR IN CHIEF

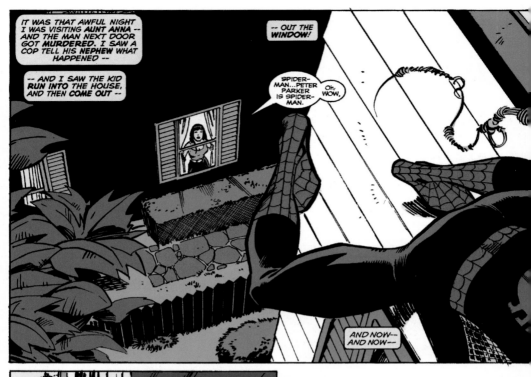

IT WAS THAT AWFUL NIGHT I WAS VISITING *AUNT ANNA* -- AND THE MAN NEXT DOOR GOT *MURDERED.* I SAW A COP TELL HIS *NEPHEW* WHAT HAPPENED --

-- AND I SAW THE KID *RUN INTO* THE HOUSE, AND THEN *COME OUT* --

-- OUT THE *WINDOW!*

SPIDER-MAN...PETER PARKER IS SPIDER-MAN.

Oh, WOW.

AND NOW-- AND NOW--

A *BLIND DATE?* AUNT ANNA, I HAVE HALF THE GUYS IN SCHOOL BACK HOME DROOLING ON MY *SHOES!*

THE *LAST* THING I NEED IS A NIGHT OUT WITH SOME *GEEK* WHO CAN'T GET A DATE ON HIS OWN!

I'D HARDLY CALL PETER PARKER A *"GEEK,"* MARY JANE. HE'S A QUIET, *SENSITIVE* BOY.

YEAH, SO WAS MY DAD. *SAVE* ME FROM SENSITIVE BOYS.

MARY JANE, YOU *CAN'T* COMPARE PETER PARKER WITH YOUR FATHER. PETER IS SO *RESPONSIBLE.*

HEY, JUST *KIDDING.* LOOK, I'M MEETING SOME KIDS AT THE *MALL.* WE'LL TALK LATER, OKAY?

MARY JANE -- DON'T GO! IF YOU'RE *UPSET* --!

Oh, DON'T YOU WORRY ABOUT *ME,* AUNT ANNA --

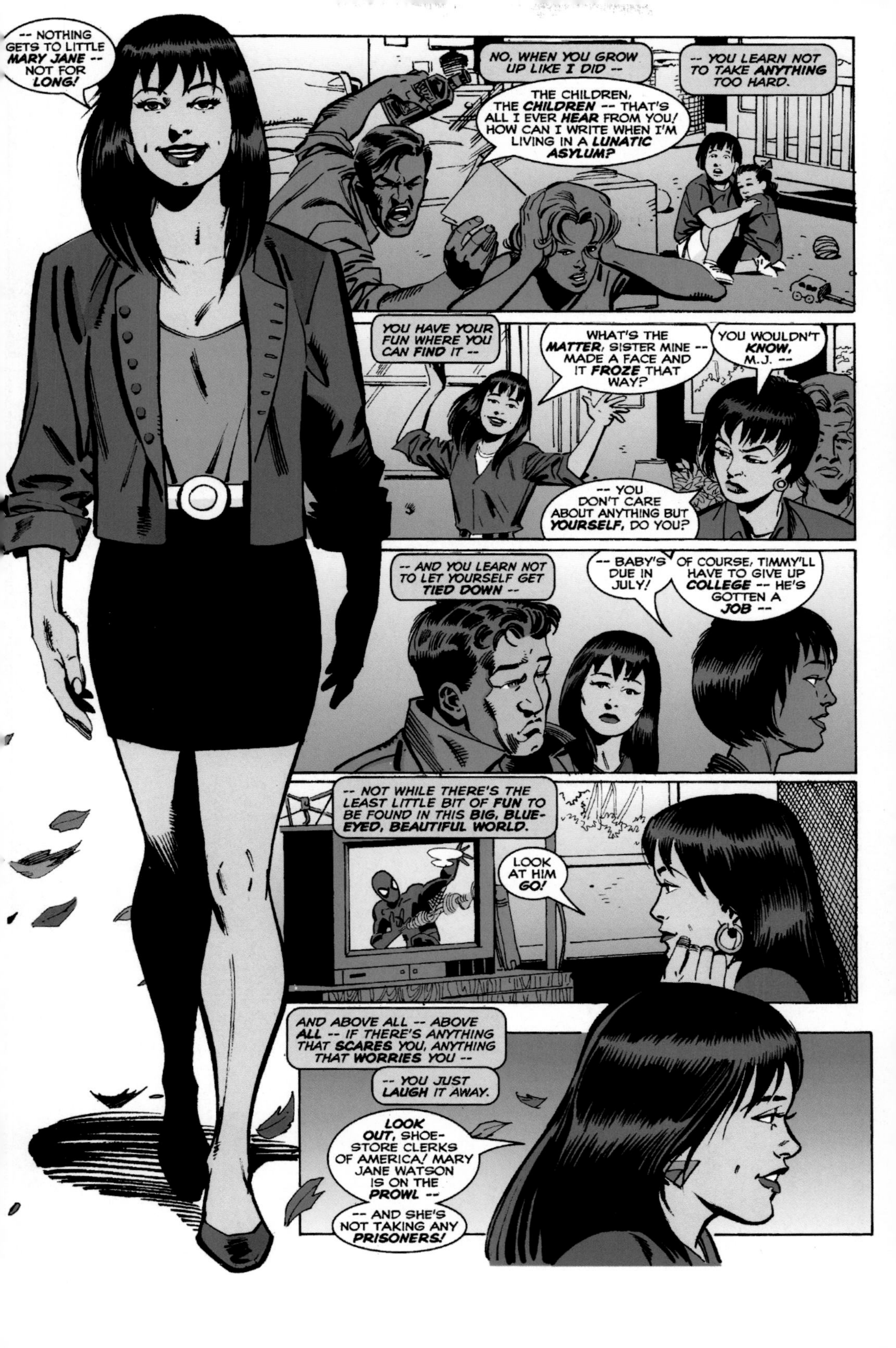
-- NOTHING GETS TO LITTLE MARY JANE -- NOT FOR LONG!
NO, WHEN YOU GROW UP LIKE I DID --
-- YOU LEARN NOT TO TAKE ANYTHING TOO HARD.
THE CHILDREN, THE CHILDREN -- THAT'S ALL I EVER HEAR FROM YOU! HOW CAN I WRITE WHEN I'M LIVING IN A LUNATIC ASYLUM?
YOU HAVE YOUR FUN WHERE YOU CAN FIND IT --
WHAT'S THE MATTER, SISTER MINE -- MADE A FACE AND IT FROZE THAT WAY?
YOU WOULDN'T KNOW, M.J. --
-- YOU DON'T CARE ABOUT ANYTHING BUT YOURSELF, DO YOU?
-- AND YOU LEARN NOT TO LET YOURSELF GET TIED DOWN --
-- BABY'S DUE IN JULY!
OF COURSE, TIMMY'LL HAVE TO GIVE UP COLLEGE -- HE'S GOTTEN A JOB --
-- NOT WHILE THERE'S THE LEAST LITTLE BIT OF FUN TO BE FOUND IN THIS BIG, BLUE-EYED, BEAUTIFUL WORLD.
LOOK AT HIM GO!
AND ABOVE ALL -- ABOVE ALL -- IF THERE'S ANYTHING THAT SCARES YOU, ANYTHING THAT WORRIES YOU --
-- YOU JUST LAUGH IT AWAY.
LOOK OUT, SHOE-STORE CLERKS OF AMERICA! MARY JANE WATSON IS ON THE PROWL --
-- AND SHE'S NOT TAKING ANY PRISONERS!

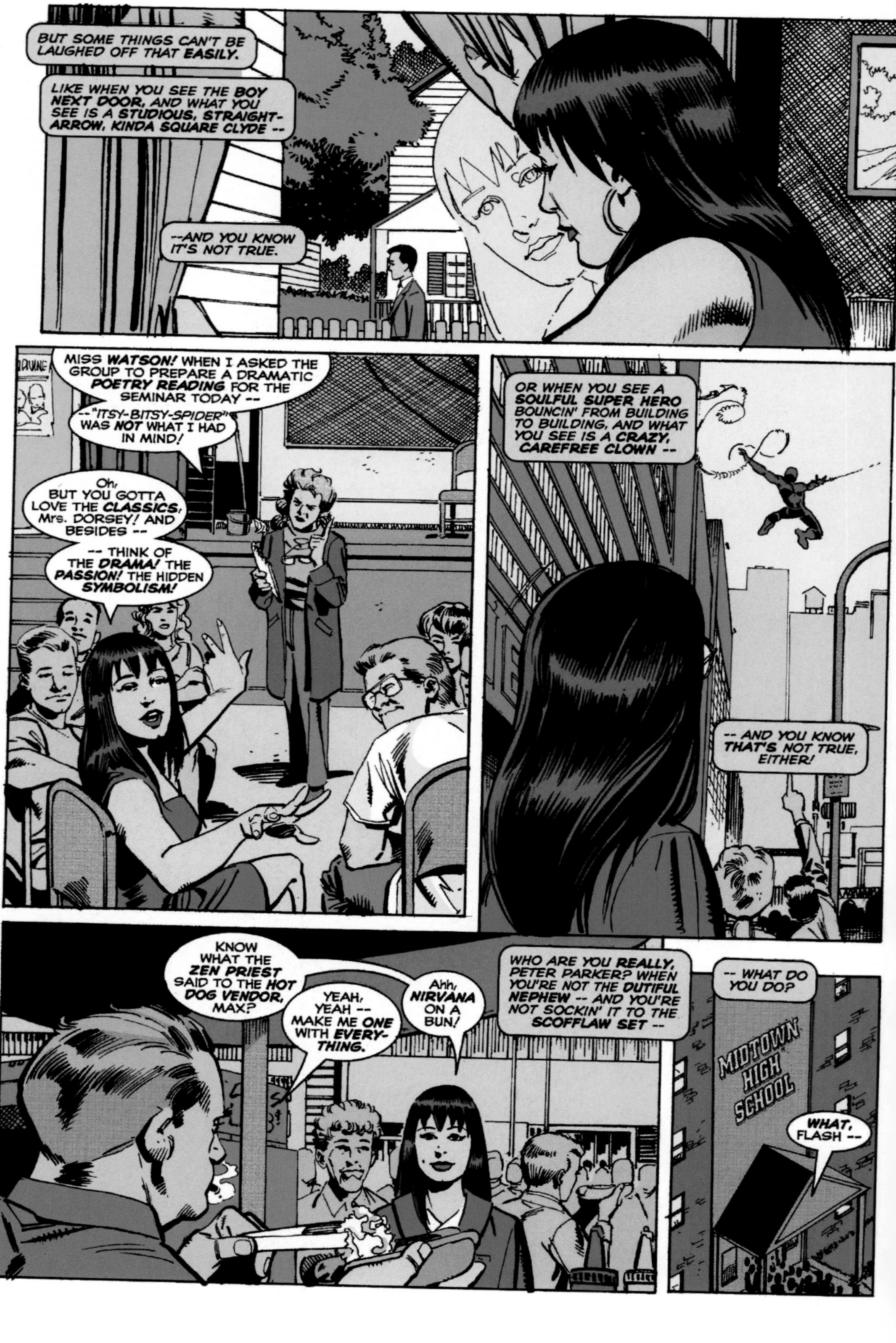
BUT SOME THINGS CAN'T BE LAUGHED OFF THAT EASILY.
LIKE WHEN YOU SEE THE BOY NEXT DOOR, AND WHAT YOU SEE IS A STUDIOUS, STRAIGHT-ARROW, KINDA SQUARE CLYDE --
--AND YOU KNOW IT'S NOT TRUE.
MISS WATSON! WHEN I ASKED THE GROUP TO PREPARE A DRAMATIC POETRY READING FOR THE SEMINAR TODAY --
--"ITSY-BITSY-SPIDER" WAS NOT WHAT I HAD IN MIND!
Oh, BUT YOU GOTTA LOVE THE CLASSICS, Mrs. DORSEY! AND BESIDES --
-- THINK OF THE DRAMA! THE PASSION! THE HIDDEN SYMBOLISM!
OR WHEN YOU SEE A SOULFUL SUPER HERO BOUNCIN' FROM BUILDING TO BUILDING, AND WHAT YOU SEE IS A CRAZY, CAREFREE CLOWN --
-- AND YOU KNOW THAT'S NOT TRUE, EITHER!
KNOW WHAT THE ZEN PRIEST SAID TO THE HOT DOG VENDOR, MAX?
YEAH, YEAH -- MAKE ME ONE WITH EVERYTHING.
Ahh, NIRVANA ON A BUN!
WHO ARE YOU REALLY, PETER PARKER? WHEN YOU'RE NOT THE DUTIFUL NEPHEW -- AND YOU'RE NOT SOCKIN' IT TO THE SCOFFLAW SET --
-- WHAT DO YOU DO?
MIDTOWN HIGH SCHOOL
WHAT, FLASH --

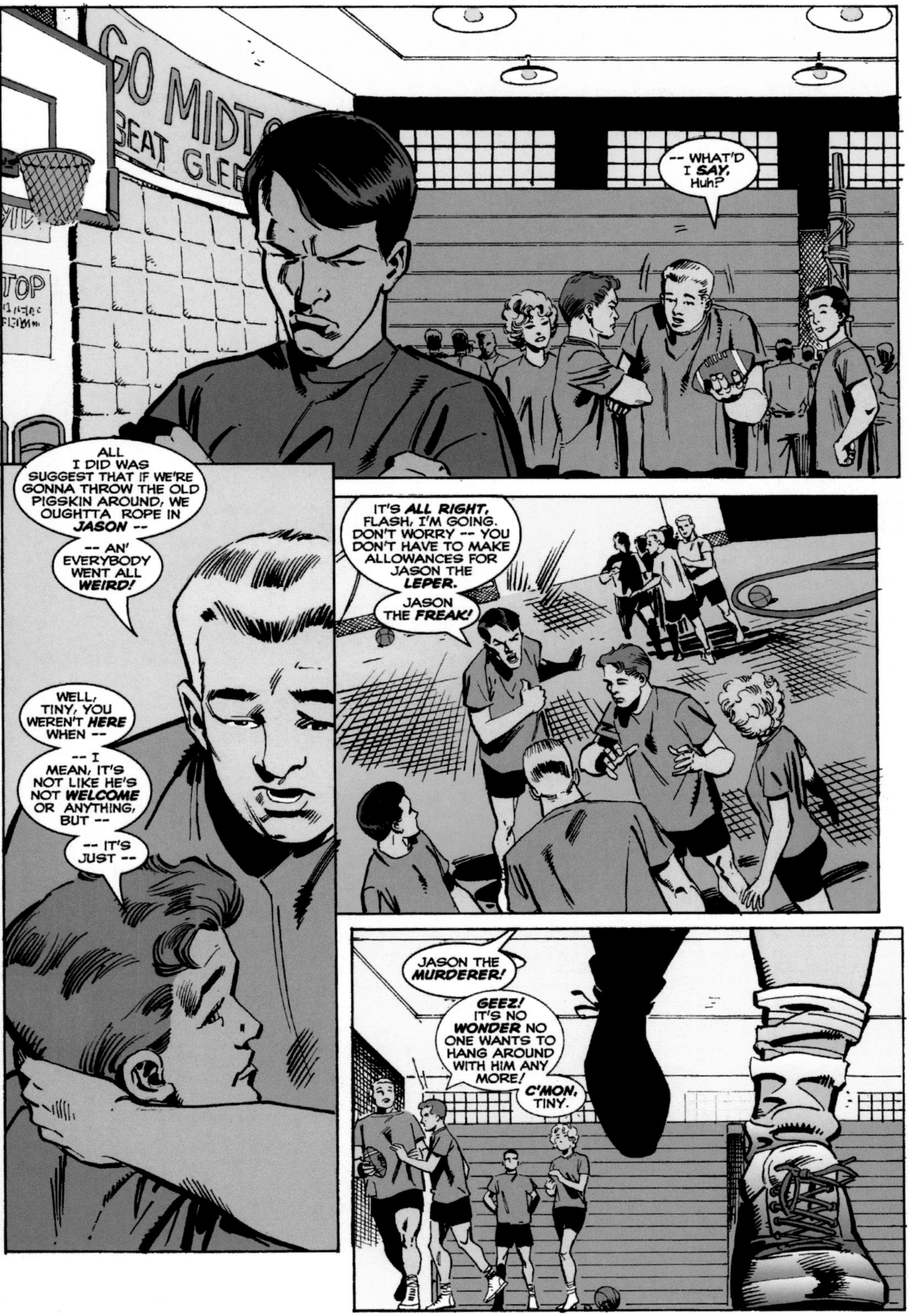
GO MIDT
BEAT GLE
-- WHAT'D I SAY, Huh?
ALL I DID WAS SUGGEST THAT IF WE'RE GONNA THROW THE OLD PIGSKIN AROUND, WE OUGHTTA ROPE IN JASON --
-- AN' EVERYBODY WENT ALL WEIRD!
WELL, TINY, YOU WEREN'T HERE WHEN --
-- I MEAN, IT'S NOT LIKE HE'S NOT WELCOME OR ANYTHING, BUT --
-- IT'S JUST --
IT'S ALL RIGHT, FLASH, I'M GOING. DON'T WORRY -- YOU DON'T HAVE TO MAKE ALLOWANCES FOR JASON THE LEPER.
JASON THE FREAK!
JASON THE MURDERER!
GEEZ! IT'S NO WONDER NO ONE WANTS TO HANG AROUND WITH HIM ANY MORE!
C'MON, TINY.

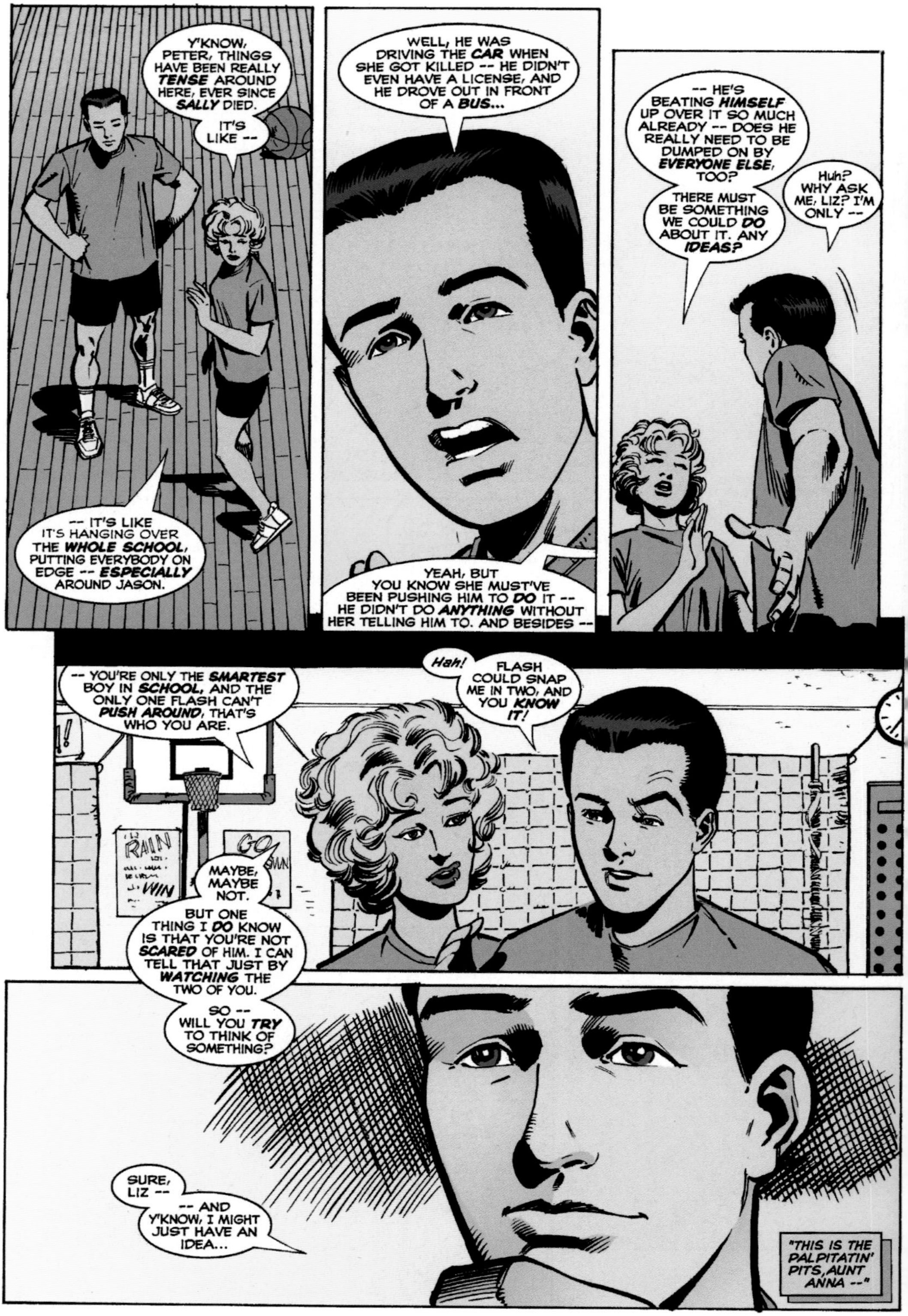
Y'KNOW, PETER, THINGS HAVE BEEN REALLY TENSE AROUND HERE, EVER SINCE SALLY DIED.
IT'S LIKE --
-- IT'S LIKE IT'S HANGING OVER THE WHOLE SCHOOL, PUTTING EVERYBODY ON EDGE -- ESPECIALLY AROUND JASON.
WELL, HE WAS DRIVING THE CAR WHEN SHE GOT KILLED -- HE DIDN'T EVEN HAVE A LICENSE, AND HE DROVE OUT IN FRONT OF A BUS...
YEAH, BUT YOU KNOW SHE MUST'VE BEEN PUSHING HIM TO DO IT -- HE DIDN'T DO ANYTHING WITHOUT HER TELLING HIM TO. AND BESIDES --
-- HE'S BEATING HIMSELF UP OVER IT SO MUCH ALREADY -- DOES HE REALLY NEED TO BE DUMPED ON BY EVERYONE ELSE, TOO?
THERE MUST BE SOMETHING WE COULD DO ABOUT IT. ANY IDEAS?
Huh? WHY ASK ME, LIZ? I'M ONLY --
-- YOU'RE ONLY THE SMARTEST BOY IN SCHOOL, AND THE ONLY ONE FLASH CAN'T PUSH AROUND, THAT'S WHO YOU ARE.
Hah!
FLASH COULD SNAP ME IN TWO, AND YOU KNOW IT!
MAYBE, MAYBE NOT.
BUT ONE THING I DO KNOW IS THAT YOU'RE NOT SCARED OF HIM. I CAN TELL THAT JUST BY WATCHING THE TWO OF YOU.
SO -- WILL YOU TRY TO THINK OF SOMETHING?
SURE, LIZ --
-- AND Y'KNOW, I MIGHT JUST HAVE AN IDEA...
"THIS IS THE PALPITATIN' PITS, AUNT ANNA --"

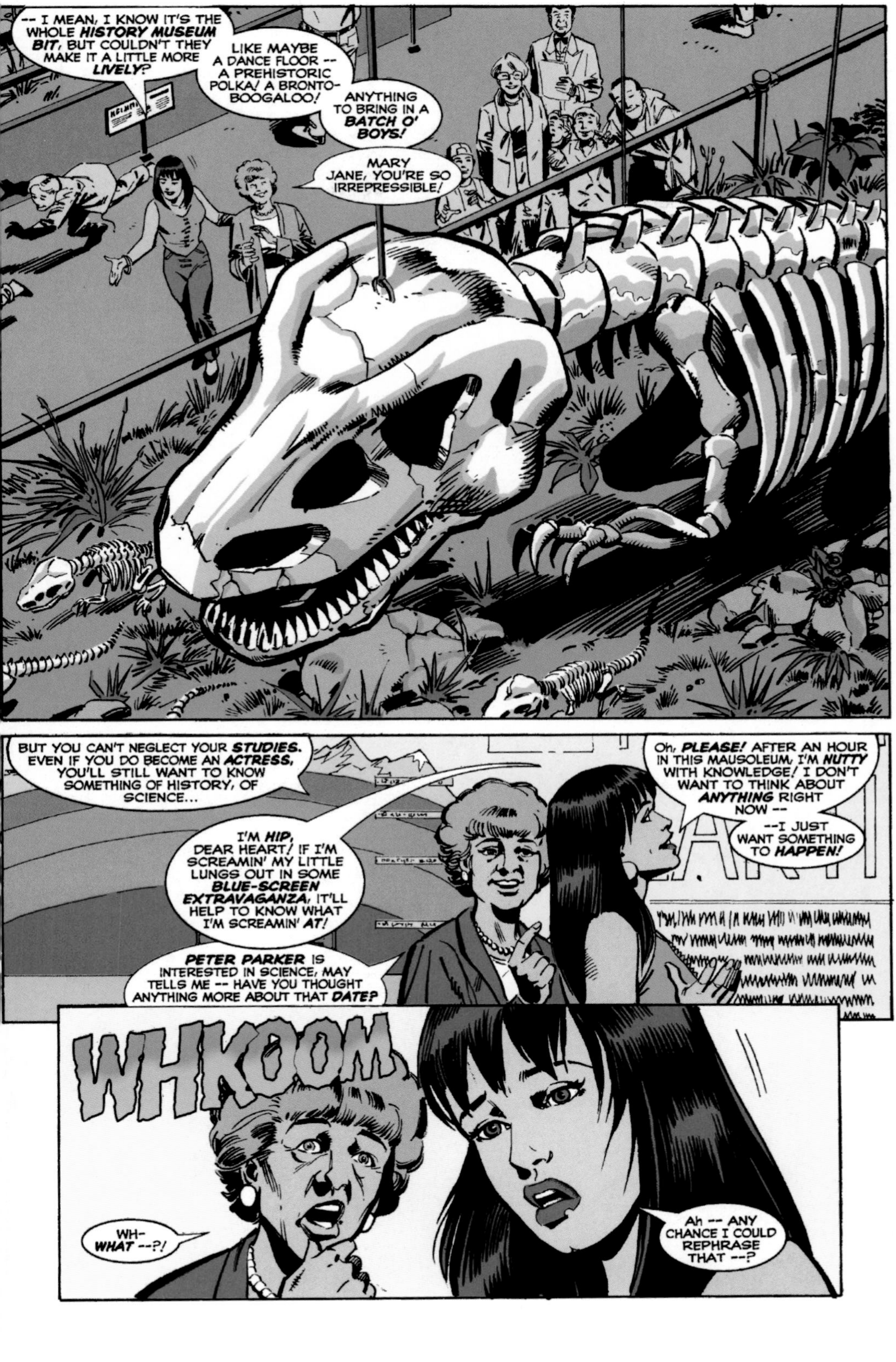
-- I MEAN, I KNOW IT'S THE WHOLE HISTORY MUSEUM BIT, BUT COULDN'T THEY MAKE IT A LITTLE MORE LIVELY?
LIKE MAYBE A DANCE FLOOR -- A PREHISTORIC POLKA! A BRONTO-BOOGALOO!
ANYTHING TO BRING IN A BATCH O' BOYS!
MARY JANE, YOU'RE SO IRREPRESSIBLE!
BUT YOU CAN'T NEGLECT YOUR STUDIES. EVEN IF YOU DO BECOME AN ACTRESS, YOU'LL STILL WANT TO KNOW SOMETHING OF HISTORY, OF SCIENCE...
I'M HIP, DEAR HEART! IF I'M SCREAMIN' MY LITTLE LUNGS OUT IN SOME BLUE-SCREEN EXTRAVAGANZA, IT'LL HELP TO KNOW WHAT I'M SCREAMIN' AT!
PETER PARKER IS INTERESTED IN SCIENCE, MAY TELLS ME -- HAVE YOU THOUGHT ANYTHING MORE ABOUT THAT DATE?
Oh, PLEASE! AFTER AN HOUR IN THIS MAUSOLEUM, I'M NUTTY WITH KNOWLEDGE! I DON'T WANT TO THINK ABOUT ANYTHING RIGHT NOW --
--I JUST WANT SOMETHING TO HAPPEN!
WHKOOM
WH- WHAT --?!
Ah -- ANY CHANCE I COULD REPHRASE THAT --?

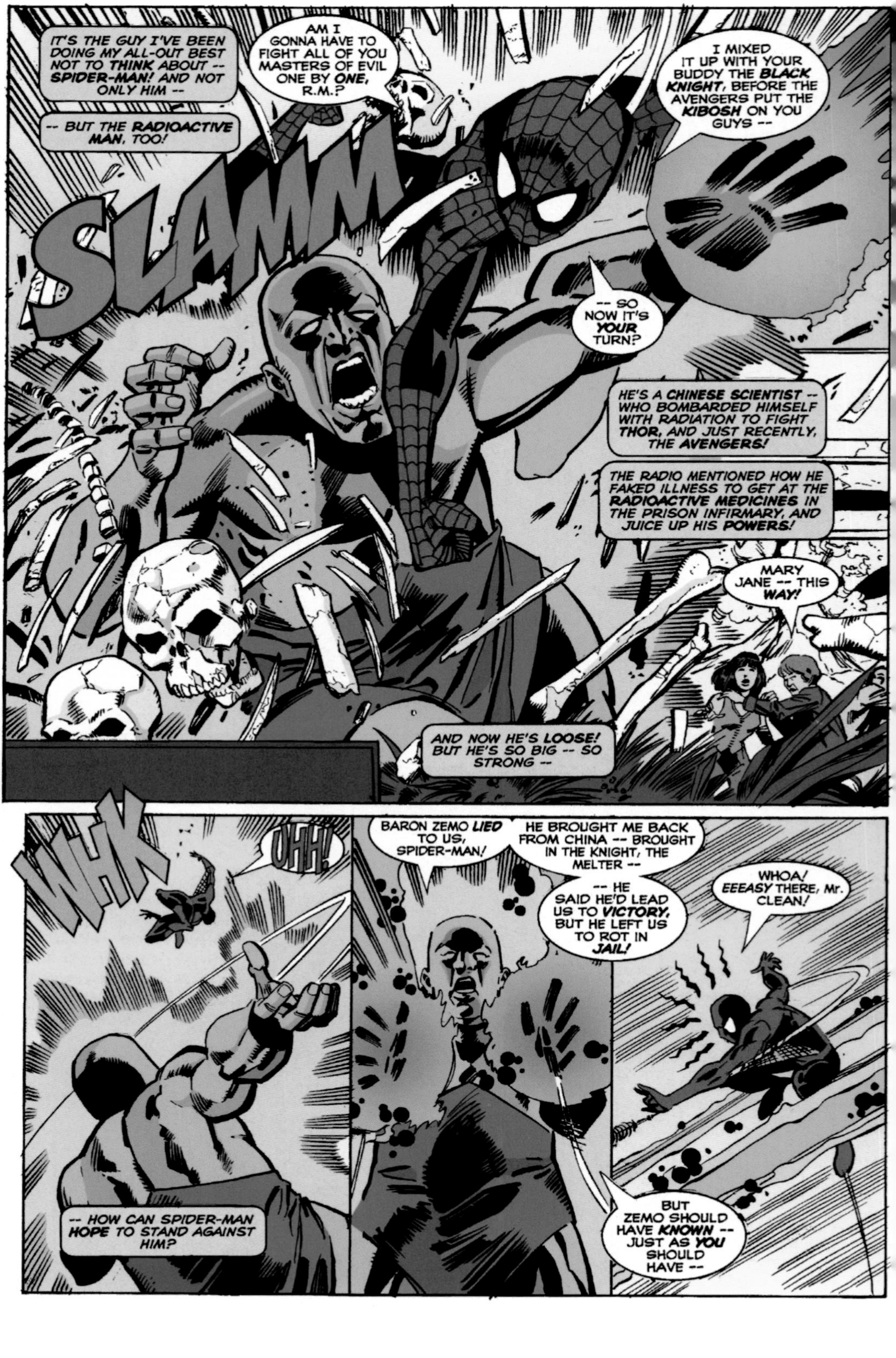
IT'S THE GUY I'VE BEEN DOING MY ALL-OUT BEST NOT TO THINK ABOUT -- SPIDER-MAN! AND NOT ONLY HIM --
-- BUT THE RADIOACTIVE MAN, TOO!
AM I GONNA HAVE TO FIGHT ALL OF YOU MASTERS OF EVIL ONE BY ONE, R.M.?
SLAMM
I MIXED IT UP WITH YOUR BUDDY THE BLACK KNIGHT, BEFORE THE AVENGERS PUT THE KIBOSH ON YOU GUYS --
-- SO NOW IT'S YOUR TURN?
HE'S A CHINESE SCIENTIST -- WHO BOMBARDED HIMSELF WITH RADIATION TO FIGHT THOR, AND JUST RECENTLY, THE AVENGERS!
THE RADIO MENTIONED HOW HE FAKED ILLNESS TO GET AT THE RADIOACTIVE MEDICINES IN THE PRISON INFIRMARY, AND JUICE UP HIS POWERS!
MARY JANE -- THIS WAY!
AND NOW HE'S LOOSE! BUT HE'S SO BIG -- SO STRONG --
WHK
UHH!
-- HOW CAN SPIDER-MAN HOPE TO STAND AGAINST HIM?
BARON ZEMO LIED TO US, SPIDER-MAN!
HE BROUGHT ME BACK FROM CHINA -- BROUGHT IN THE KNIGHT, THE MELTER --
-- HE SAID HE'D LEAD US TO VICTORY, BUT HE LEFT US TO ROT IN JAIL!
BUT ZEMO SHOULD HAVE KNOWN -- JUST AS YOU SHOULD HAVE --
WHOA! EEEASY THERE, Mr. CLEAN!

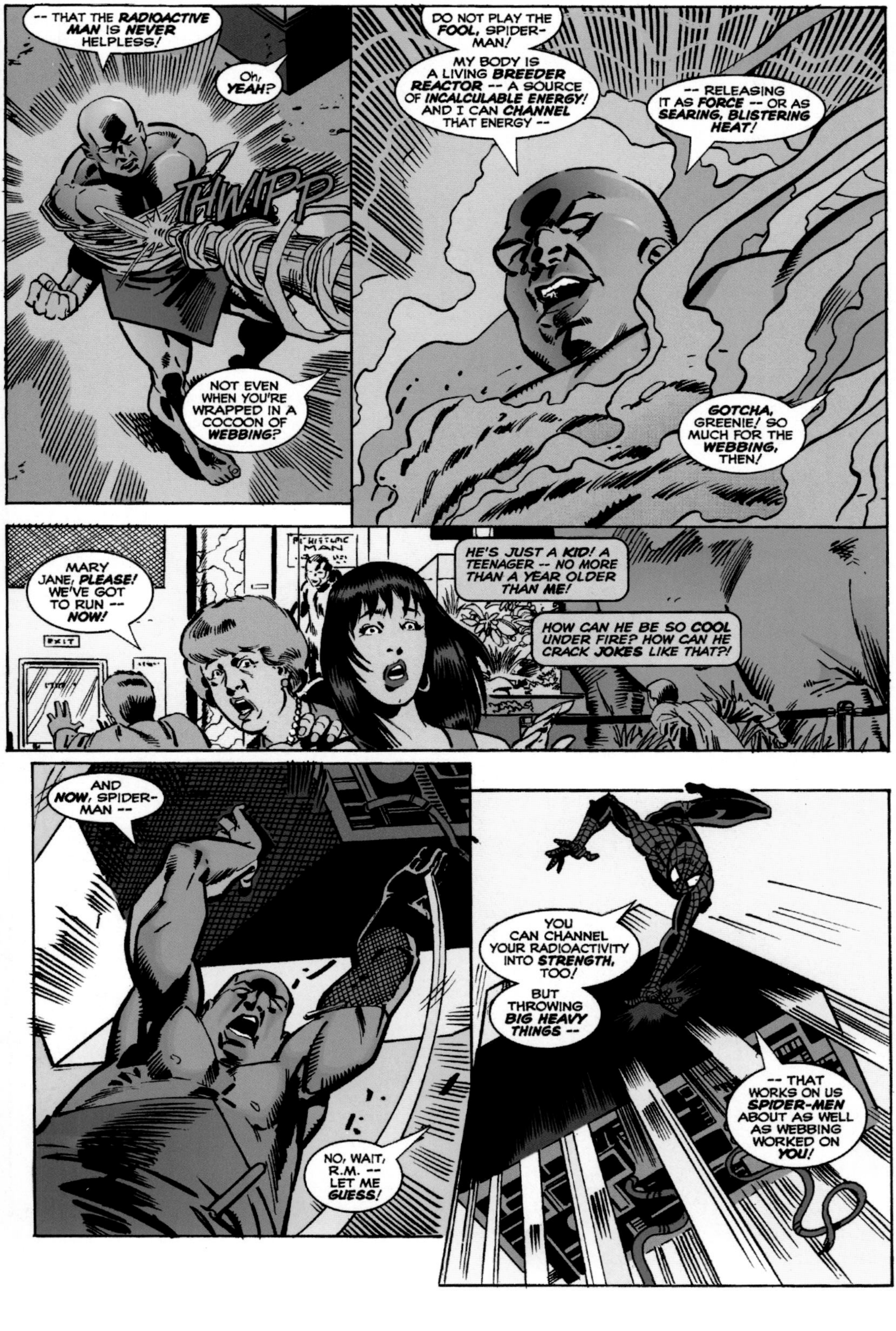
-- THAT THE RADIOACTIVE MAN IS NEVER HELPLESS!
Oh, YEAH?
THWIPP
NOT EVEN WHEN YOU'RE WRAPPED IN A COCOON OF WEBBING?
DO NOT PLAY THE FOOL, SPIDER-MAN!
MY BODY IS A LIVING BREEDER REACTOR -- A SOURCE OF INCALCULABLE ENERGY! AND I CAN CHANNEL THAT ENERGY --
-- RELEASING IT AS FORCE -- OR AS SEARING, BLISTERING HEAT!
GOTCHA, GREENIE! SO MUCH FOR THE WEBBING, THEN!
MARY JANE, PLEASE! WE'VE GOT TO RUN -- NOW!
HE'S JUST A KID! A TEENAGER -- NO MORE THAN A YEAR OLDER THAN ME!
HOW CAN HE BE SO COOL UNDER FIRE? HOW CAN HE CRACK JOKES LIKE THAT?!
EXIT
AND NOW, SPIDER-MAN --
NO, WAIT, R.M. -- LET ME GUESS!
YOU CAN CHANNEL YOUR RADIOACTIVITY INTO STRENGTH, TOO!
BUT THROWING BIG HEAVY THINGS --
-- THAT WORKS ON US SPIDER-MEN ABOUT AS WELL AS WEBBING WORKED ON YOU!

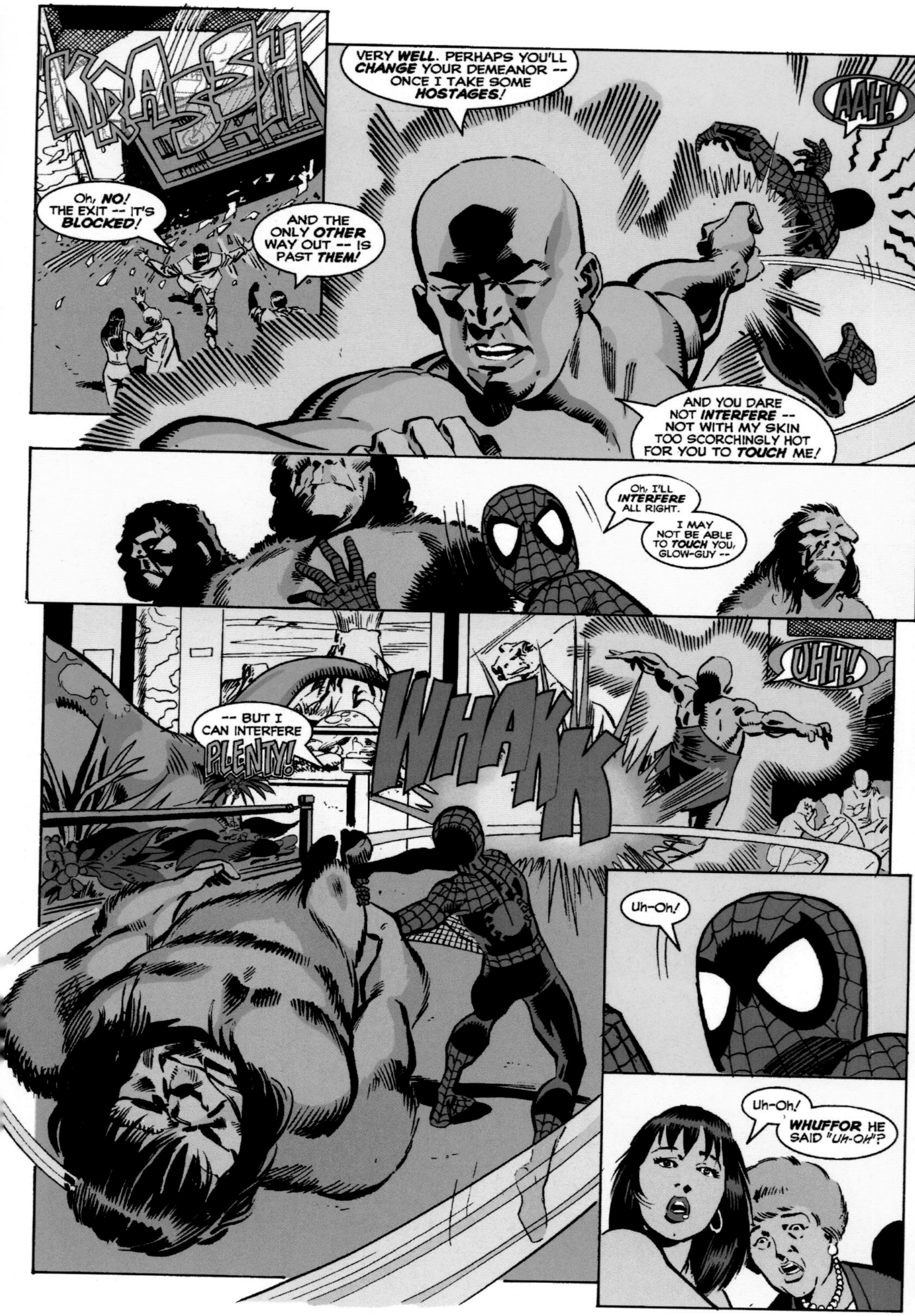
KRAASH
Oh, NO! THE EXIT -- IT'S BLOCKED!
AND THE ONLY OTHER WAY OUT -- IS PAST THEM!
VERY WELL. PERHAPS YOU'LL CHANGE YOUR DEMEANOR -- ONCE I TAKE SOME HOSTAGES!
AAH!
AND YOU DARE NOT INTERFERE -- NOT WITH MY SKIN TOO SCORCHINGLY HOT FOR YOU TO TOUCH ME!
Oh, I'LL INTERFERE ALL RIGHT.
I MAY NOT BE ABLE TO TOUCH YOU, GLOW-GUY --
-- BUT I CAN INTERFERE PLENTY!
WHAKK
OHH!
Uh-Oh!
Uh-Oh! WHUFFOR HE SAID "UH-OH"?

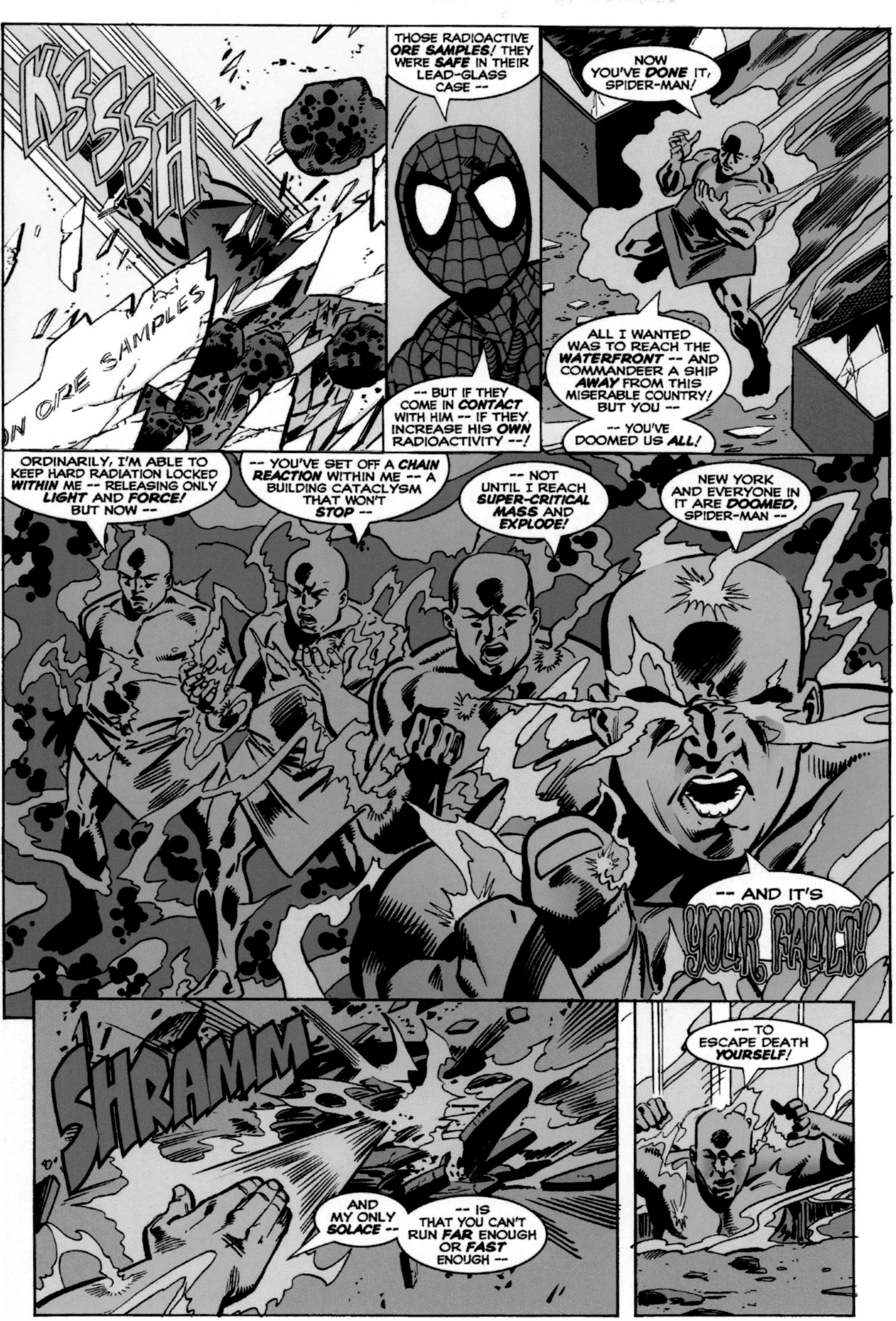
KSSSH
ON ORE SAMPLES
THOSE RADIOACTIVE ORE SAMPLES! THEY WERE SAFE IN THEIR LEAD-GLASS CASE --
-- BUT IF THEY COME IN CONTACT WITH HIM -- IF THEY INCREASE HIS OWN RADIOACTIVITY --!
NOW YOU'VE DONE IT, SPIDER-MAN!
ALL I WANTED WAS TO REACH THE WATERFRONT -- AND COMMANDEER A SHIP AWAY FROM THIS MISERABLE COUNTRY! BUT YOU --
-- YOU'VE DOOMED US ALL!
ORDINARILY, I'M ABLE TO KEEP HARD RADIATION LOCKED WITHIN ME -- RELEASING ONLY LIGHT AND FORCE! BUT NOW --
-- YOU'VE SET OFF A CHAIN REACTION WITHIN ME -- A BUILDING CATACLYSM THAT WON'T STOP --
-- NOT UNTIL I REACH SUPER-CRITICAL MASS AND EXPLODE!
NEW YORK AND EVERYONE IN IT ARE DOOMED, SPIDER-MAN --
-- AND IT'S YOUR FAULT!
SHRAMM
AND MY ONLY SOLACE --
-- IS THAT YOU CAN'T RUN FAR ENOUGH OR FAST ENOUGH --
-- TO ESCAPE DEATH YOURSELF!

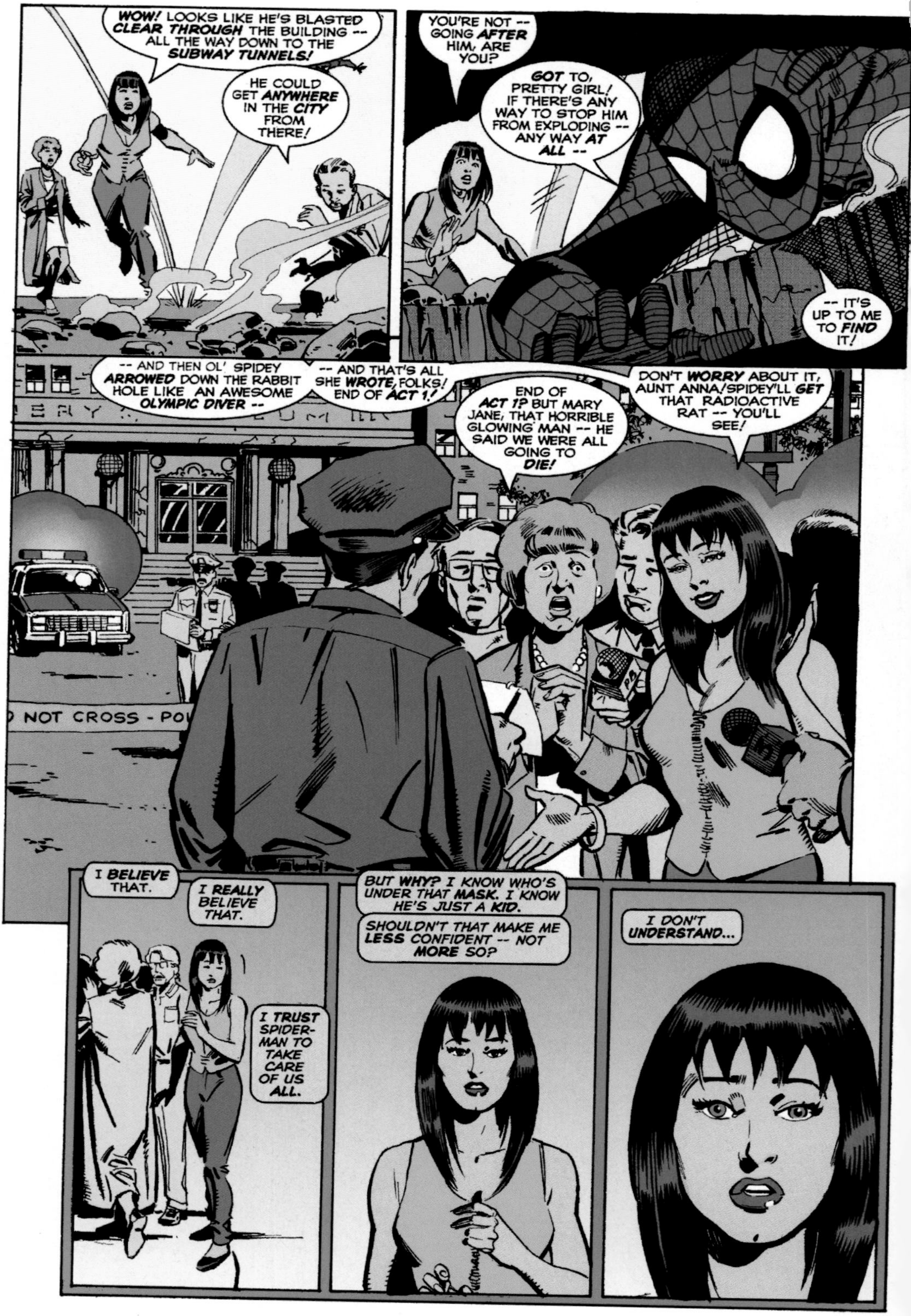
WOW! LOOKS LIKE HE'S BLASTED CLEAR THROUGH THE BUILDING -- ALL THE WAY DOWN TO THE SUBWAY TUNNELS!
HE COULD GET ANYWHERE IN THE CITY FROM THERE!
YOU'RE NOT -- GOING AFTER HIM, ARE YOU?
GOT TO, PRETTY GIRL! IF THERE'S ANY WAY TO STOP HIM FROM EXPLODING -- ANY WAY AT ALL --
-- IT'S UP TO ME TO FIND IT!
-- AND THEN OL' SPIDEY ARROWED DOWN THE RABBIT HOLE LIKE AN AWESOME OLYMPIC DIVER --
-- AND THAT'S ALL SHE WROTE, FOLKS! END OF ACT 1.!
END OF ACT 1!? BUT MARY JANE, THAT HORRIBLE GLOWING MAN -- HE SAID WE WERE ALL GOING TO DIE!
DON'T WORRY ABOUT IT, AUNT ANNA! SPIDEY'LL GET THAT RADIOACTIVE RAT -- YOU'LL SEE!
NOT CROSS - PO
I BELIEVE THAT.
I REALLY BELIEVE THAT.
I TRUST SPIDER-MAN TO TAKE CARE OF US ALL.
BUT WHY? I KNOW WHO'S UNDER THAT MASK. I KNOW HE'S JUST A KID.
SHOULDN'T THAT MAKE ME LESS CONFIDENT -- NOT MORE SO?
I DON'T UNDERSTAND...

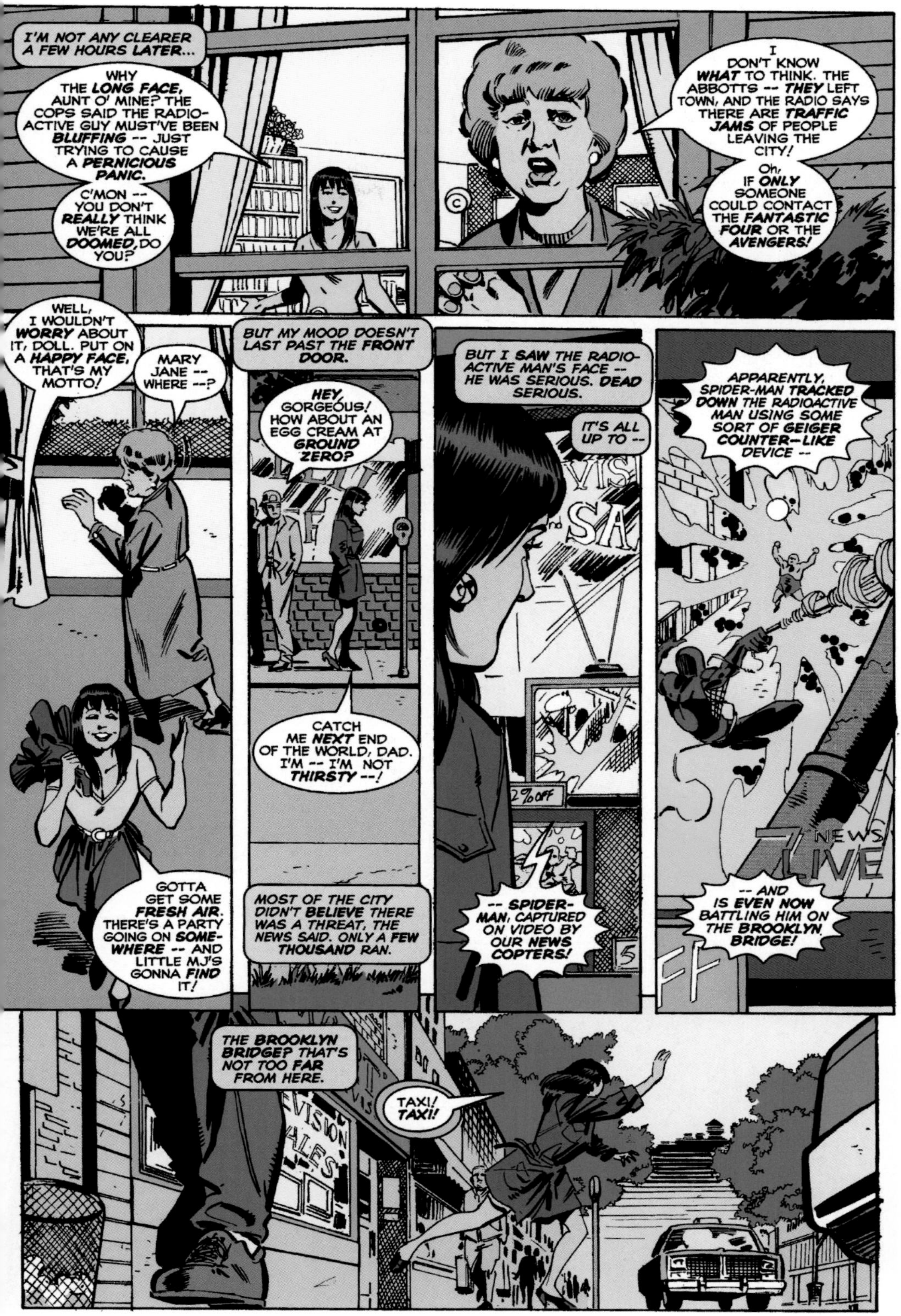
I'M NOT ANY CLEARER A FEW HOURS LATER...
WHY THE LONG FACE, AUNT O' MINE? THE COPS SAID THE RADIO-ACTIVE GUY MUST'VE BEEN BLUFFING -- JUST TRYING TO CAUSE A PERNICIOUS PANIC.
C'MON -- YOU DON'T REALLY THINK WE'RE ALL DOOMED, DO YOU?
I DON'T KNOW WHAT TO THINK. THE ABBOTTS -- THEY LEFT TOWN, AND THE RADIO SAYS THERE ARE TRAFFIC JAMS OF PEOPLE LEAVING THE CITY!
Oh, IF ONLY SOMEONE COULD CONTACT THE FANTASTIC FOUR OR THE AVENGERS!
WELL, I WOULDN'T WORRY ABOUT IT, DOLL. PUT ON A HAPPY FACE, THAT'S MY MOTTO!
MARY JANE -- WHERE --?
GOTTA GET SOME FRESH AIR. THERE'S A PARTY GOING ON SOME-WHERE -- AND LITTLE MJ'S GONNA FIND IT!
BUT MY MOOD DOESN'T LAST PAST THE FRONT DOOR.
HEY, GORGEOUS! HOW ABOUT AN EGG CREAM AT GROUND ZERO?
CATCH ME NEXT END OF THE WORLD, DAD. I'M -- I'M NOT THIRSTY --!
MOST OF THE CITY DIDN'T BELIEVE THERE WAS A THREAT, THE NEWS SAID. ONLY A FEW THOUSAND RAN.
BUT I SAW THE RADIO-ACTIVE MAN'S FACE -- HE WAS SERIOUS. DEAD SERIOUS.
IT'S ALL UP TO --
-- SPIDER-MAN, CAPTURED ON VIDEO BY OUR NEWS COPTERS!
APPARENTLY, SPIDER-MAN TRACKED DOWN THE RADIOACTIVE MAN USING SOME SORT OF GEIGER COUNTER-LIKE DEVICE --
7 NEWS LIVE
-- AND IS EVEN NOW BATTLING HIM ON THE BROOKLYN BRIDGE!
THE BROOKLYN BRIDGE? THAT'S NOT TOO FAR FROM HERE.
TAXI! TAXI!

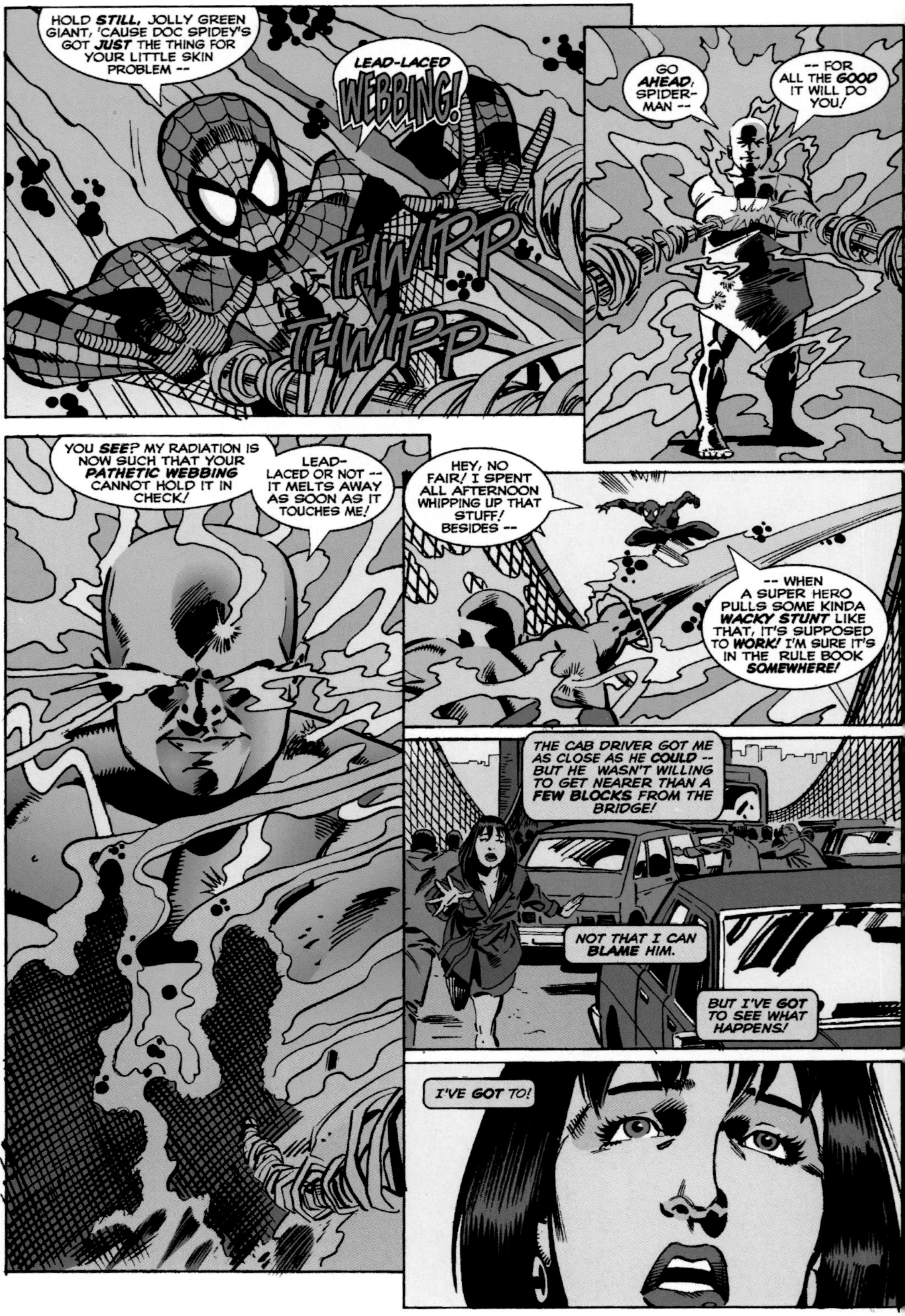

HOLD **STILL,** JOLLY GREEN GIANT, 'CAUSE DOC SPIDEY'S GOT **JUST** THE THING FOR YOUR LITTLE SKIN PROBLEM --
LEAD-LACED WEBBING!
THWIPP
THWIPP
GO **AHEAD,** SPIDER-MAN --
-- FOR ALL THE **GOOD** IT WILL DO YOU!
YOU **SEE?** MY RADIATION IS NOW SUCH THAT YOUR **PATHETIC WEBBING** CANNOT HOLD IT IN CHECK!
LEAD-LACED OR NOT -- IT MELTS AWAY AS SOON AS IT TOUCHES ME!
HEY, NO FAIR! I SPENT ALL AFTERNOON WHIPPING UP THAT STUFF! BESIDES --
-- WHEN A SUPER HERO PULLS SOME KINDA **WACKY STUNT** LIKE THAT, IT'S SUPPOSED TO **WORK!** I'M SURE IT'S IN THE RULE BOOK **SOMEWHERE!**
THE CAB DRIVER GOT ME AS CLOSE AS HE **COULD** -- BUT HE WASN'T WILLING TO GET NEARER THAN A **FEW BLOCKS** FROM THE BRIDGE!
NOT THAT I CAN **BLAME** HIM.
BUT I'VE **GOT** TO SEE WHAT HAPPENS!
I'VE **GOT** TO!

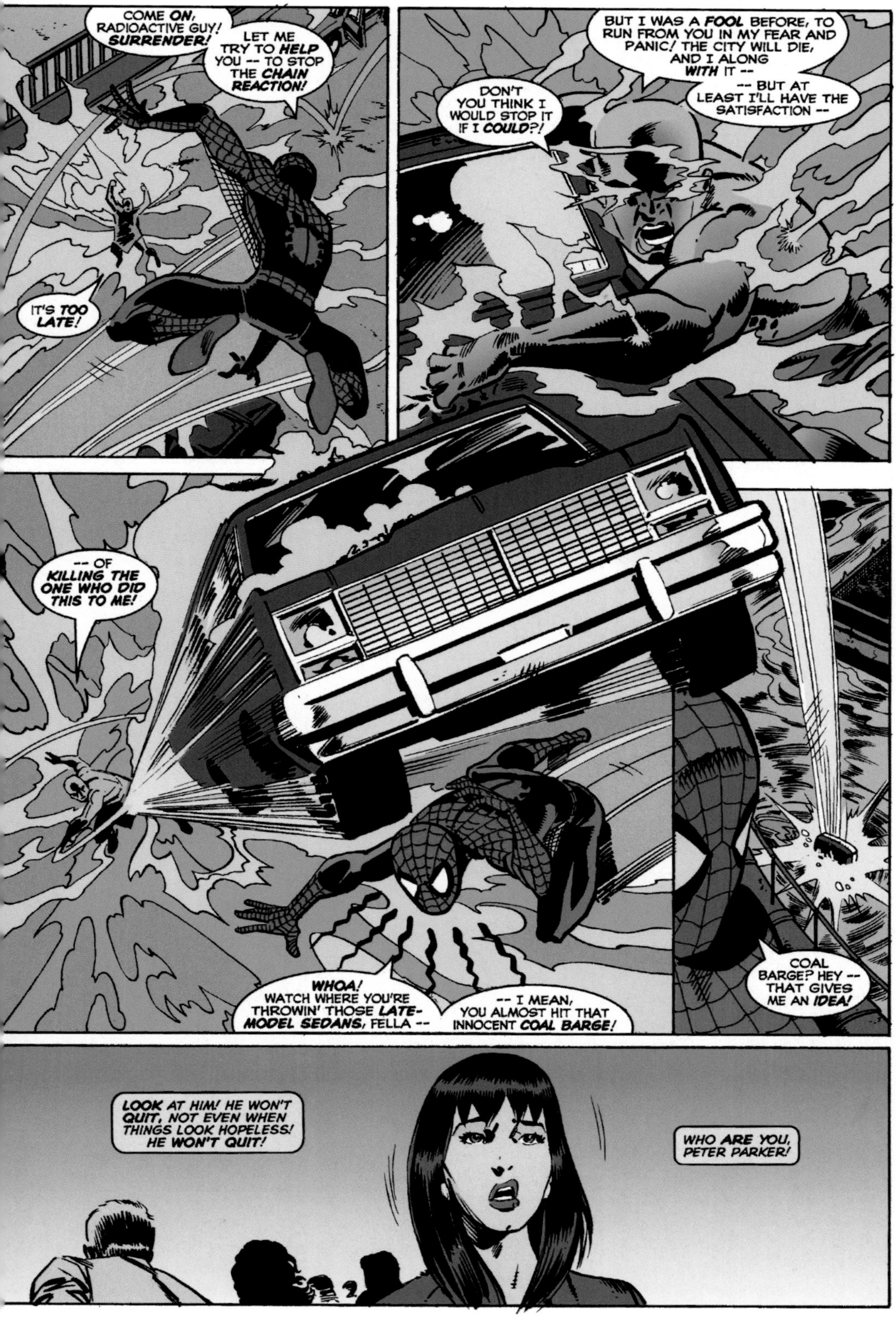

COME ON, RADIOACTIVE GUY! SURRENDER!
LET ME TRY TO HELP YOU -- TO STOP THE CHAIN REACTION!
IT'S TOO LATE!
BUT I WAS A FOOL BEFORE, TO RUN FROM YOU IN MY FEAR AND PANIC! THE CITY WILL DIE, AND I ALONG WITH IT --
DON'T YOU THINK I WOULD STOP IT IF I COULD?!
-- BUT AT LEAST I'LL HAVE THE SATISFACTION --
-- OF KILLING THE ONE WHO DID THIS TO ME!
WHOA! WATCH WHERE YOU'RE THROWIN' THOSE LATE-MODEL SEDANS, FELLA --
-- I MEAN, YOU ALMOST HIT THAT INNOCENT COAL BARGE!
COAL BARGE? HEY -- THAT GIVES ME AN IDEA!
LOOK AT HIM! HE WON'T QUIT, NOT EVEN WHEN THINGS LOOK HOPELESS! HE WON'T QUIT!
WHO ARE YOU, PETER PARKER!

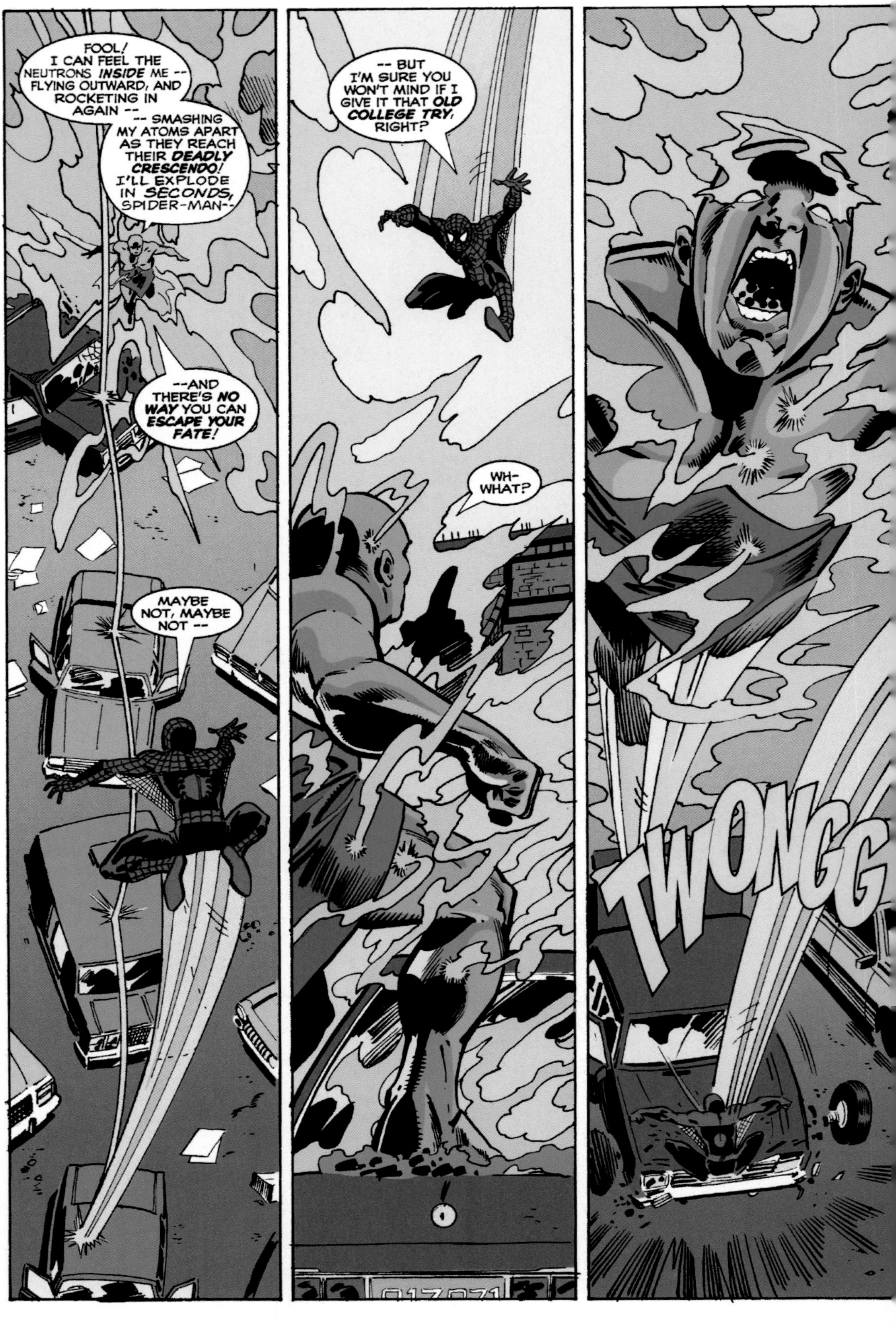
FOOL! I CAN FEEL THE NEUTRONS INSIDE ME -- FLYING OUTWARD, AND ROCKETING IN AGAIN --
-- SMASHING MY ATOMS APART AS THEY REACH THEIR DEADLY CRESCENDO! I'LL EXPLODE IN SECONDS, SPIDER-MAN--
--AND THERE'S NO WAY YOU CAN ESCAPE YOUR FATE!
MAYBE NOT, MAYBE NOT --
-- BUT I'M SURE YOU WON'T MIND IF I GIVE IT THAT OLD COLLEGE TRY, RIGHT?
WH- WHAT?
TWONGG

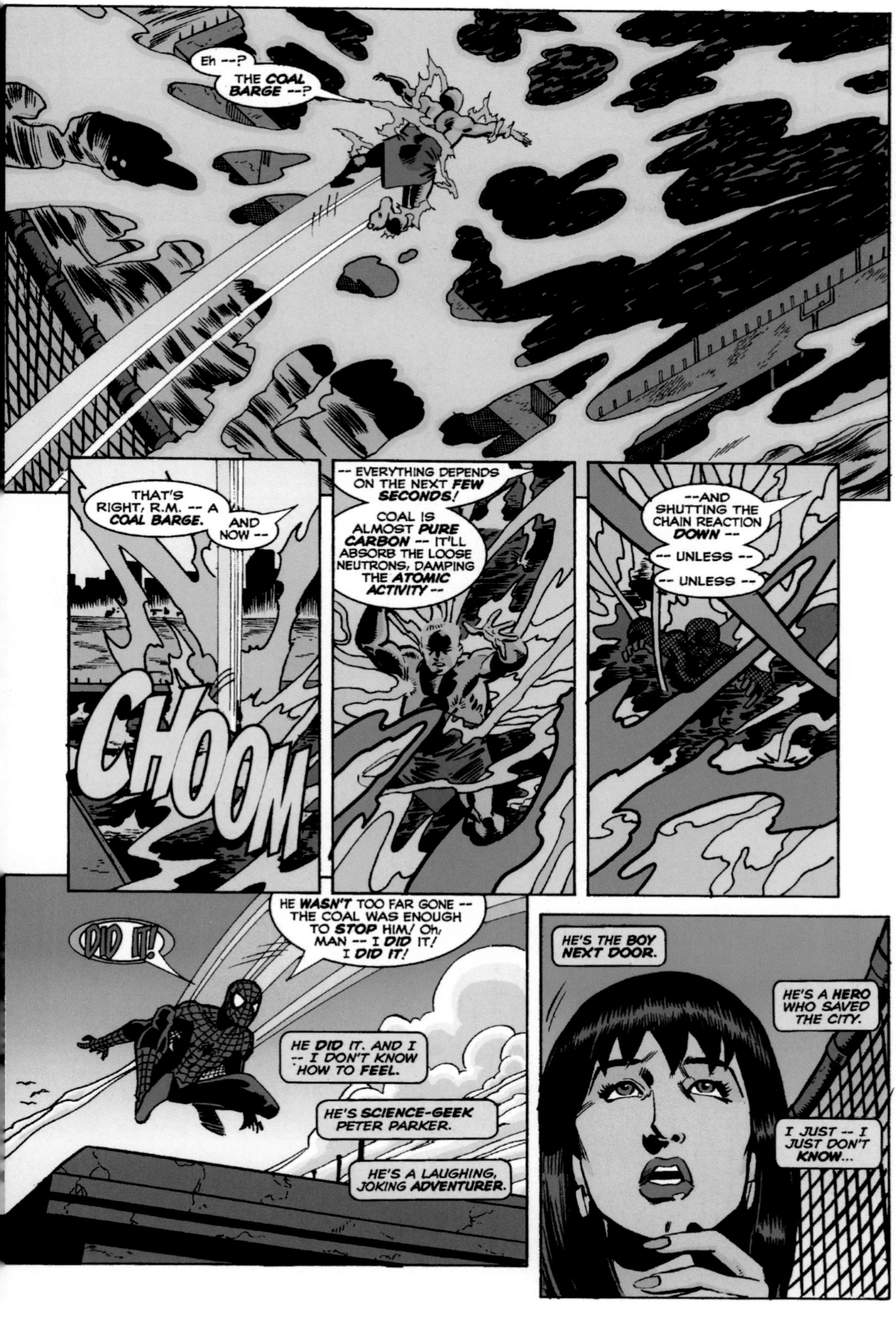
Eh --? THE COAL BARGE --?
THAT'S RIGHT, R.M. -- A COAL BARGE.
AND NOW --
CHOOM
-- EVERYTHING DEPENDS ON THE NEXT FEW SECONDS!
COAL IS ALMOST PURE CARBON -- IT'LL ABSORB THE LOOSE NEUTRONS, DAMPING THE ATOMIC ACTIVITY --
--AND SHUTTING THE CHAIN REACTION DOWN --
-- UNLESS --
-- UNLESS --
DID IT!
HE WASN'T TOO FAR GONE -- THE COAL WAS ENOUGH TO STOP HIM! Oh, MAN -- I DID IT! I DID IT!
HE DID IT. AND I -- I DON'T KNOW HOW TO FEEL.
HE'S SCIENCE-GEEK PETER PARKER.
HE'S A LAUGHING, JOKING ADVENTURER.
HE'S THE BOY NEXT DOOR.
HE'S A HERO WHO SAVED THE CITY.
I JUST -- I JUST DON'T KNOW...

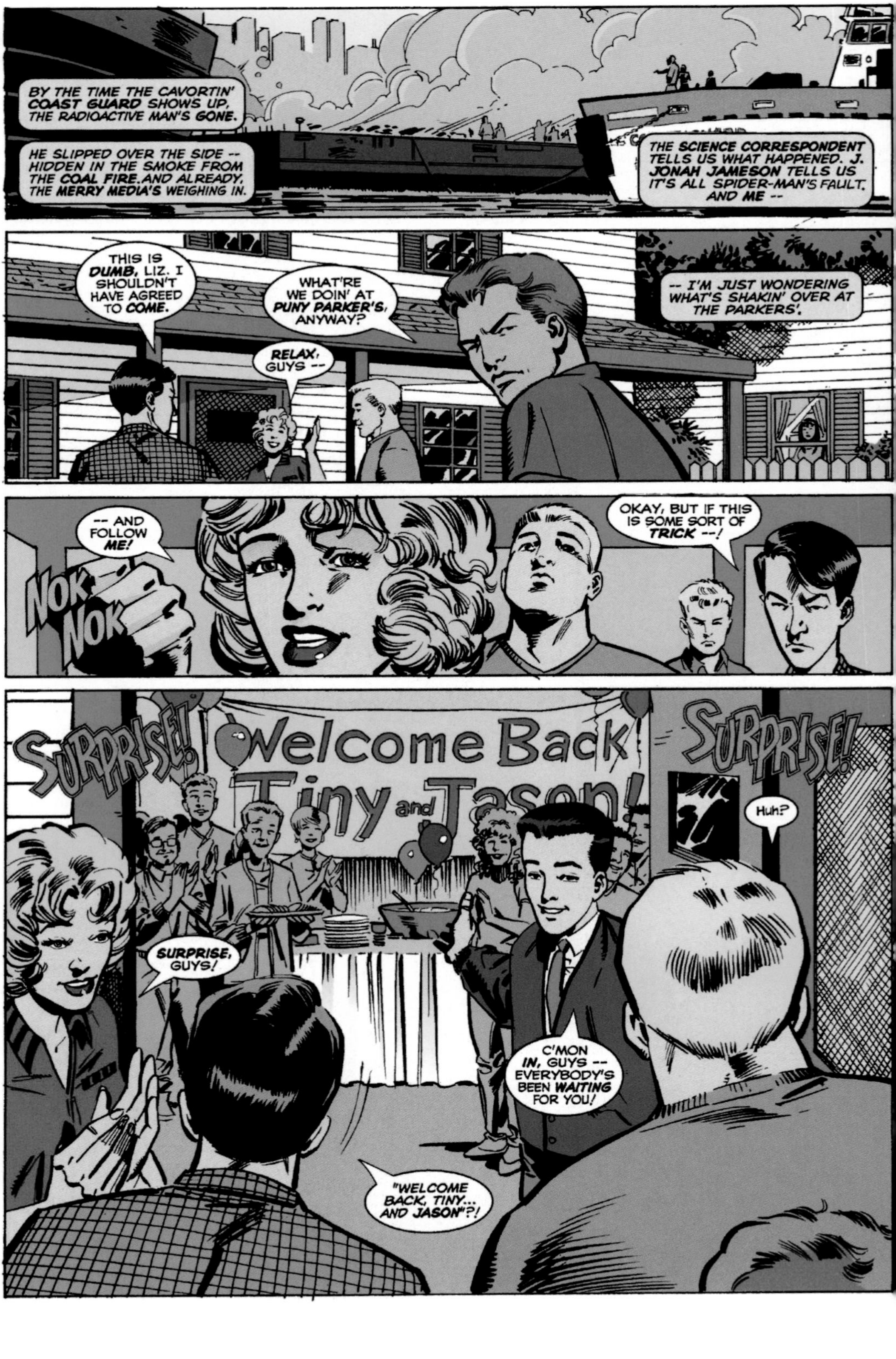
BY THE TIME THE CAVORTIN' COAST GUARD SHOWS UP, THE RADIOACTIVE MAN'S GONE.
HE SLIPPED OVER THE SIDE -- HIDDEN IN THE SMOKE FROM THE COAL FIRE. AND ALREADY, THE MERRY MEDIA'S WEIGHING IN.
THE SCIENCE CORRESPONDENT TELLS US WHAT HAPPENED. J. JONAH JAMESON TELLS US IT'S ALL SPIDER-MAN'S FAULT. AND ME --
THIS IS DUMB, LIZ. I SHOULDN'T HAVE AGREED TO COME.
WHAT'RE WE DOIN' AT PUNY PARKER'S, ANYWAY?
RELAX, GUYS --
-- I'M JUST WONDERING WHAT'S SHAKIN' OVER AT THE PARKERS'.
-- AND FOLLOW ME!
NOK NOK
OKAY, BUT IF THIS IS SOME SORT OF TRICK --!
SURPRISE!
Welcome Back Tiny and Jason!
SURPRISE!
Huh?
SURPRISE, GUYS!
C'MON IN, GUYS -- EVERYBODY'S BEEN WAITING FOR YOU!
"WELCOME BACK, TINY... AND JASON"?!

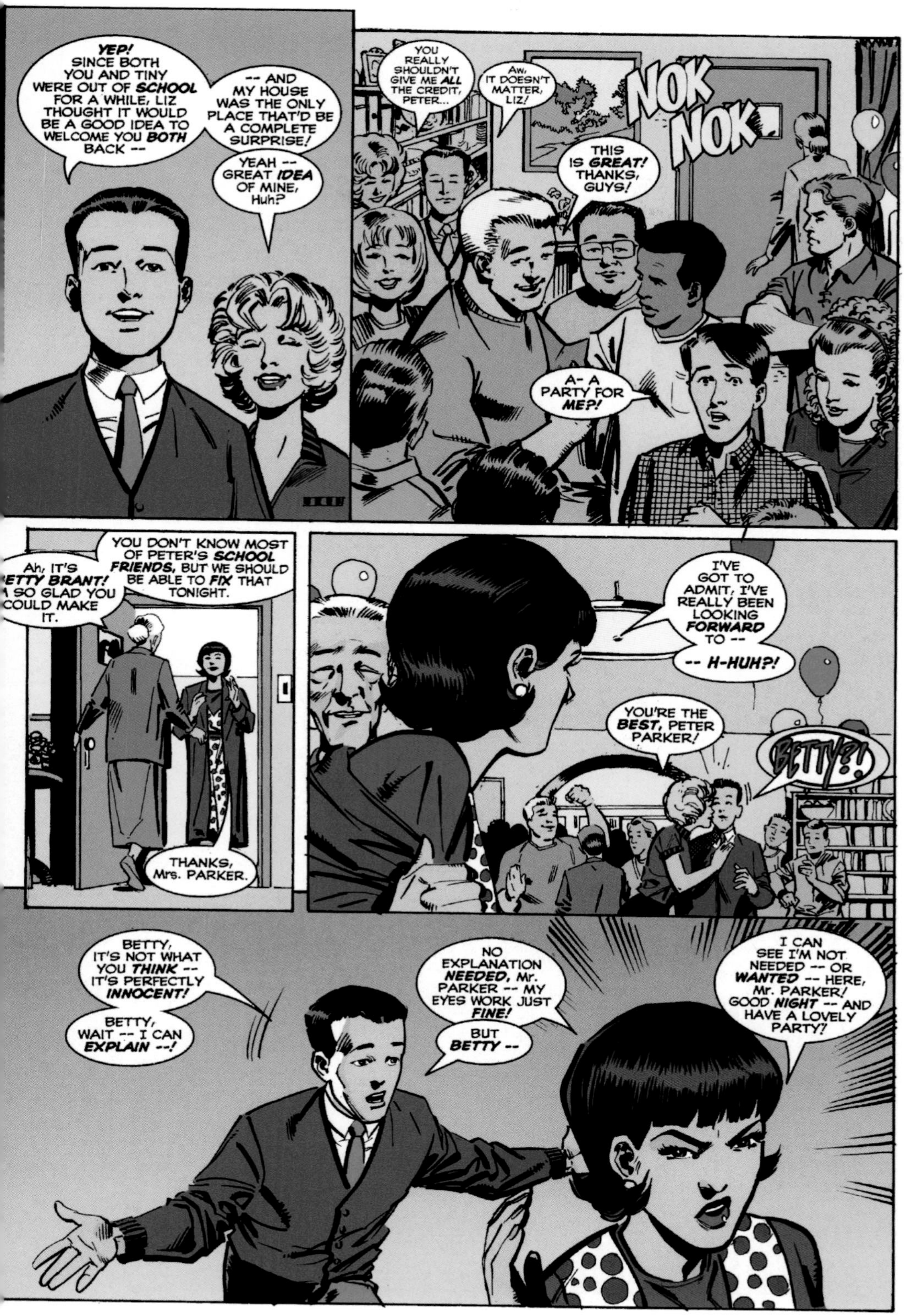
YEP! SINCE BOTH YOU AND TINY WERE OUT OF SCHOOL FOR A WHILE, LIZ THOUGHT IT WOULD BE A GOOD IDEA TO WELCOME YOU BOTH BACK --
-- AND MY HOUSE WAS THE ONLY PLACE THAT'D BE A COMPLETE SURPRISE!
YEAH -- GREAT IDEA OF MINE, Huh?
YOU REALLY SHOULDN'T GIVE ME ALL THE CREDIT, PETER...
Aw, IT DOESN'T MATTER, LIZ!
NOK NOK
THIS IS GREAT! THANKS, GUYS!
A- A PARTY FOR ME?!
Ah, IT'S BETTY BRANT! I'M SO GLAD YOU COULD MAKE IT.
YOU DON'T KNOW MOST OF PETER'S SCHOOL FRIENDS, BUT WE SHOULD BE ABLE TO FIX THAT TONIGHT.
THANKS, Mrs. PARKER.
I'VE GOT TO ADMIT, I'VE REALLY BEEN LOOKING FORWARD TO --
-- H-HUH?!
YOU'RE THE BEST, PETER PARKER!
BETTY?!
BETTY, IT'S NOT WHAT YOU THINK -- IT'S PERFECTLY INNOCENT!
BETTY, WAIT -- I CAN EXPLAIN --!
NO EXPLANATION NEEDED, Mr. PARKER -- MY EYES WORK JUST FINE!
BUT BETTY --
I CAN SEE I'M NOT NEEDED -- OR WANTED -- HERE, Mr. PARKER! GOOD NIGHT -- AND HAVE A LOVELY PARTY!

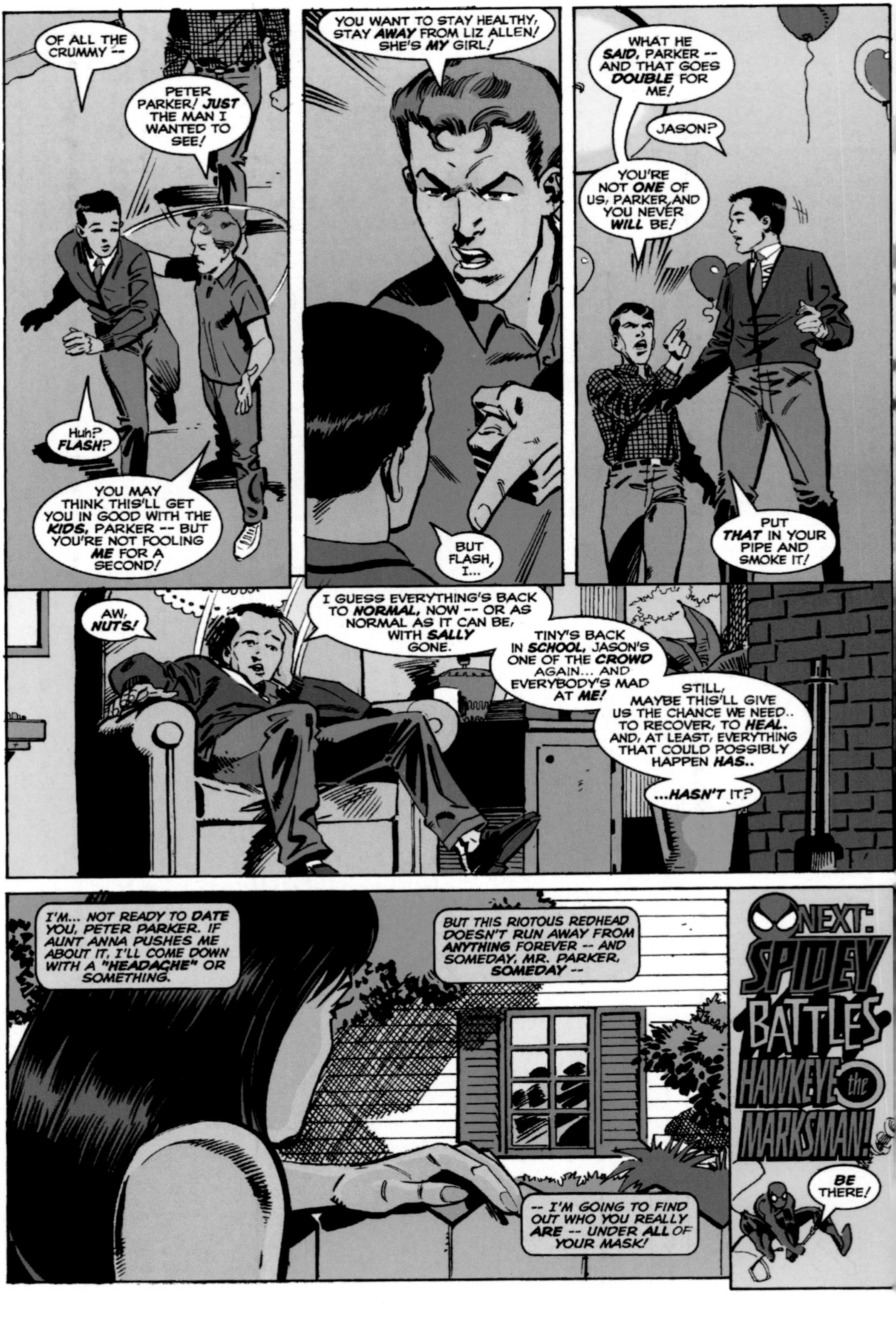

OF ALL THE CRUMMY --
PETER PARKER! JUST THE MAN I WANTED TO SEE!
Huh? FLASH?
YOU MAY THINK THIS'LL GET YOU IN GOOD WITH THE KIDS, PARKER -- BUT YOU'RE NOT FOOLING ME FOR A SECOND!
YOU WANT TO STAY HEALTHY, STAY AWAY FROM LIZ ALLEN! SHE'S MY GIRL!
BUT FLASH, I...
WHAT HE SAID, PARKER -- AND THAT GOES DOUBLE FOR ME!
JASON?
YOU'RE NOT ONE OF US, PARKER, AND YOU NEVER WILL BE!
PUT THAT IN YOUR PIPE AND SMOKE IT!
AW, NUTS!
I GUESS EVERYTHING'S BACK TO NORMAL, NOW -- OR AS NORMAL AS IT CAN BE, WITH SALLY GONE.
TINY'S BACK IN SCHOOL, JASON'S ONE OF THE CROWD AGAIN... AND EVERYBODY'S MAD AT ME!
STILL, MAYBE THIS'LL GIVE US THE CHANCE WE NEED.. TO RECOVER, TO HEAL. AND, AT LEAST, EVERYTHING THAT COULD POSSIBLY HAPPEN HAS..
...HASN'T IT?
I'M... NOT READY TO DATE YOU, PETER PARKER. IF AUNT ANNA PUSHES ME ABOUT IT, I'LL COME DOWN WITH A "HEADACHE" OR SOMETHING.
BUT THIS RIOTOUS REDHEAD DOESN'T RUN AWAY FROM ANYTHING FOREVER -- AND SOMEDAY, MR. PARKER, SOMEDAY --
-- I'M GOING TO FIND OUT WHO YOU REALLY ARE -- UNDER ALL OF YOUR MASK!
NEXT: SPIDEY BATTLES HAWKEYE the MARKSMAN!
BE THERE!

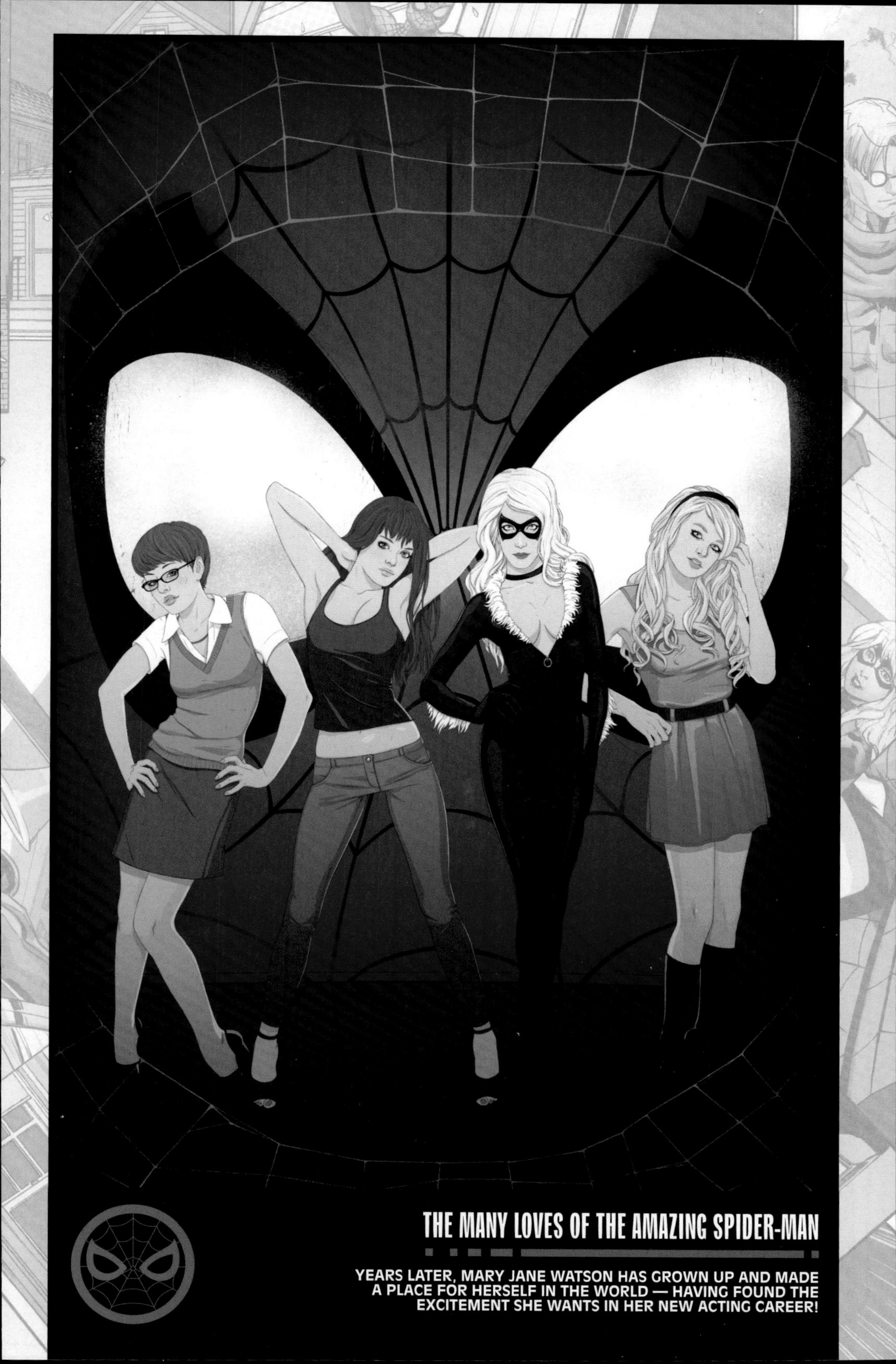
THE MANY LOVES OF THE AMAZING SPIDER-MAN
YEARS LATER, MARY JANE WATSON HAS GROWN UP AND MADE A PLACE FOR HERSELF IN THE WORLD — HAVING FOUND THE EXCITEMENT SHE WANTS IN HER NEW ACTING CAREER!

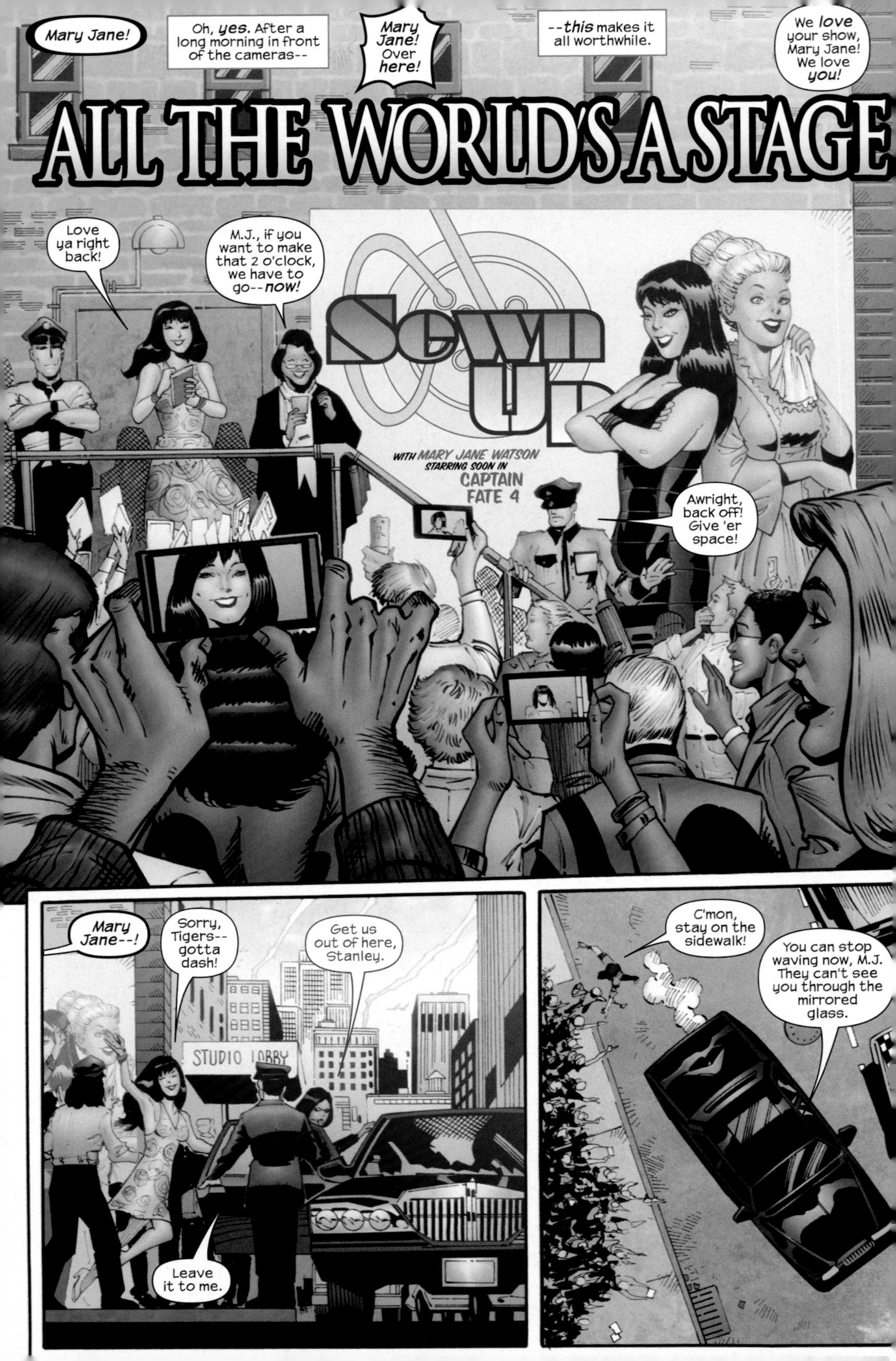
Mary Jane!
Oh, *yes.* After a long morning in front of the cameras--
Mary Jane! Over *here!*
--*this* makes it all worthwhile.
We *love* your show, Mary Jane! We love *you!*
ALL THE WORLD'S A STAGE
Love ya right back!
M.J., if you want to make that 2 o'clock, we have to go--*now!*
Sewn Up
WITH MARY JANE WATSON
STARRING SOON IN
CAPTAIN FATE 4
Awright, back off! Give 'er space!
Mary Jane--!
Sorry, Tigers-- gotta dash!
Get us out of here, Stanley.
STUDIO LOBBY
Leave it to me.
C'mon, stay on the sidewalk!
You can stop waving now, M.J. They can't see you through the mirrored glass.

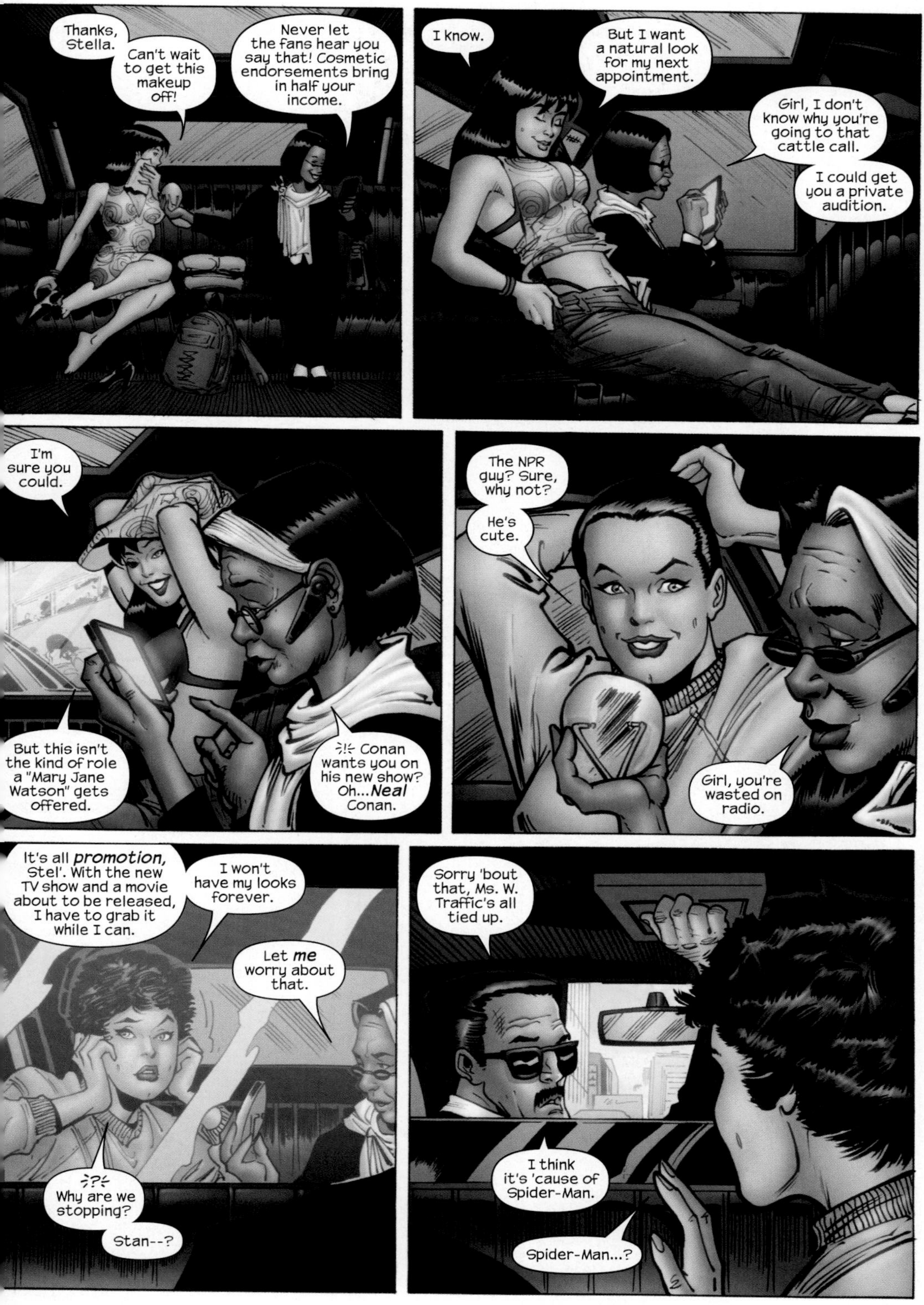
Thanks, Stella.
Can't wait to get this makeup off!
Never let the fans hear you say that! Cosmetic endorsements bring in half your income.
I know.
But I want a natural look for my next appointment.
Girl, I don't know why you're going to that cattle call.
I could get you a private audition.
I'm sure you could.
But this isn't the kind of role a "Mary Jane Watson" gets offered.
Conan wants you on his new show? Oh...*Neal* Conan.
The NPR guy? Sure, why not?
He's cute.
Girl, you're wasted on radio.
It's all ***promotion,*** Stel'. With the new TV show and a movie about to be released, I have to grab it while I can.
I won't have my looks forever.
Let ***me*** worry about that.
Why are we stopping?
Stan--?
Sorry 'bout that, Ms. W. Traffic's all tied up.
I think it's 'cause of Spider-Man.
Spider-Man...?

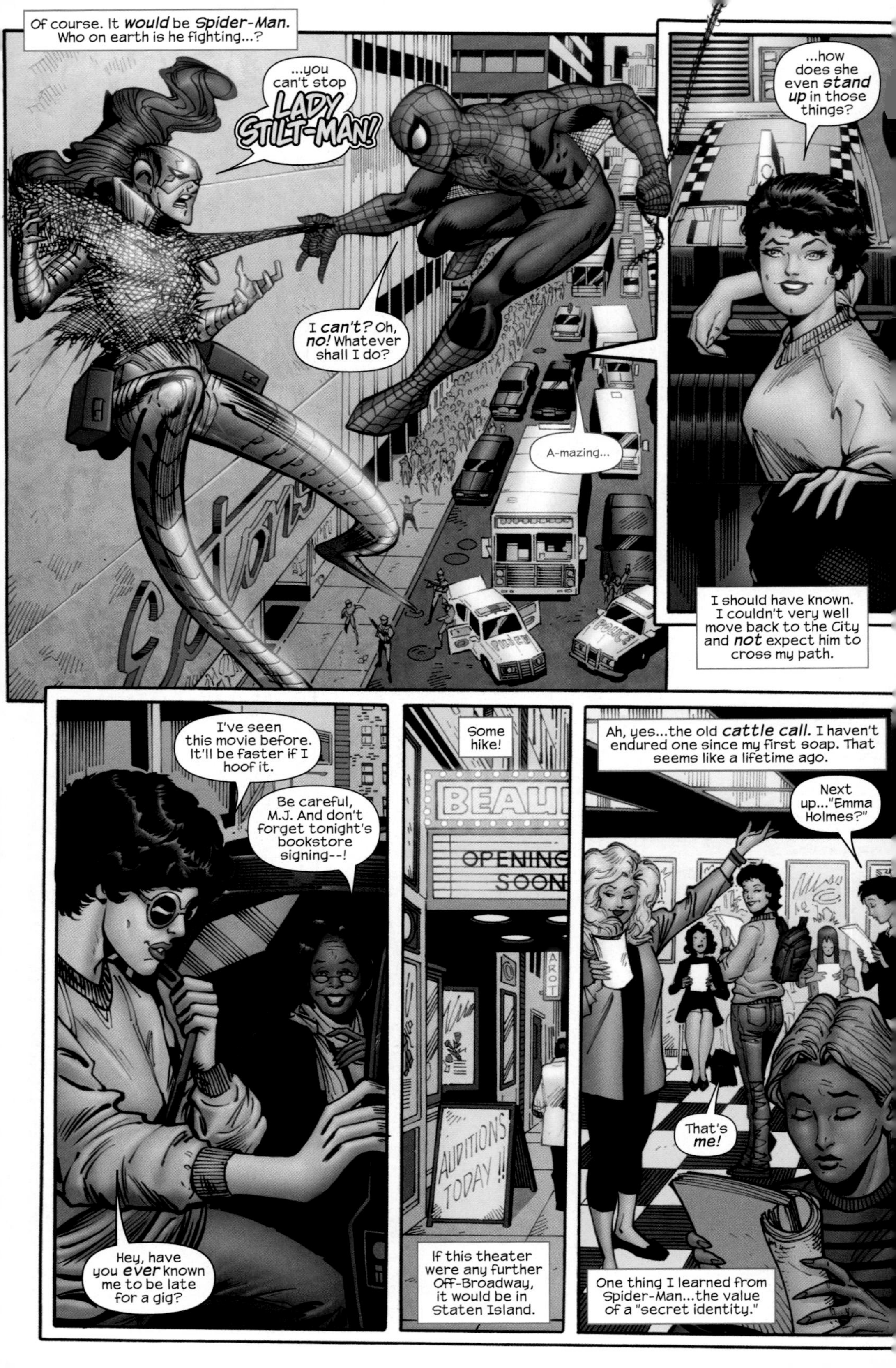
Of course. It *would* be *Spider-Man.* Who on earth is he fighting...?
...you can't stop LADY STILT-MAN!
I *can't?* Oh, *no!* Whatever shall I do?
A-mazing...
...how does she even *stand up* in those things?
I should have known. I couldn't very well move back to the City and *not* expect him to cross my path.
I've seen this movie before. It'll be faster if I hoof it.
Be careful, M.J. And don't forget tonight's bookstore signing--!
Hey, have you *ever* known me to be late for a gig?
Some hike!
BEAU
OPENING SOON
AUDITIONS TODAY!!
If this theater were any further Off-Broadway, it would be in Staten Island.
Ah, yes...the old *cattle call.* I haven't endured one since my first soap. That seems like a lifetime ago.
Next up..."Emma Holmes?"
That's *me!*
One thing I learned from Spider-Man...the value of a "secret identity."

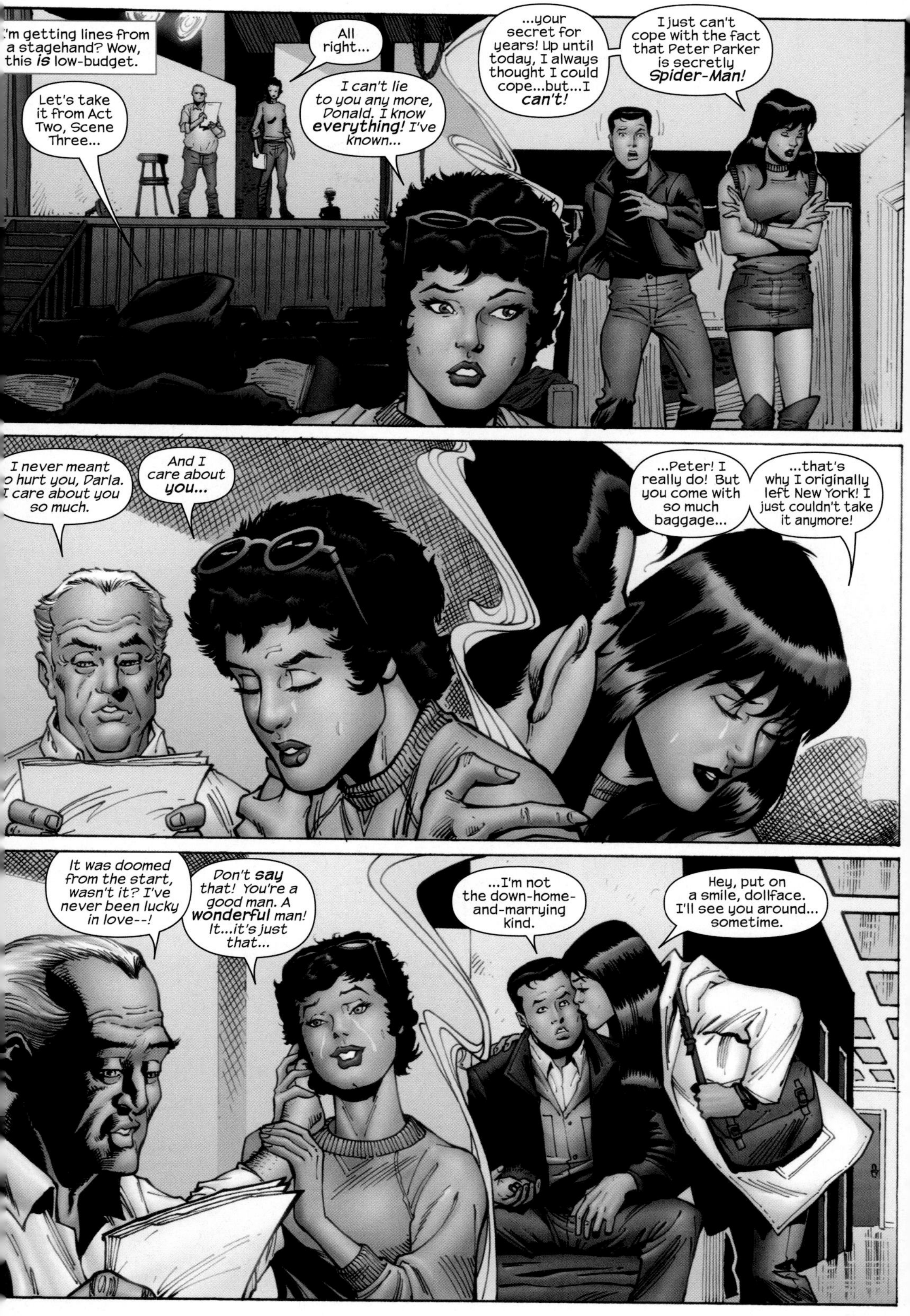
I'm getting lines from a stagehand? Wow, this *is* low-budget.
Let's take it from Act Two, Scene Three...
All right...
I can't lie to you any more, Donald. I know **everything!** I've known...
...your secret for years! Up until today, I always thought I could cope...but...I **can't!**
I just can't cope with the fact that Peter Parker is secretly **Spider-Man!**
I never meant to hurt you, Darla. I care about you so much.
And I care about **you...**
...Peter! I really do! But you come with so much baggage...
...that's why I originally left New York! I just couldn't take it anymore!
It was doomed from the start, wasn't it? I've never been lucky in love--!
Don't **say** that! You're a good man. A **wonderful** man! It...it's just that...
...I'm not the down-home-and-marrying kind.
Hey, put on a smile, dollface. I'll see you around... sometime.

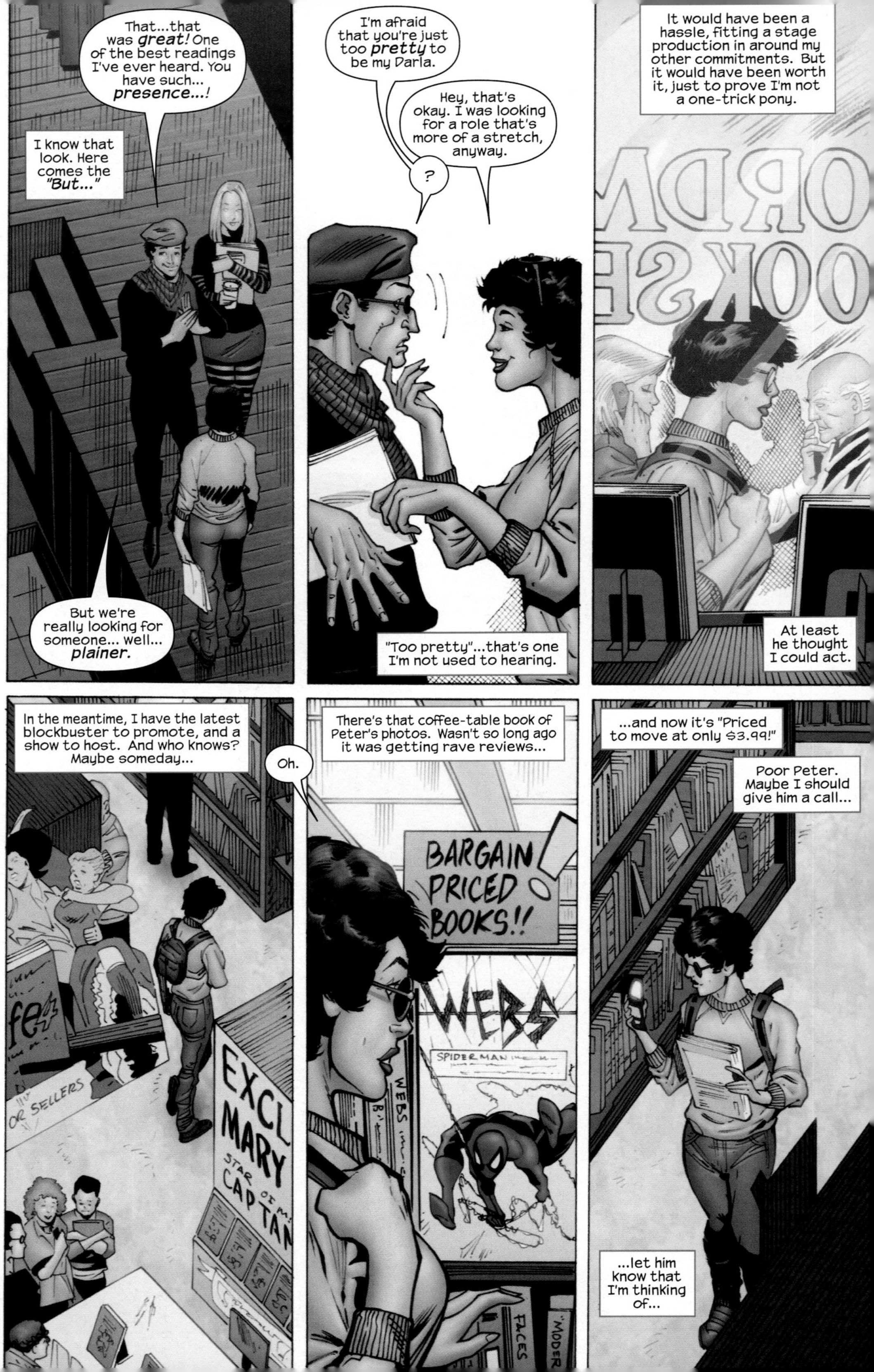

That...that was great! One of the best readings I've ever heard. You have such... presence...!
I know that look. Here comes the "But..."
But we're really looking for someone... well... plainer.
I'm afraid that you're just too pretty to be my Darla.
Hey, that's okay. I was looking for a role that's more of a stretch, anyway.
?
"Too pretty"...that's one I'm not used to hearing.
It would have been a hassle, fitting a stage production in around my other commitments. But it would have been worth it, just to prove I'm not a one-trick pony.
At least he thought I could act.
In the meantime, I have the latest blockbuster to promote, and a show to host. And who knows? Maybe someday...
OR SELLERS
EXCL
MARY
STAR
CAPTAN
There's that coffee-table book of Peter's photos. Wasn't so long ago it was getting rave reviews...
Oh.
BARGAIN PRICED BOOKS!!
WEBS
SPIDERMAN
WEBS
FACES
MODER
...and now it's "Priced to move at only $3.99!"
Poor Peter. Maybe I should give him a call...
...let him know that I'm thinking of...

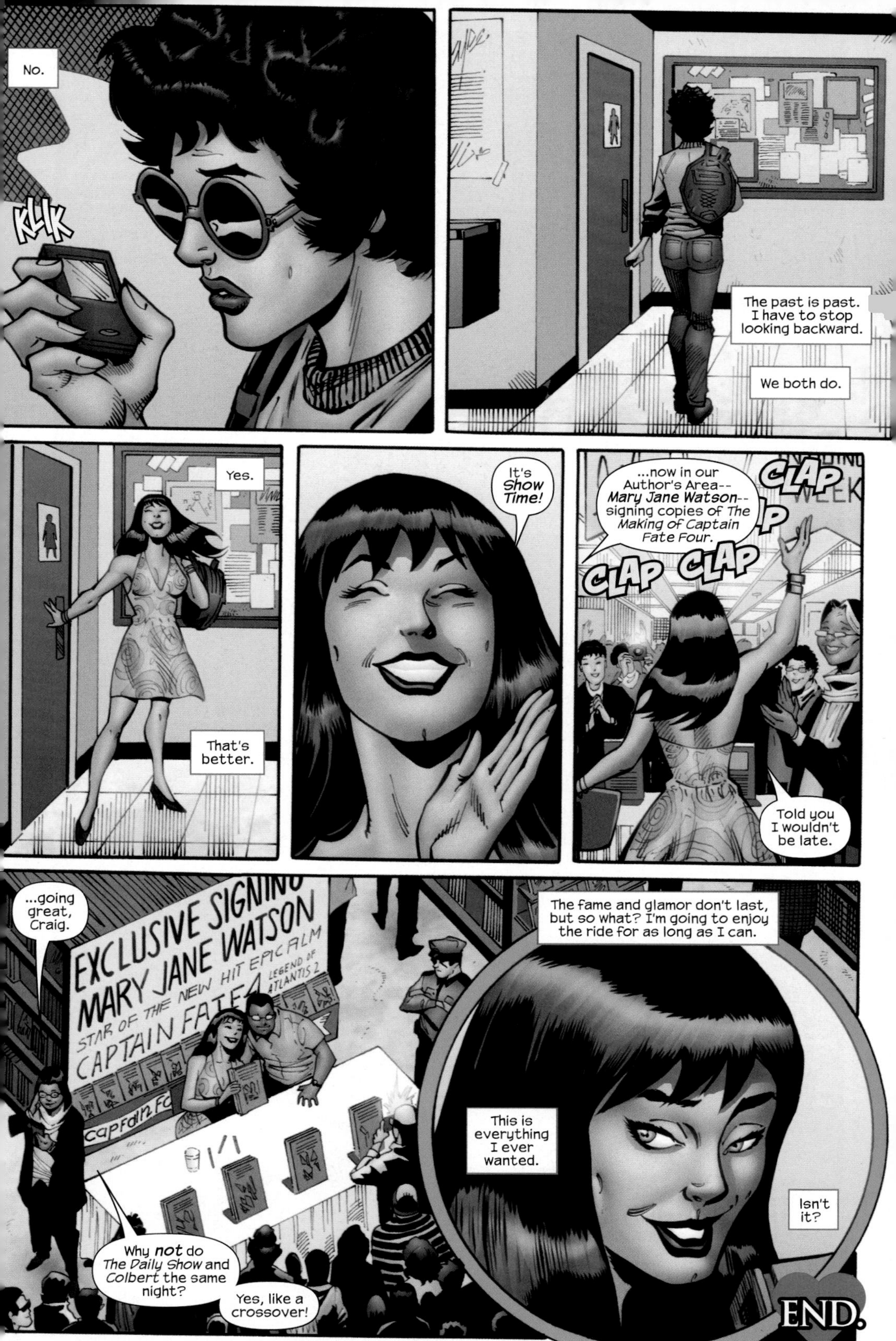

No.
KLIK
The past is past. I have to stop looking backward.
We both do.
Yes.
That's better.
It's *Show Time!*
...now in our Author's Area-- **Mary Jane Watson**-- signing copies of *The Making of Captain Fate Four.*
CLAP
CLAP
CLAP
CLAP
Told you I wouldn't be late.
...going great, Craig.
EXCLUSIVE SIGNING
MARY JANE WATSON
STAR OF THE NEW HIT EPIC FILM
CAPTAIN FATE 4
LEGEND OF ATLANTIS 2
The fame and glamor don't last, but so what? I'm going to enjoy the ride for as long as I can.
This is everything I ever wanted.
Isn't it?
Why **not** do *The Daily Show* and *Colbert* the same night?
Yes, like a crossover!
END.

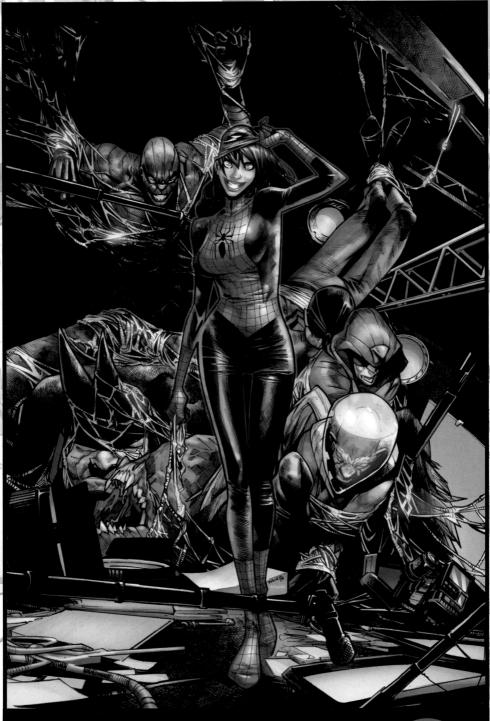

AMAZING MARY JANE #5

MARY JANE AND THE REFORMED VILLAIN MYSTERIO ARE TRYING TO MAKE
A BLOCKBUSTER HOLLYWOOD FILM... THAT IS, IF THE SAVAGE SIX DON'T

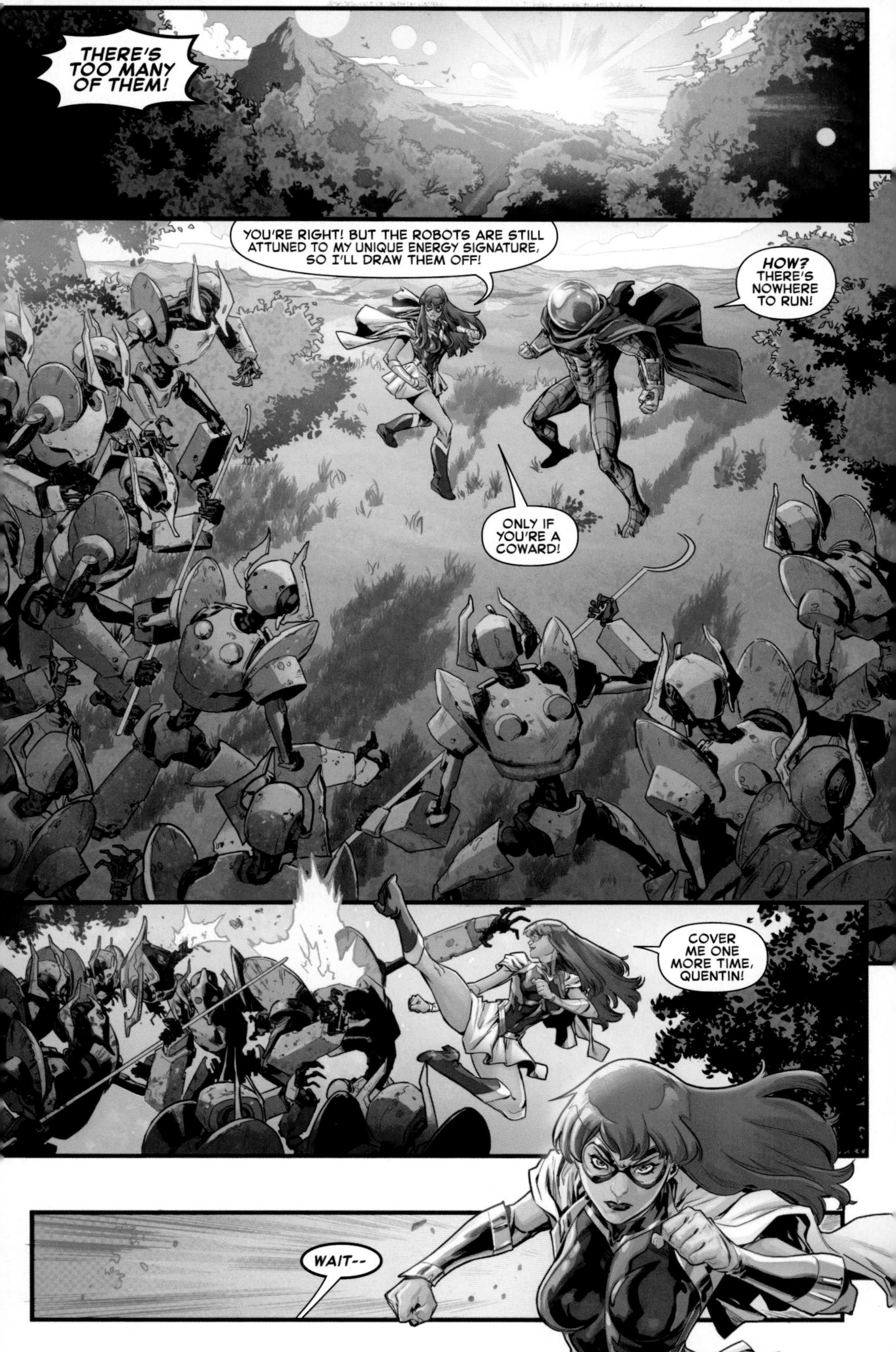
THERE'S TOO MANY OF THEM!
YOU'RE RIGHT! BUT THE ROBOTS ARE STILL ATTUNED TO MY UNIQUE ENERGY SIGNATURE, SO I'LL DRAW THEM OFF!
HOW? THERE'S NOWHERE TO RUN!
ONLY IF YOU'RE A COWARD!
COVER ME ONE MORE TIME, QUENTIN!
WAIT--

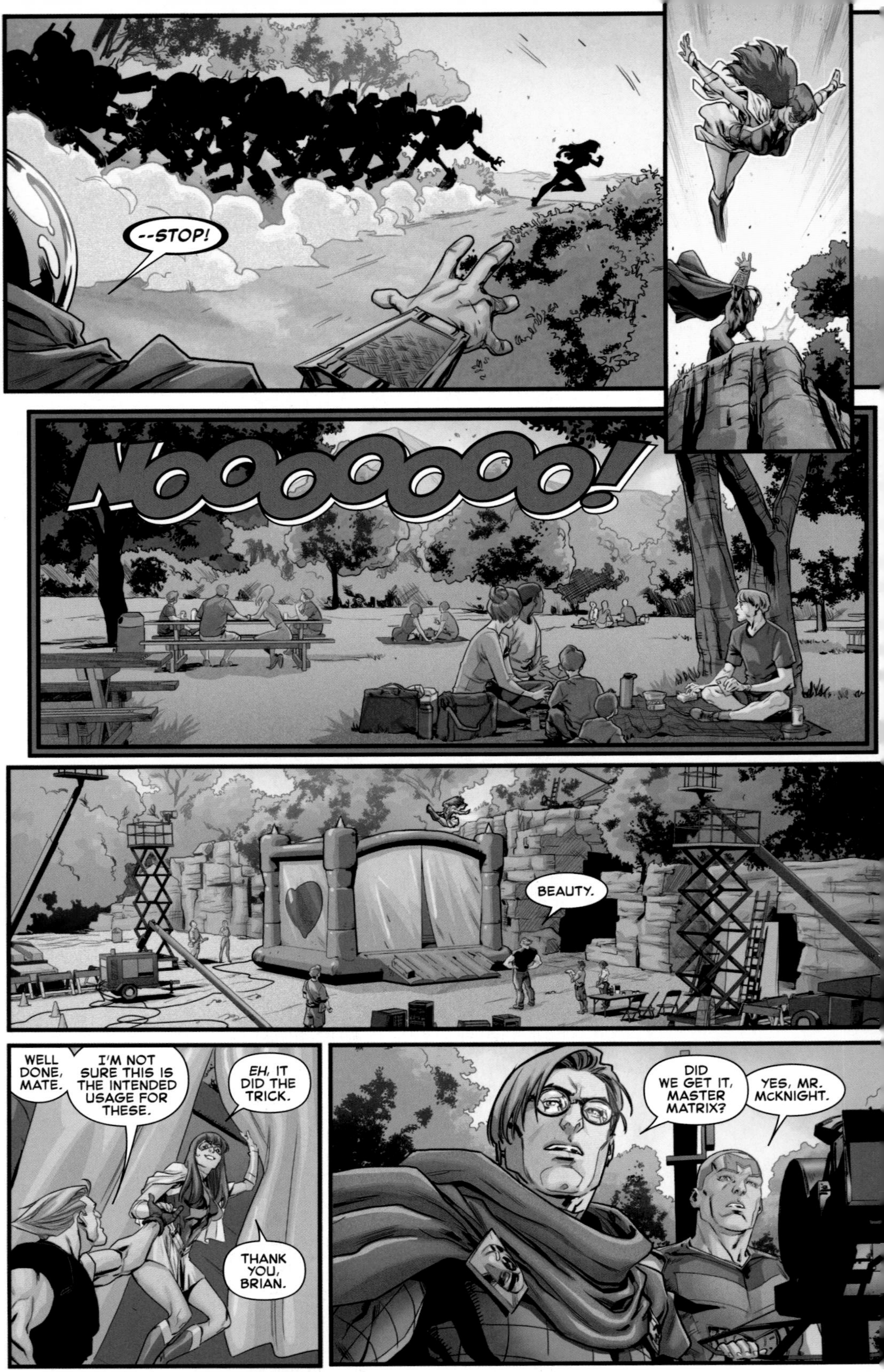

--STOP!
NOOOOOOO!
BEAUTY.
WELL DONE, MATE.
I'M NOT SURE THIS IS THE INTENDED USAGE FOR THESE.
EH, IT DID THE TRICK.
THANK YOU, BRIAN.
DID WE GET IT, MASTER MATRIX?
YES, MR. McKNIGHT.

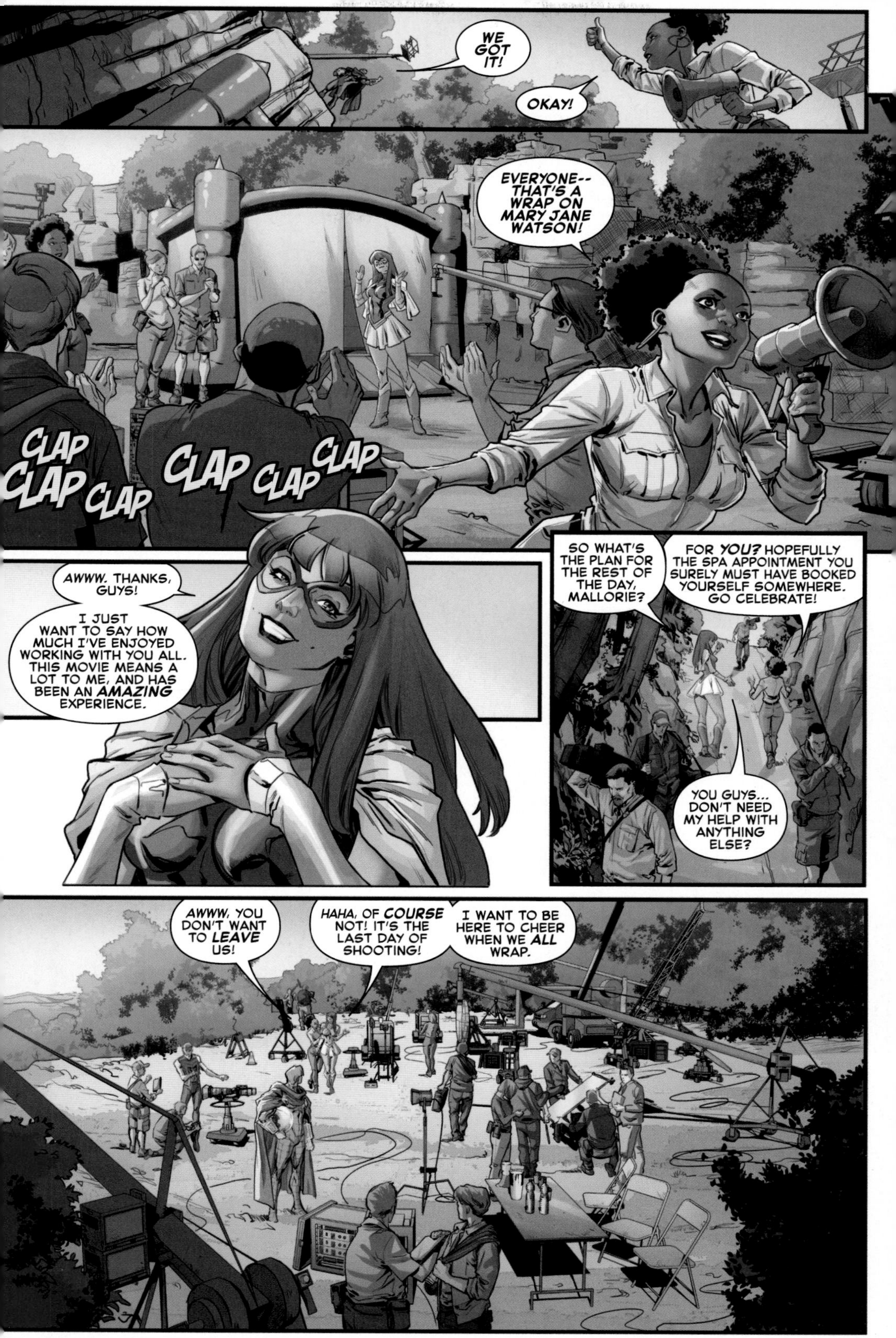
WE GOT IT!
OKAY!
EVERYONE-- THAT'S A WRAP ON MARY JANE WATSON!
CLAP CLAP CLAP CLAP CLAP CLAP
AWWW. THANKS, GUYS!
I JUST WANT TO SAY HOW MUCH I'VE ENJOYED WORKING WITH YOU ALL. THIS MOVIE MEANS A LOT TO ME, AND HAS BEEN AN AMAZING EXPERIENCE.
SO WHAT'S THE PLAN FOR THE REST OF THE DAY, MALLORIE?
FOR YOU? HOPEFULLY THE SPA APPOINTMENT YOU SURELY MUST HAVE BOOKED YOURSELF SOMEWHERE. GO CELEBRATE!
YOU GUYS... DON'T NEED MY HELP WITH ANYTHING ELSE?
AWWW, YOU DON'T WANT TO LEAVE US!
HAHA, OF COURSE NOT! IT'S THE LAST DAY OF SHOOTING!
I WANT TO BE HERE TO CHEER WHEN WE ALL WRAP.

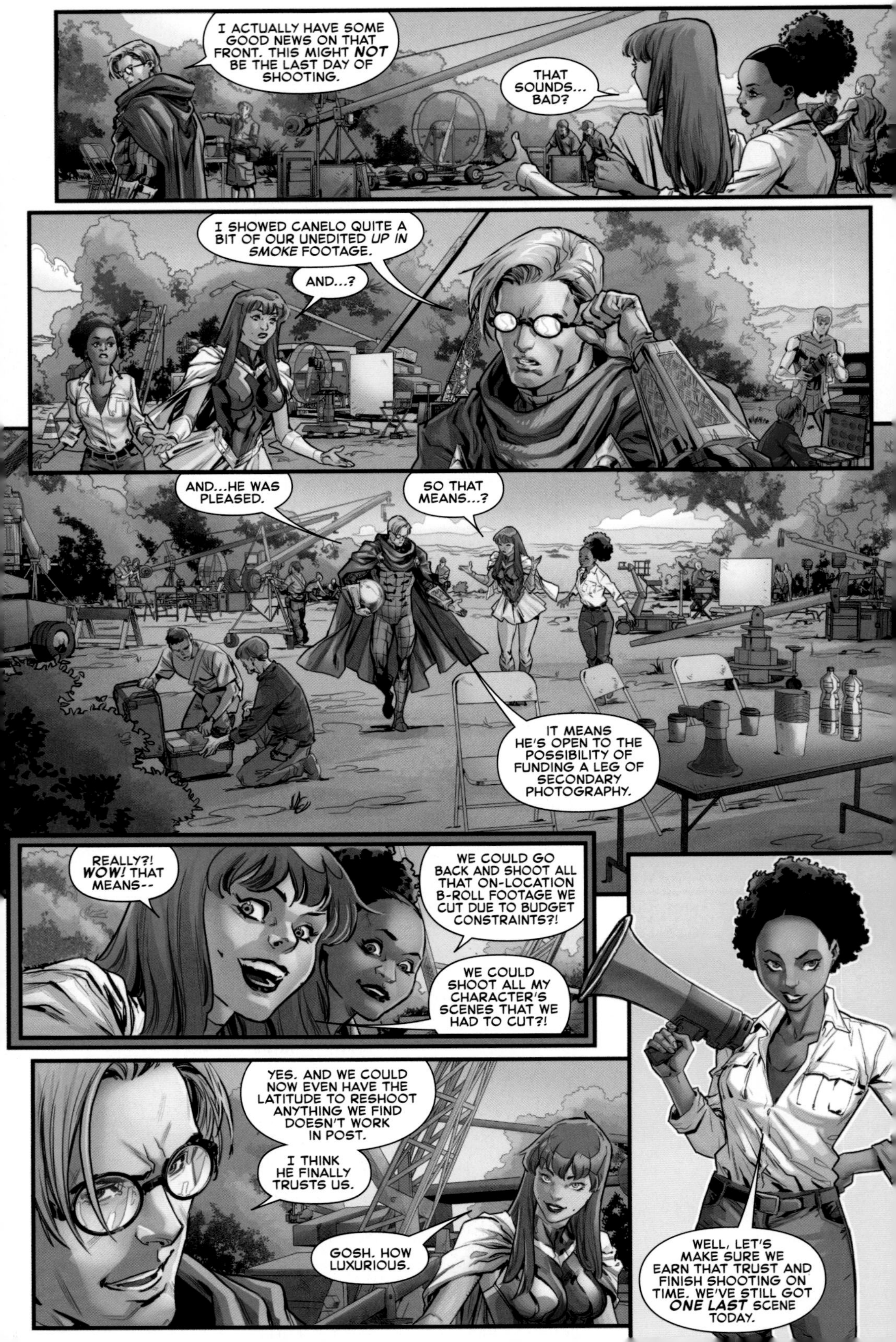
I ACTUALLY HAVE SOME GOOD NEWS ON THAT FRONT. THIS MIGHT NOT BE THE LAST DAY OF SHOOTING.
THAT SOUNDS... BAD?
I SHOWED CANELO QUITE A BIT OF OUR UNEDITED UP IN SMOKE FOOTAGE.
AND...?
AND...HE WAS PLEASED.
SO THAT MEANS...?
IT MEANS HE'S OPEN TO THE POSSIBILITY OF FUNDING A LEG OF SECONDARY PHOTOGRAPHY.
REALLY?! WOW! THAT MEANS--
WE COULD GO BACK AND SHOOT ALL THAT ON-LOCATION B-ROLL FOOTAGE WE CUT DUE TO BUDGET CONSTRAINTS?!
WE COULD SHOOT ALL MY CHARACTER'S SCENES THAT WE HAD TO CUT?!
YES. AND WE COULD NOW EVEN HAVE THE LATITUDE TO RESHOOT ANYTHING WE FIND DOESN'T WORK IN POST.
I THINK HE FINALLY TRUSTS US.
GOSH. HOW LUXURIOUS.
WELL, LET'S MAKE SURE WE EARN THAT TRUST AND FINISH SHOOTING ON TIME. WE'VE STILL GOT ONE LAST SCENE TODAY.

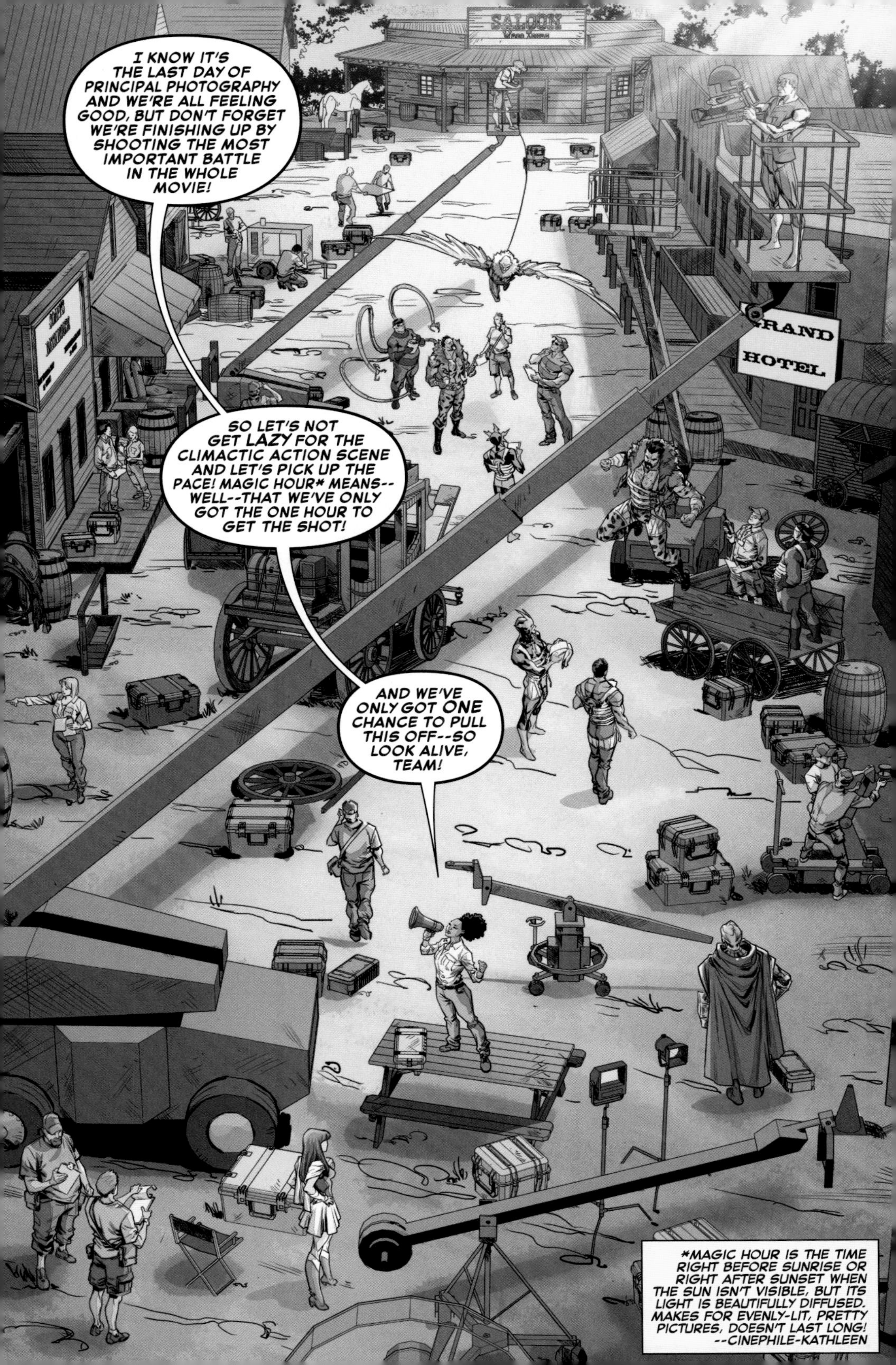
SALOON
I KNOW IT'S THE LAST DAY OF PRINCIPAL PHOTOGRAPHY AND WE'RE ALL FEELING GOOD, BUT DON'T FORGET WE'RE FINISHING UP BY SHOOTING THE MOST IMPORTANT BATTLE IN THE WHOLE MOVIE!
GRAND HOTEL
SO LET'S NOT GET LAZY FOR THE CLIMACTIC ACTION SCENE AND LET'S PICK UP THE PACE! MAGIC HOUR* MEANS--WELL--THAT WE'VE ONLY GOT THE ONE HOUR TO GET THE SHOT!
AND WE'VE ONLY GOT ONE CHANCE TO PULL THIS OFF--SO LOOK ALIVE, TEAM!
*MAGIC HOUR IS THE TIME RIGHT BEFORE SUNRISE OR RIGHT AFTER SUNSET WHEN THE SUN ISN'T VISIBLE, BUT ITS LIGHT IS BEAUTIFULLY DIFFUSED. MAKES FOR EVENLY-LIT, PRETTY PICTURES, DOESN'T LAST LONG! --CINEPHILE-KATHLEEN

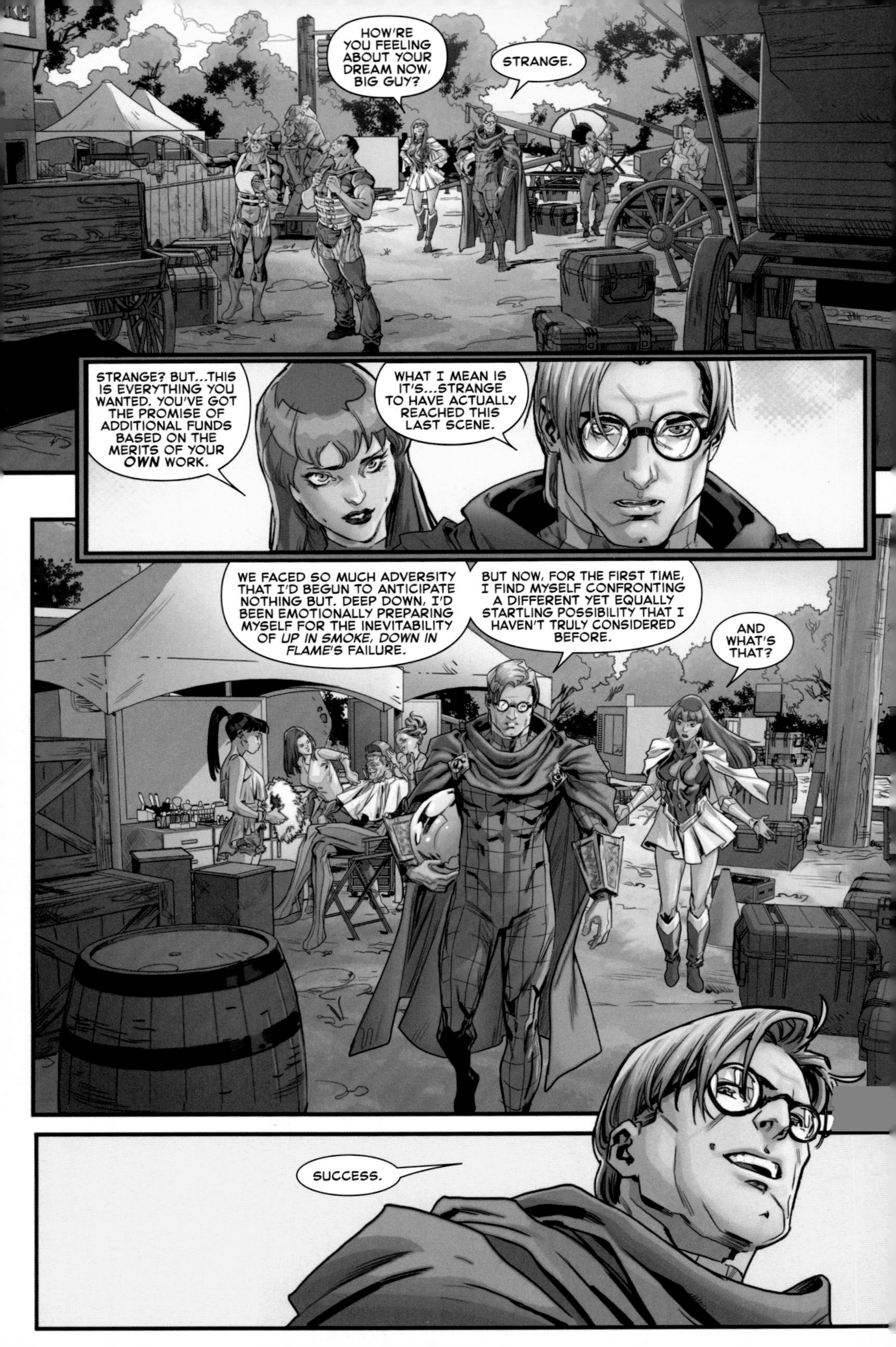
HOW'RE YOU FEELING ABOUT YOUR DREAM NOW, BIG GUY?
STRANGE.
STRANGE? BUT...THIS IS EVERYTHING YOU WANTED. YOU'VE GOT THE PROMISE OF ADDITIONAL FUNDS BASED ON THE MERITS OF YOUR OWN WORK.
WHAT I MEAN IS IT'S...STRANGE TO HAVE ACTUALLY REACHED THIS LAST SCENE.
WE FACED SO MUCH ADVERSITY THAT I'D BEGUN TO ANTICIPATE NOTHING BUT. DEEP DOWN, I'D BEEN EMOTIONALLY PREPARING MYSELF FOR THE INEVITABILITY OF UP IN SMOKE, DOWN IN FLAME'S FAILURE.
BUT NOW, FOR THE FIRST TIME, I FIND MYSELF CONFRONTING A DIFFERENT YET EQUALLY STARTLING POSSIBILITY THAT I HAVEN'T TRULY CONSIDERED BEFORE.
AND WHAT'S THAT?
SUCCESS.

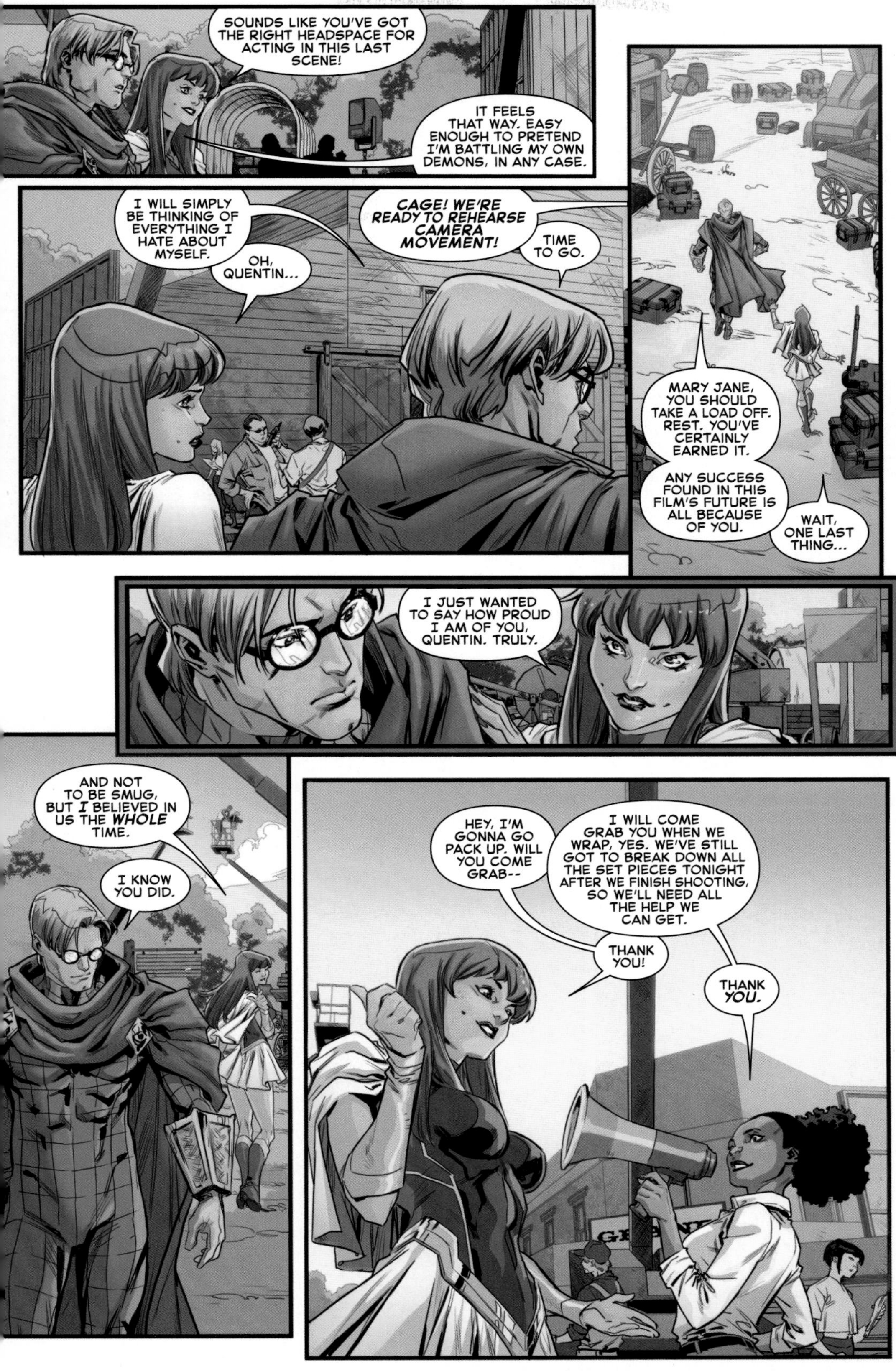
SOUNDS LIKE YOU'VE GOT THE RIGHT HEADSPACE FOR ACTING IN THIS LAST SCENE!
IT FEELS THAT WAY. EASY ENOUGH TO PRETEND I'M BATTLING MY OWN DEMONS, IN ANY CASE.
I WILL SIMPLY BE THINKING OF EVERYTHING I HATE ABOUT MYSELF.
OH, QUENTIN...
CAGE! WE'RE READY TO REHEARSE CAMERA MOVEMENT!
TIME TO GO.
MARY JANE, YOU SHOULD TAKE A LOAD OFF. REST. YOU'VE CERTAINLY EARNED IT.
ANY SUCCESS FOUND IN THIS FILM'S FUTURE IS ALL BECAUSE OF YOU.
WAIT, ONE LAST THING...
I JUST WANTED TO SAY HOW PROUD I AM OF YOU, QUENTIN. TRULY.
AND NOT TO BE SMUG, BUT I BELIEVED IN US THE WHOLE TIME.
I KNOW YOU DID.
HEY, I'M GONNA GO PACK UP. WILL YOU COME GRAB--
I WILL COME GRAB YOU WHEN WE WRAP, YES. WE'VE STILL GOT TO BREAK DOWN ALL THE SET PIECES TONIGHT AFTER WE FINISH SHOOTING, SO WE'LL NEED ALL THE HELP WE CAN GET.
THANK YOU!
THANK YOU.

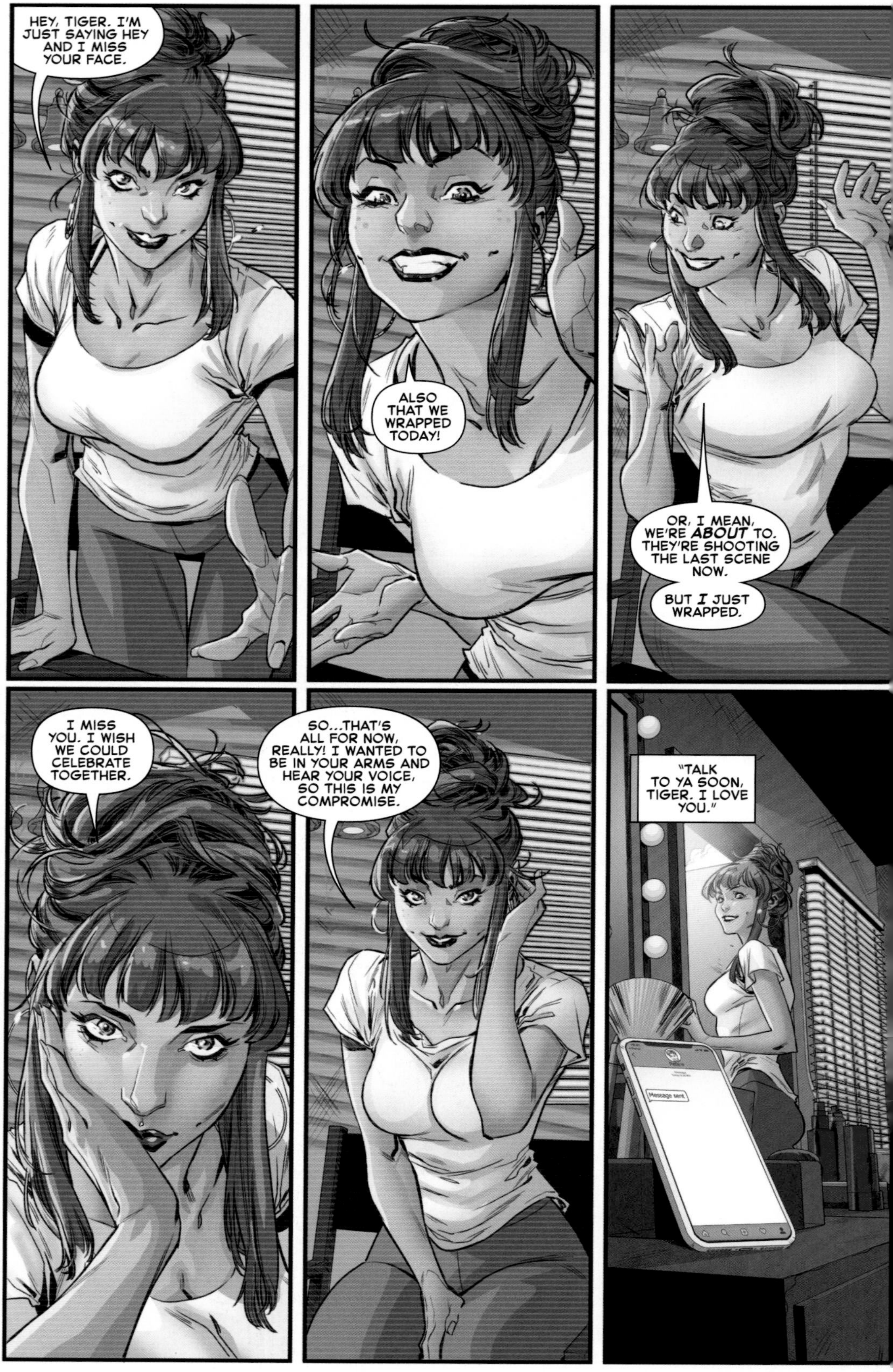
HEY, TIGER. I'M JUST SAYING HEY AND I MISS YOUR FACE.
ALSO THAT WE WRAPPED TODAY!
OR, I MEAN, WE'RE *ABOUT* TO. THEY'RE SHOOTING THE LAST SCENE NOW.
BUT *I* JUST WRAPPED.
I MISS YOU. I WISH WE COULD CELEBRATE TOGETHER.
SO...THAT'S ALL FOR NOW, REALLY! I WANTED TO BE IN YOUR ARMS AND HEAR YOUR VOICE, SO THIS IS MY COMPROMISE.
"TALK TO YA SOON, TIGER. I LOVE YOU."
Message sent

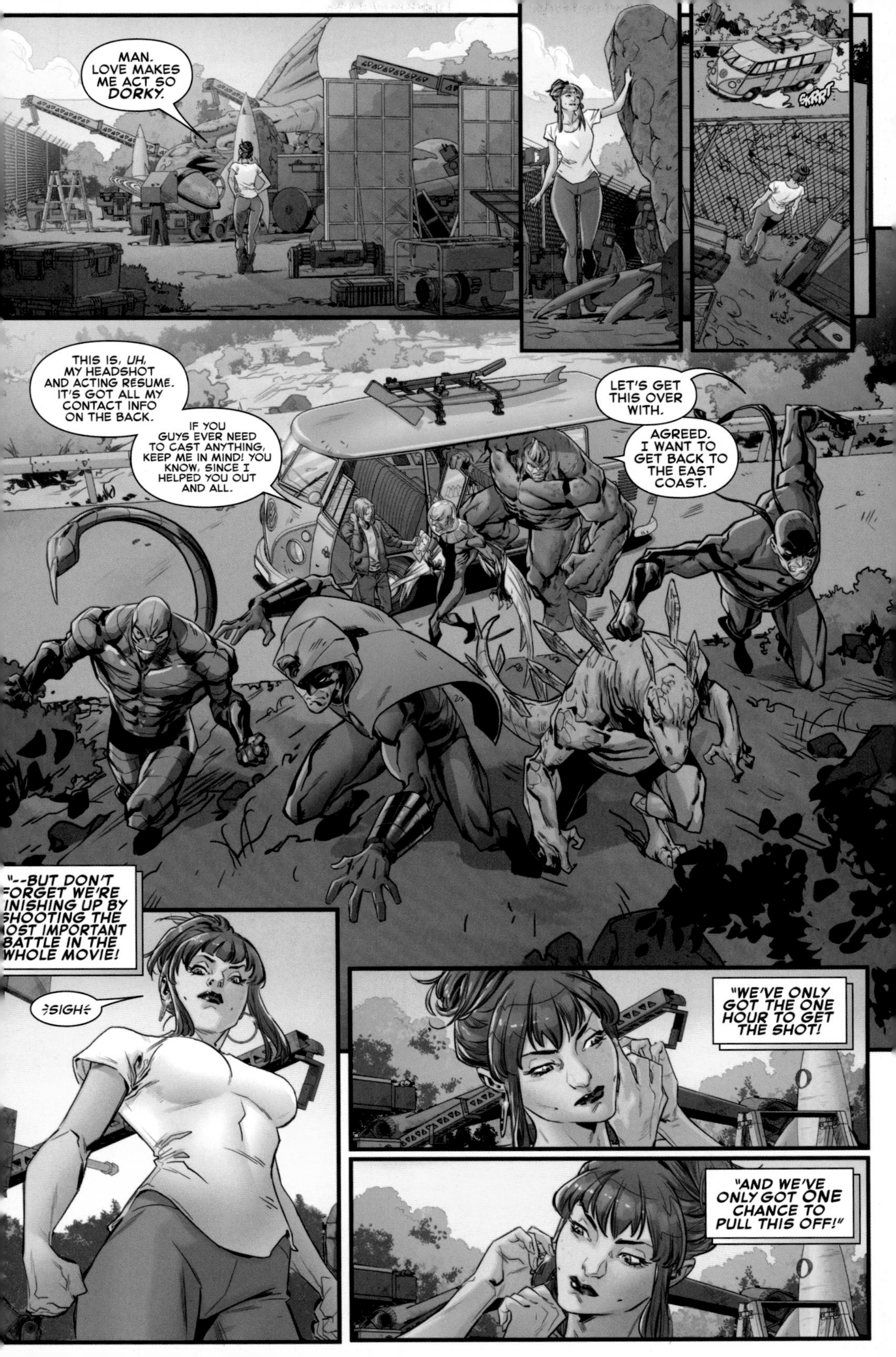
MAN. LOVE MAKES ME ACT SO DORKY.
SKRRT
THIS IS, UH, MY HEADSHOT AND ACTING RESUME. IT'S GOT ALL MY CONTACT INFO ON THE BACK.
IF YOU GUYS EVER NEED TO CAST ANYTHING, KEEP ME IN MIND! YOU KNOW, SINCE I HELPED YOU OUT AND ALL.
LET'S GET THIS OVER WITH.
AGREED. I WANT TO GET BACK TO THE EAST COAST.
"--BUT DON'T FORGET WE'RE FINISHING UP BY SHOOTING THE MOST IMPORTANT BATTLE IN THE WHOLE MOVIE!
SIGH
"WE'VE ONLY GOT THE ONE HOUR TO GET THE SHOT!
"AND WE'VE ONLY GOT ONE CHANCE TO PULL THIS OFF!"

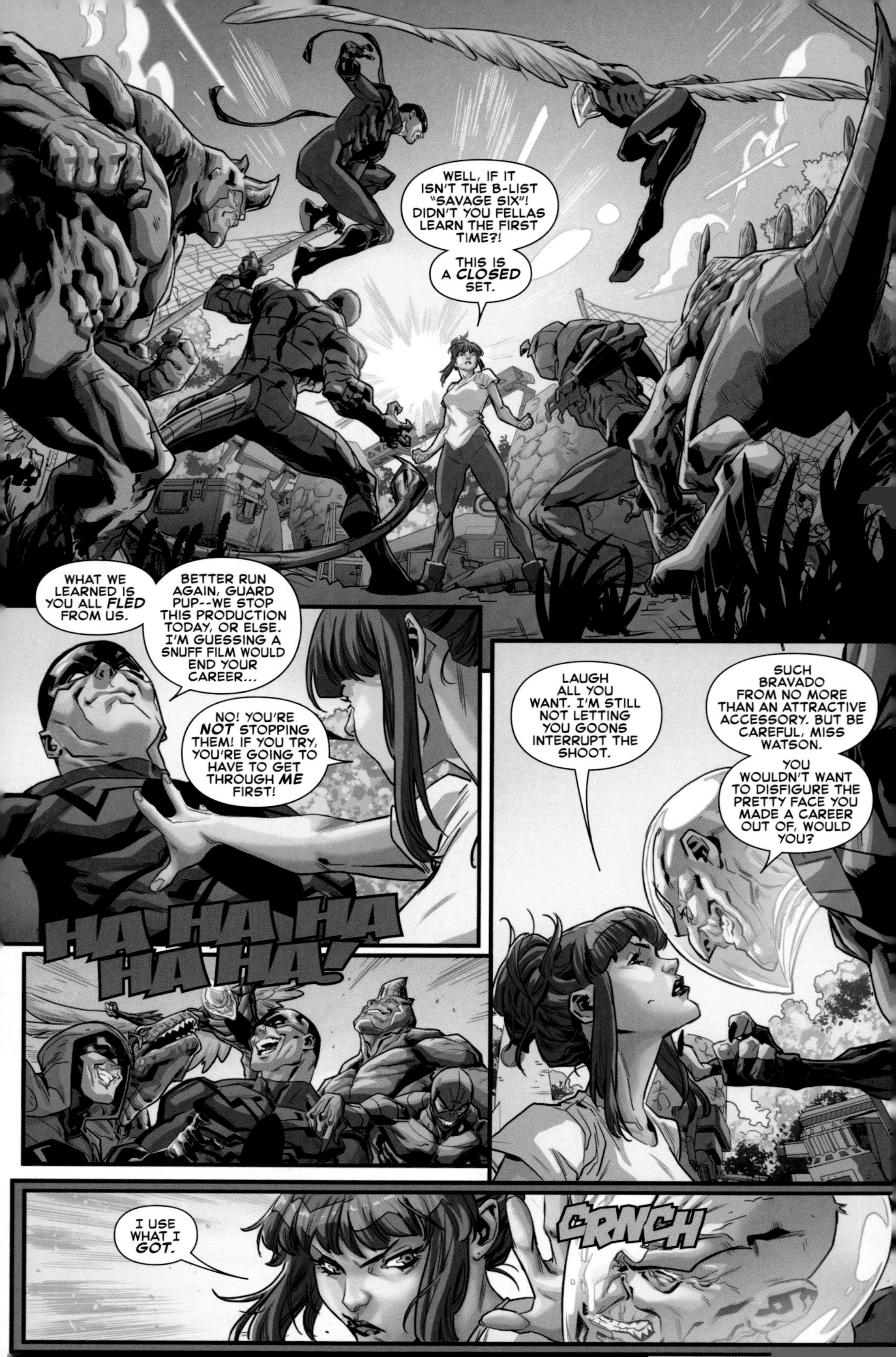
WELL, IF IT ISN'T THE B-LIST "SAVAGE SIX"! DIDN'T YOU FELLAS LEARN THE FIRST TIME?!
THIS IS A *CLOSED* SET.
WHAT WE LEARNED IS YOU ALL *FLED* FROM US.
BETTER RUN AGAIN, GUARD PUP--WE STOP THIS PRODUCTION TODAY, OR ELSE. I'M GUESSING A SNUFF FILM WOULD END YOUR CAREER...
NO! YOU'RE *NOT* STOPPING THEM! IF YOU TRY, YOU'RE GOING TO HAVE TO GET THROUGH *ME* FIRST!
HA HA HA HA HA HA!
LAUGH ALL YOU WANT. I'M STILL NOT LETTING YOU GOONS INTERRUPT THE SHOOT.
SUCH BRAVADO FROM NO MORE THAN AN ATTRACTIVE ACCESSORY. BUT BE CAREFUL, MISS WATSON.
YOU WOULDN'T WANT TO DISFIGURE THE PRETTY FACE YOU MADE A CAREER OUT OF, WOULD YOU?
I USE WHAT I *GOT*.
CRNCH

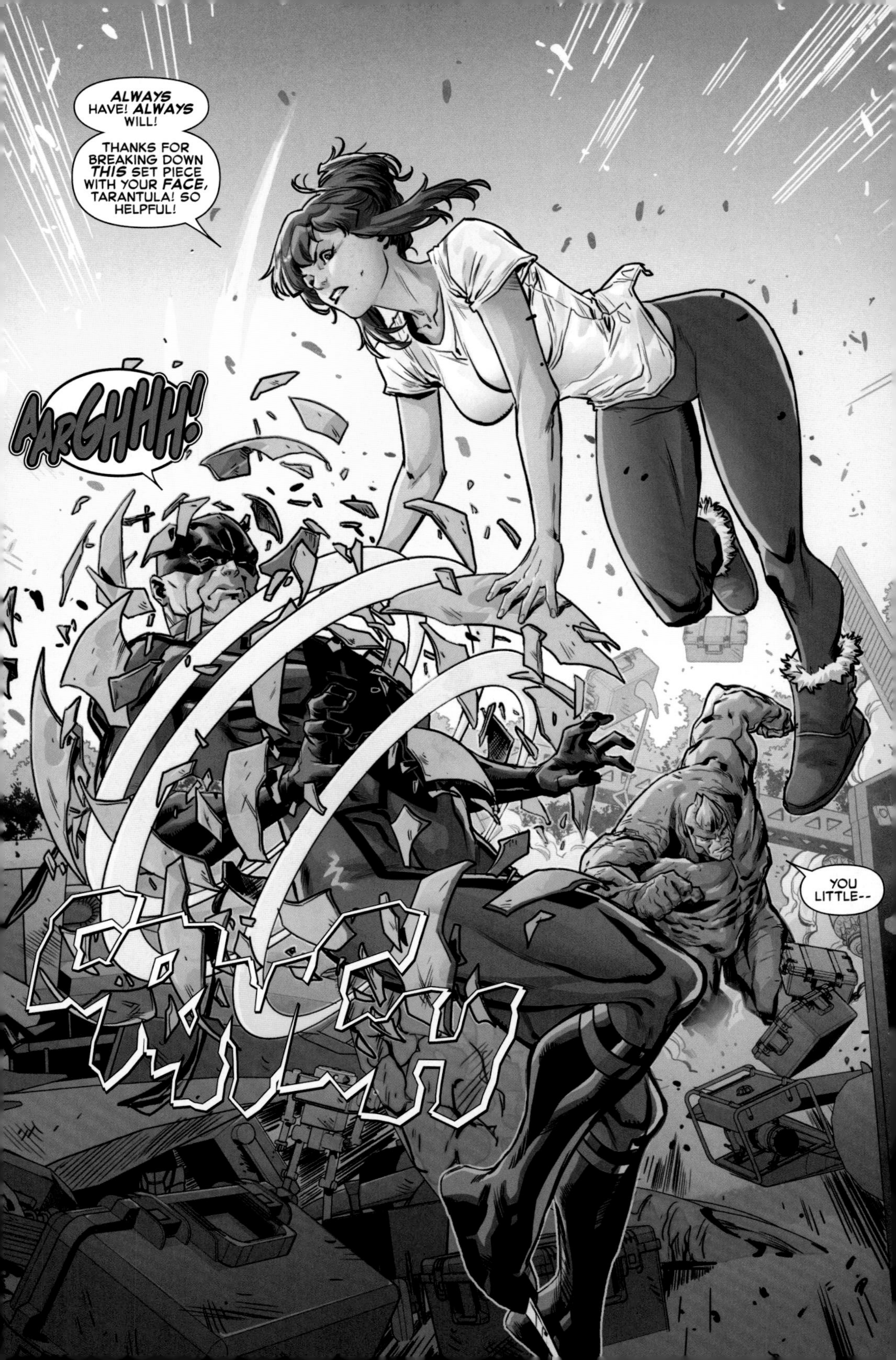

ALWAYS HAVE! ALWAYS WILL!
THANKS FOR BREAKING DOWN THIS SET PIECE WITH YOUR FACE, TARANTULA! SO HELPFUL!
AARGHHH!
YOU LITTLE--

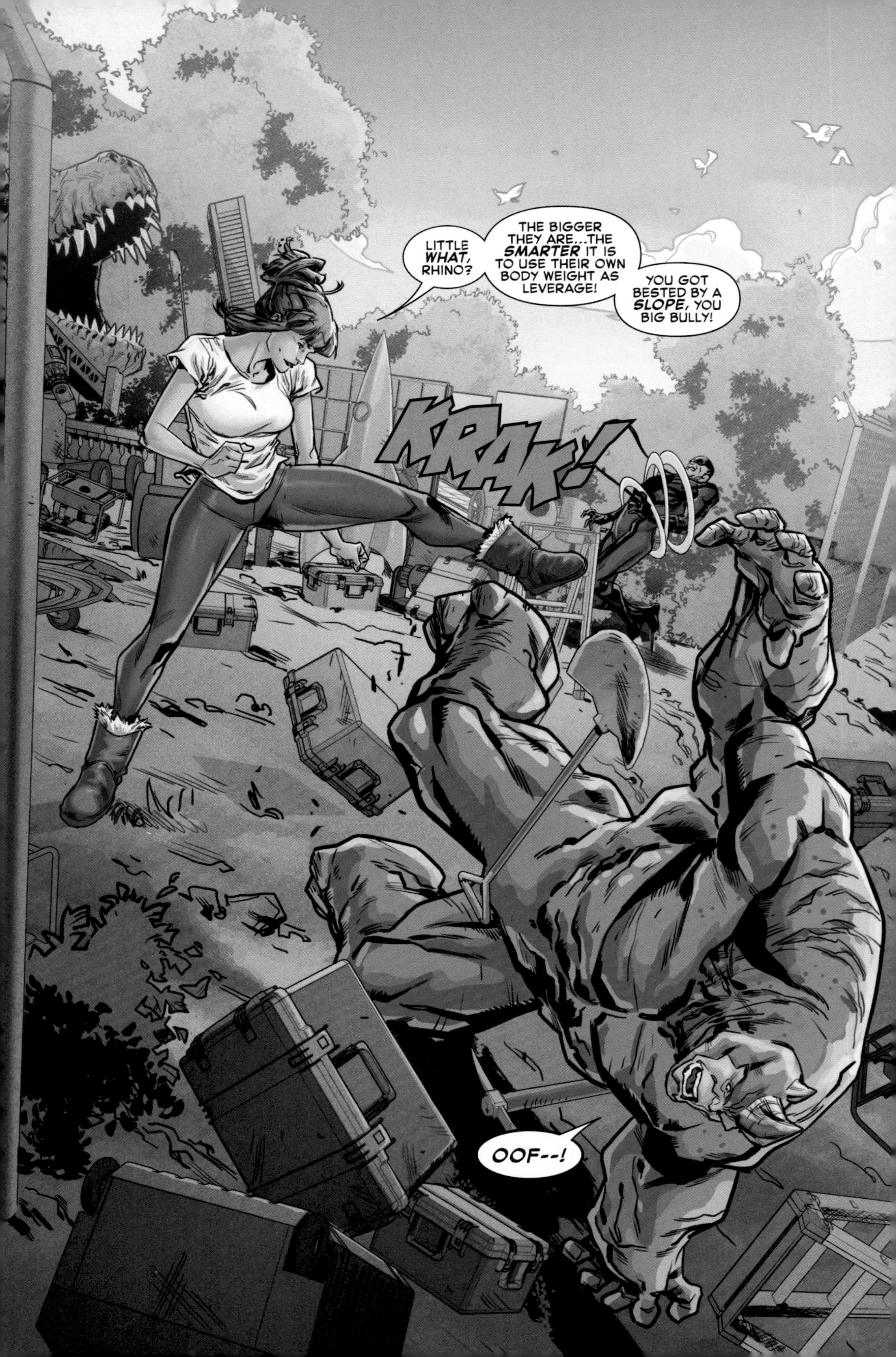
LITTLE WHAT, RHINO?
THE BIGGER THEY ARE...THE SMARTER IT IS TO USE THEIR OWN BODY WEIGHT AS LEVERAGE!
YOU GOT BESTED BY A SLOPE, YOU BIG BULLY!
KRAK!
OOF--!

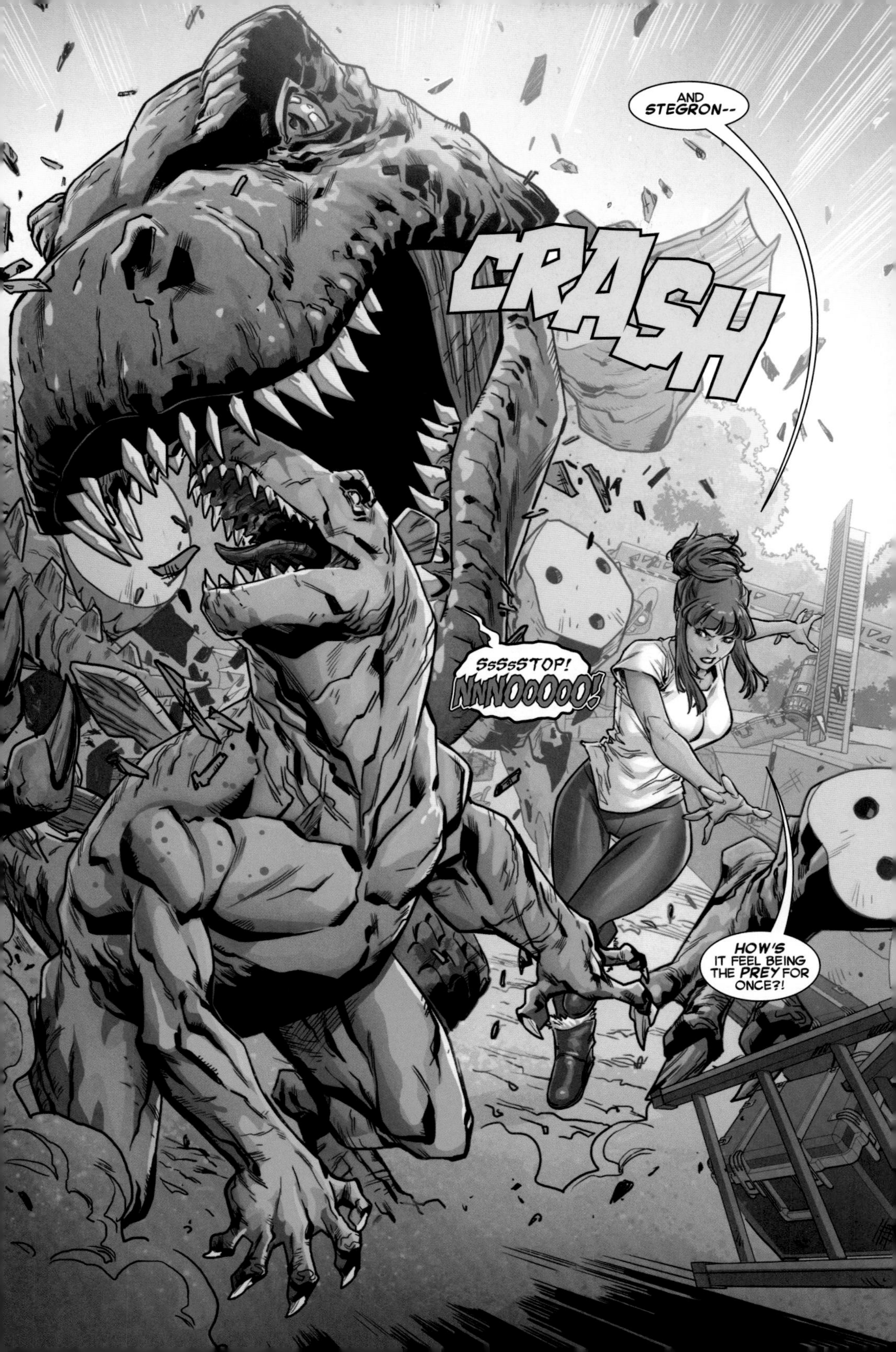
AND STEGRON--
CRASH
SsSsSTOP! NNNOOOOO!
HOW'S IT FEEL BEING THE PREY FOR ONCE?!

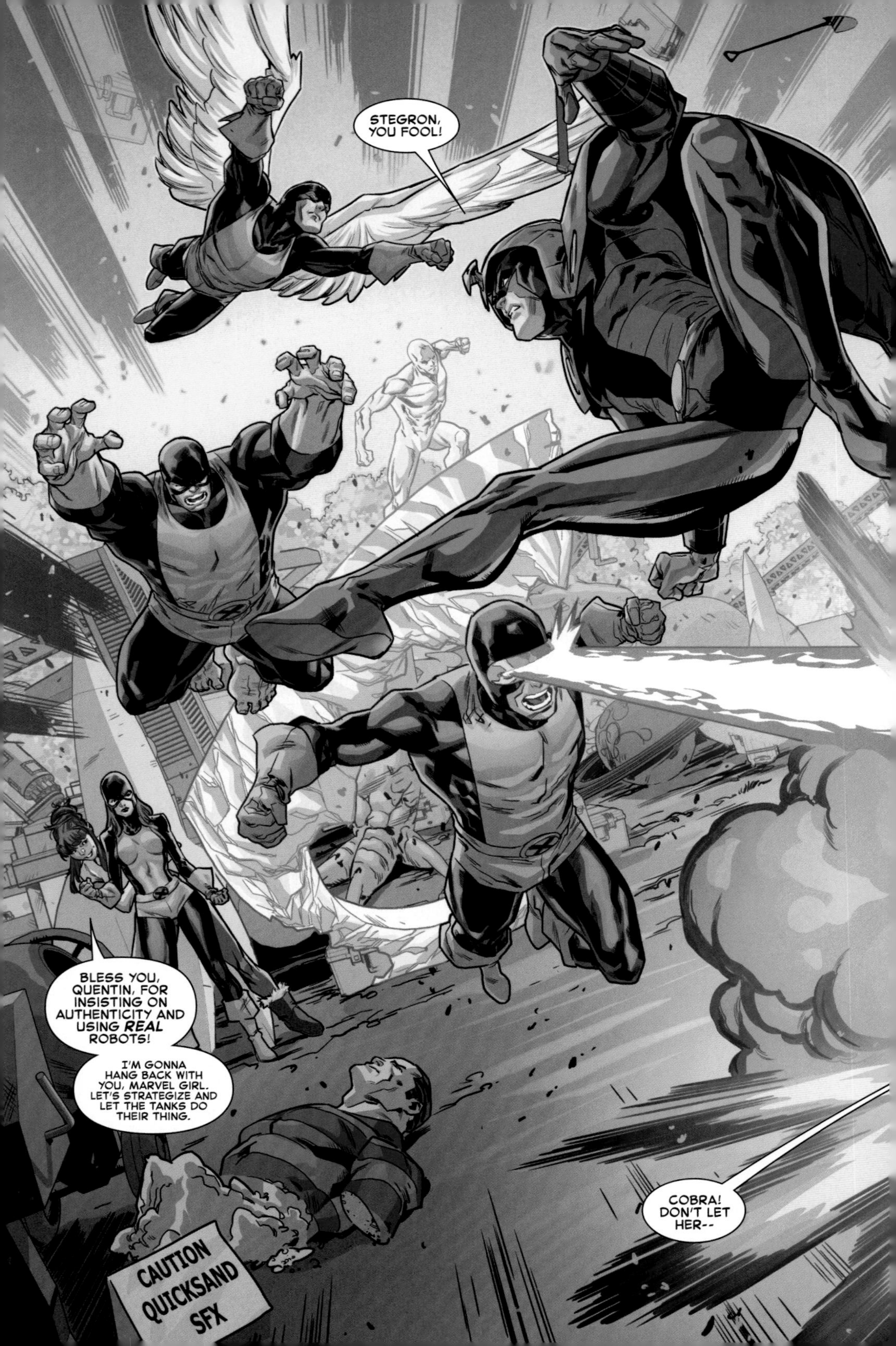
STEGRON, YOU FOOL!
BLESS YOU, QUENTIN, FOR INSISTING ON AUTHENTICITY AND USING *REAL* ROBOTS!
I'M GONNA HANG BACK WITH YOU, MARVEL GIRL. LET'S STRATEGIZE AND LET THE TANKS DO THEIR THING.
COBRA! DON'T LET HER--
CAUTION QUICKSAND SFX

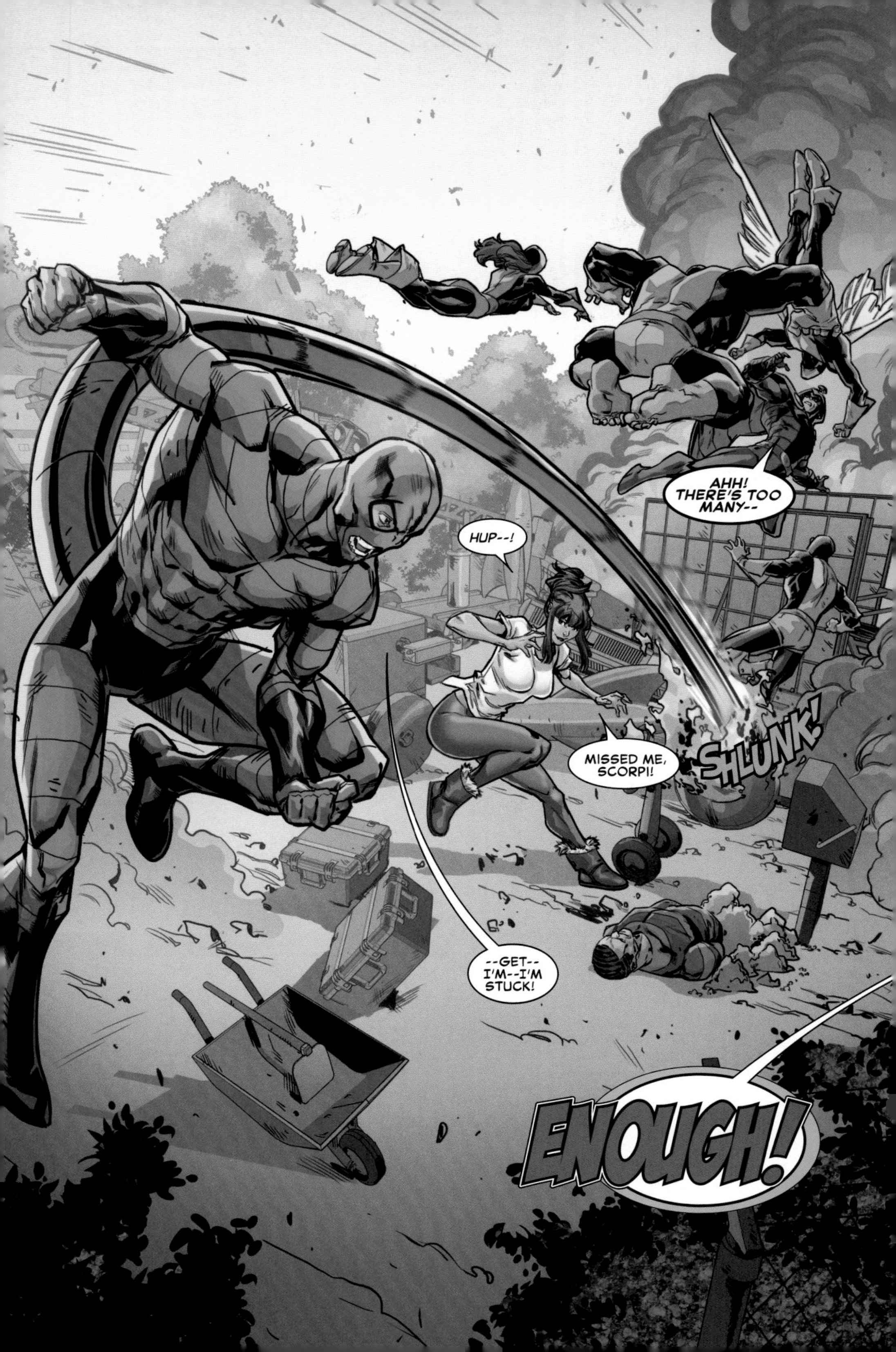
AHH! THERE'S TOO MANY--
HUP--!
MISSED ME, SCORPI!
SHLUNK!
--GET-- I'M--I'M STUCK!
ENOUGH!

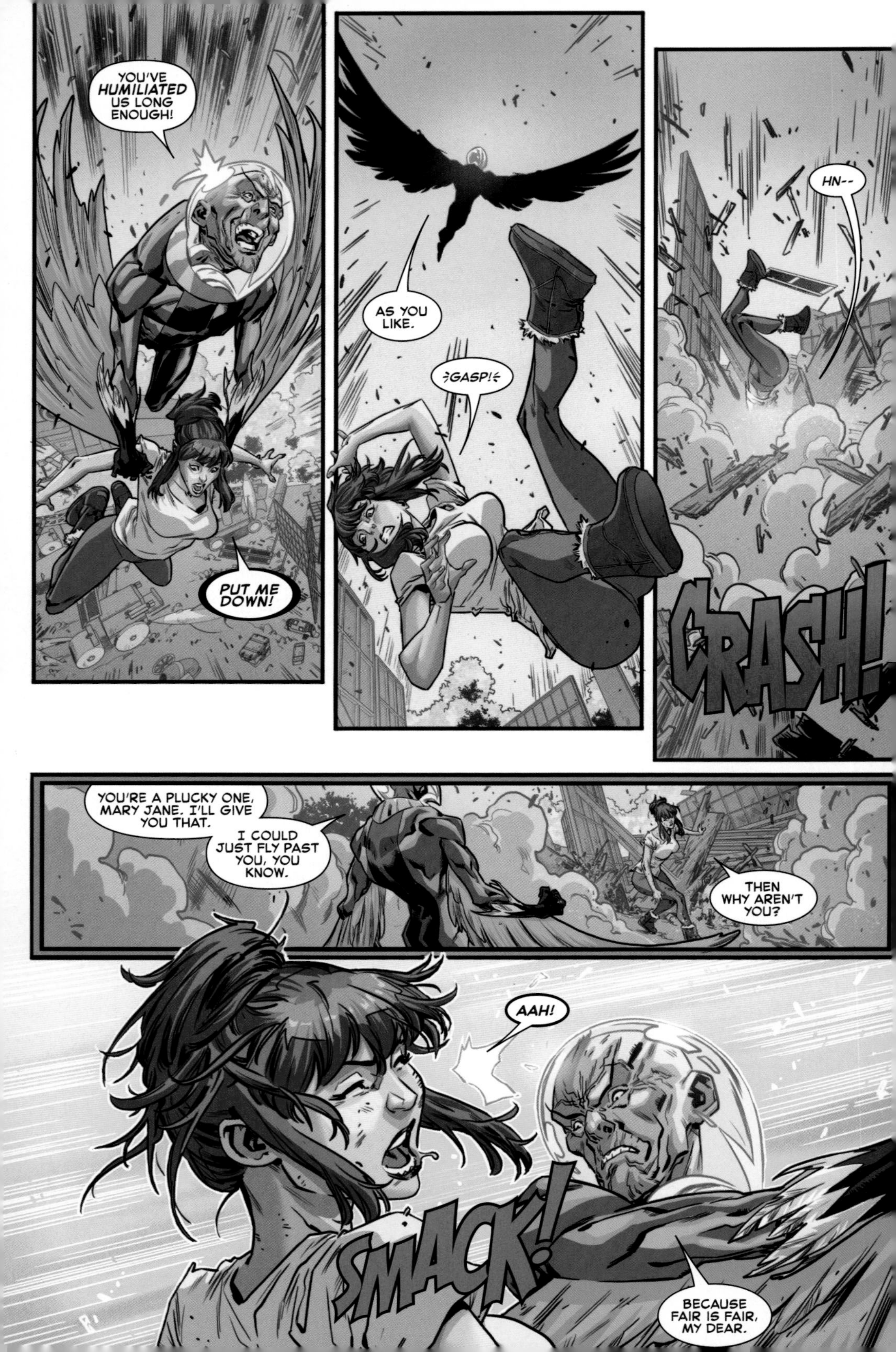
YOU'VE HUMILIATED US LONG ENOUGH!
PUT ME DOWN!
AS YOU LIKE.
GASP!
HN--
CRASH!
YOU'RE A PLUCKY ONE, MARY JANE. I'LL GIVE YOU THAT.
I COULD JUST FLY PAST YOU, YOU KNOW.
THEN WHY AREN'T YOU?
AAH!
SMACK!
BECAUSE FAIR IS FAIR, MY DEAR.

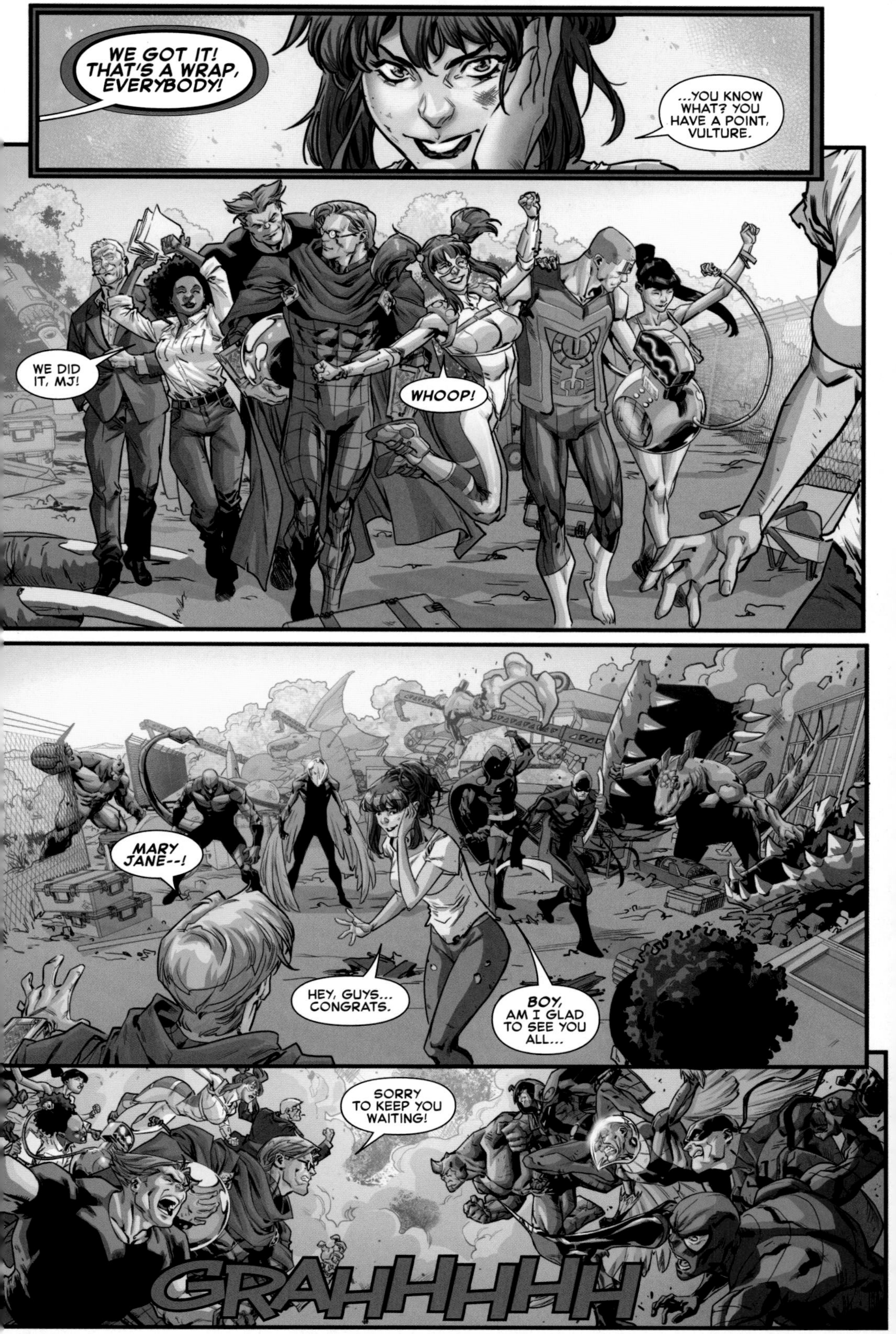
WE GOT IT! THAT'S A WRAP, EVERYBODY!
...YOU KNOW WHAT? YOU HAVE A POINT, VULTURE.
WE DID IT, MJ!
WHOOP!
MARY JANE--!
HEY, GUYS... CONGRATS.
BOY, AM I GLAD TO SEE YOU ALL...
SORRY TO KEEP YOU WAITING!
GRAHHHHH

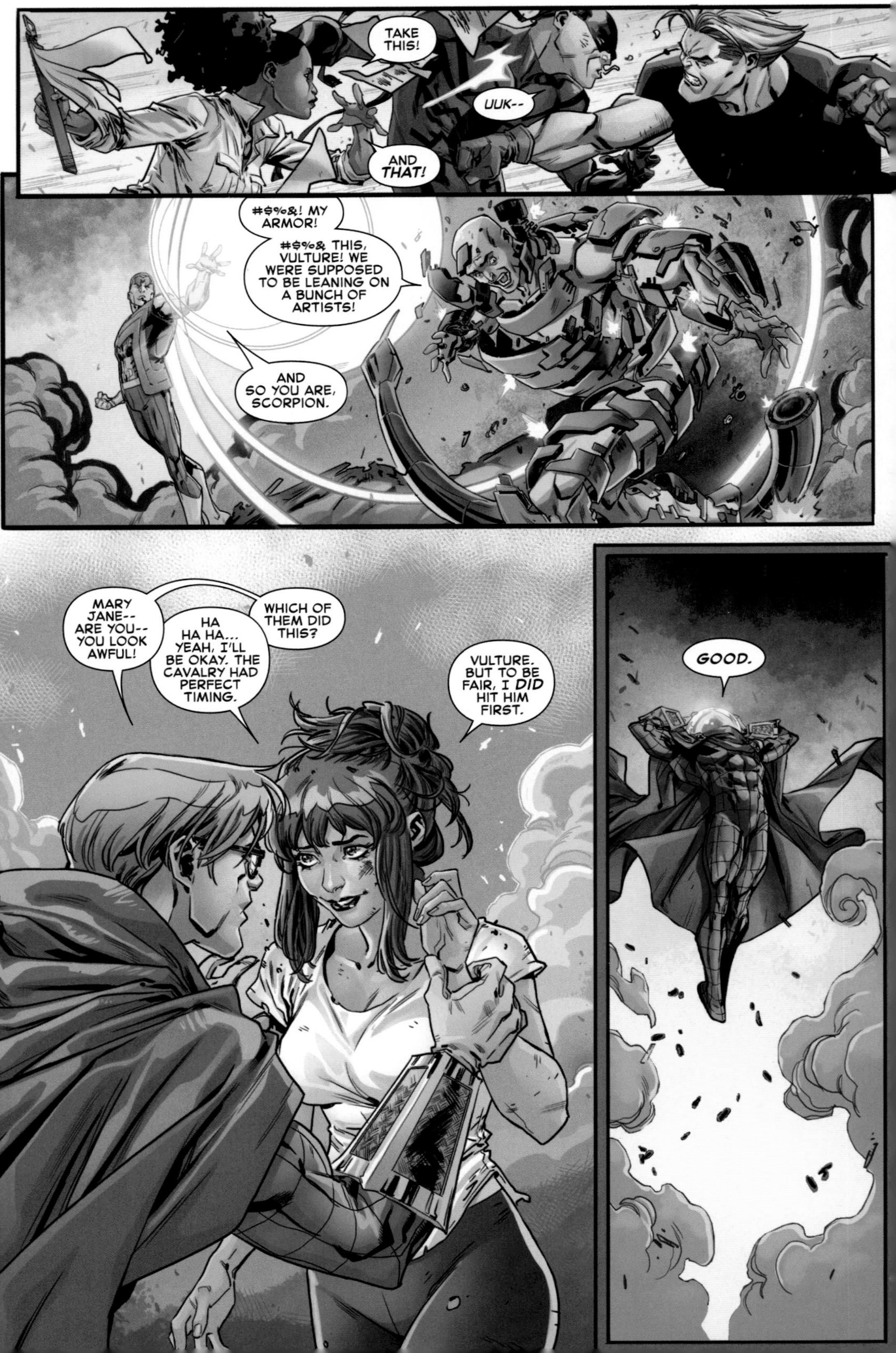
TAKE THIS!
UUK--
AND THAT!
#$%&! MY ARMOR!
#$%& THIS, VULTURE! WE WERE SUPPOSED TO BE LEANING ON A BUNCH OF ARTISTS!
AND SO YOU ARE, SCORPION.
MARY JANE-- ARE YOU-- YOU LOOK AWFUL!
WHICH OF THEM DID THIS?
HA HA HA... YEAH, I'LL BE OKAY. THE CAVALRY HAD PERFECT TIMING.
VULTURE. BUT TO BE FAIR, I DID HIT HIM FIRST.
GOOD.

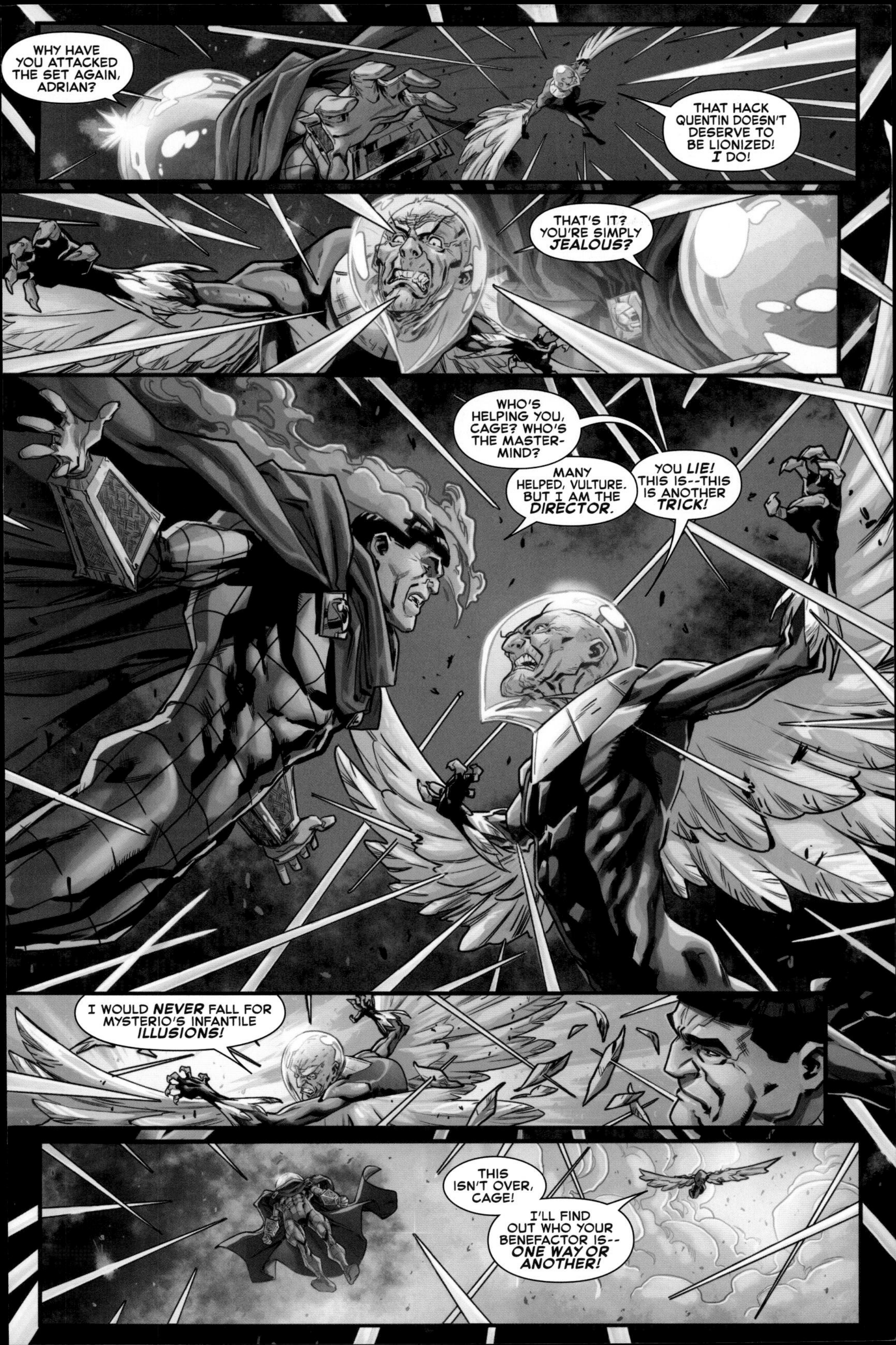
WHY HAVE YOU ATTACKED THE SET AGAIN, ADRIAN?
THAT HACK QUENTIN DOESN'T DESERVE TO BE LIONIZED! *I* DO!
THAT'S IT? YOU'RE SIMPLY *JEALOUS?*
WHO'S HELPING YOU, CAGE? WHO'S THE MASTER-MIND?
MANY HELPED, VULTURE. BUT I AM THE *DIRECTOR*.
YOU *LIE!* THIS IS--THIS IS ANOTHER *TRICK!*
I WOULD *NEVER* FALL FOR MYSTERIO'S INFANTILE *ILLUSIONS!*
THIS ISN'T OVER, CAGE!
I'LL FIND OUT WHO YOUR BENEFACTOR IS-- *ONE WAY OR ANOTHER!*

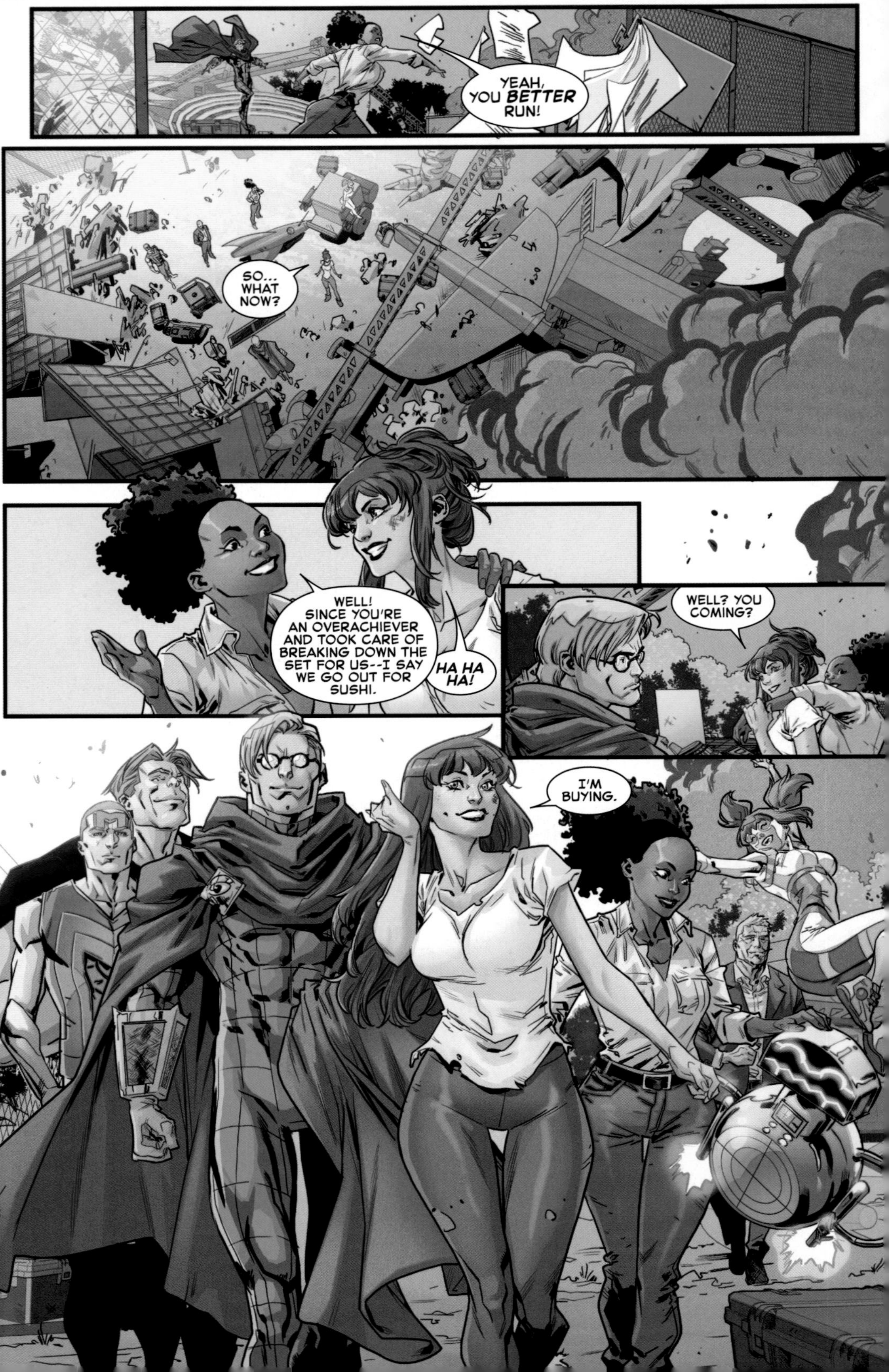
YEAH, YOU BETTER RUN!
SO... WHAT NOW?
WELL! SINCE YOU'RE AN OVERACHIEVER AND TOOK CARE OF BREAKING DOWN THE SET FOR US--I SAY WE GO OUT FOR SUSHI.
HA HA HA!
WELL? YOU COMING?
I'M BUYING.

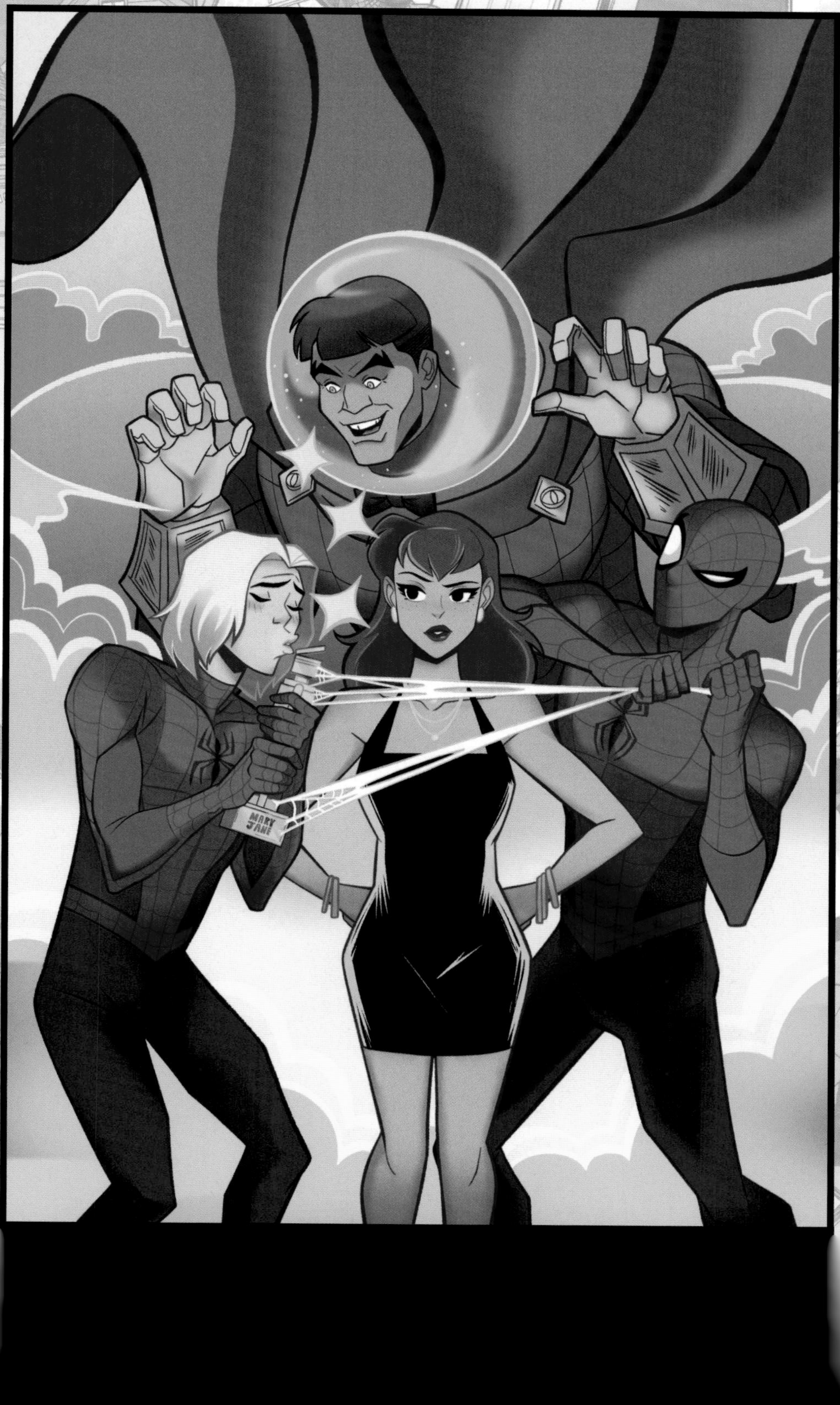
MARY JANE

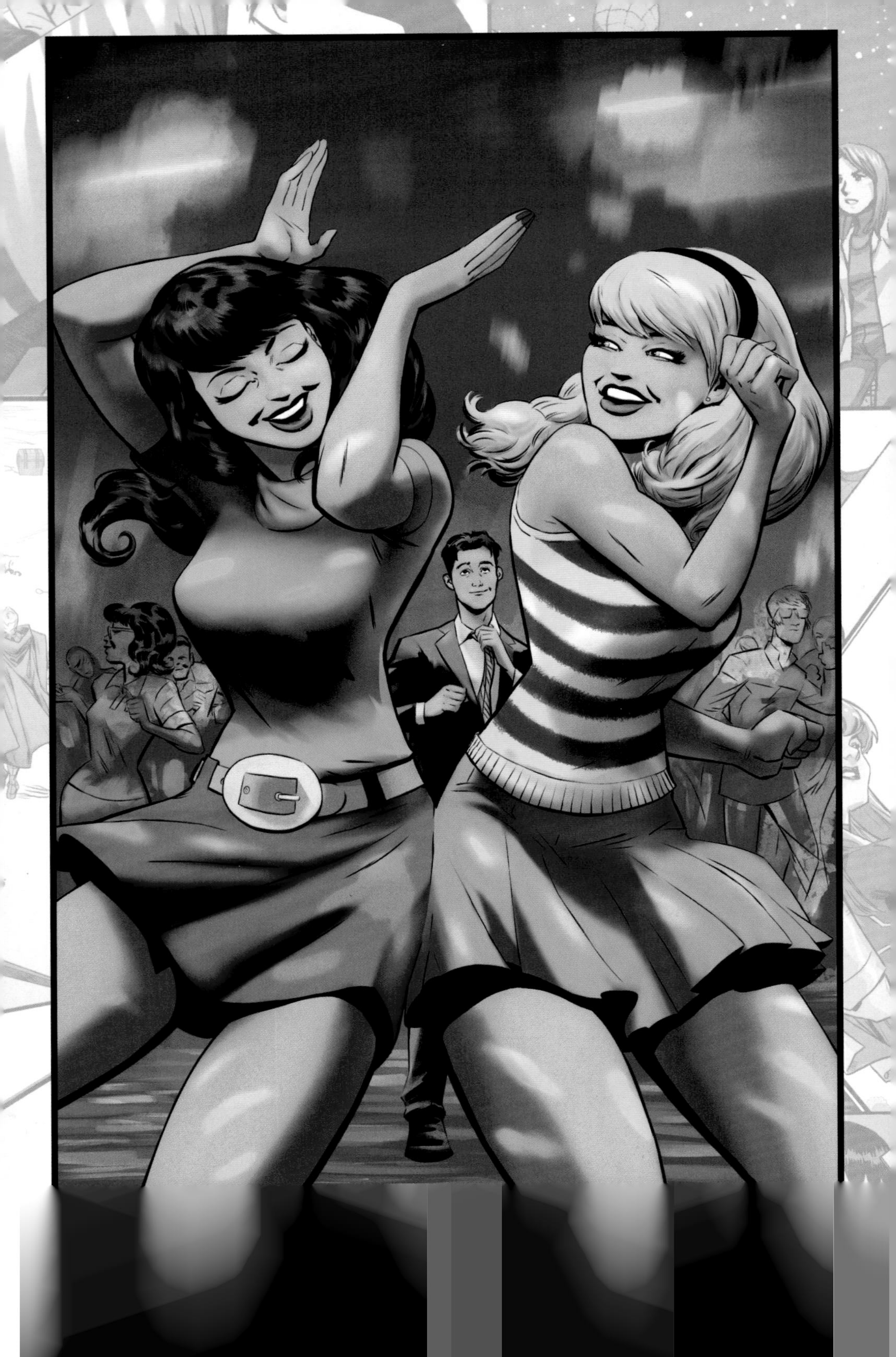

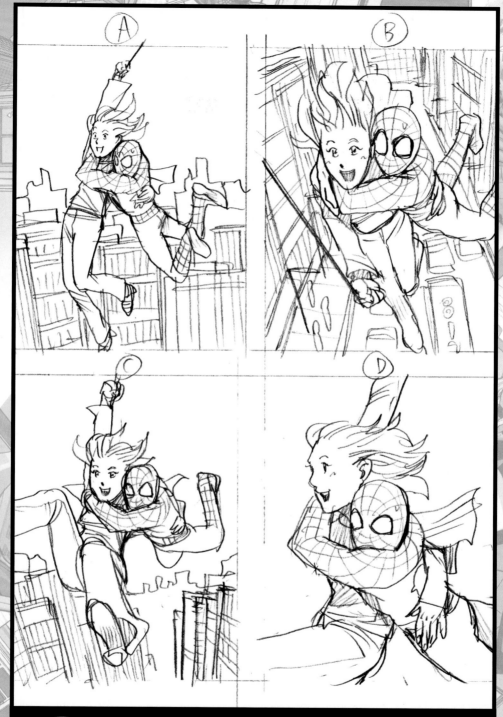

SPIDER-MAN LOVES MARY JANE #1

COVER SKETCHES BY TAKESHI MIYAZAWA

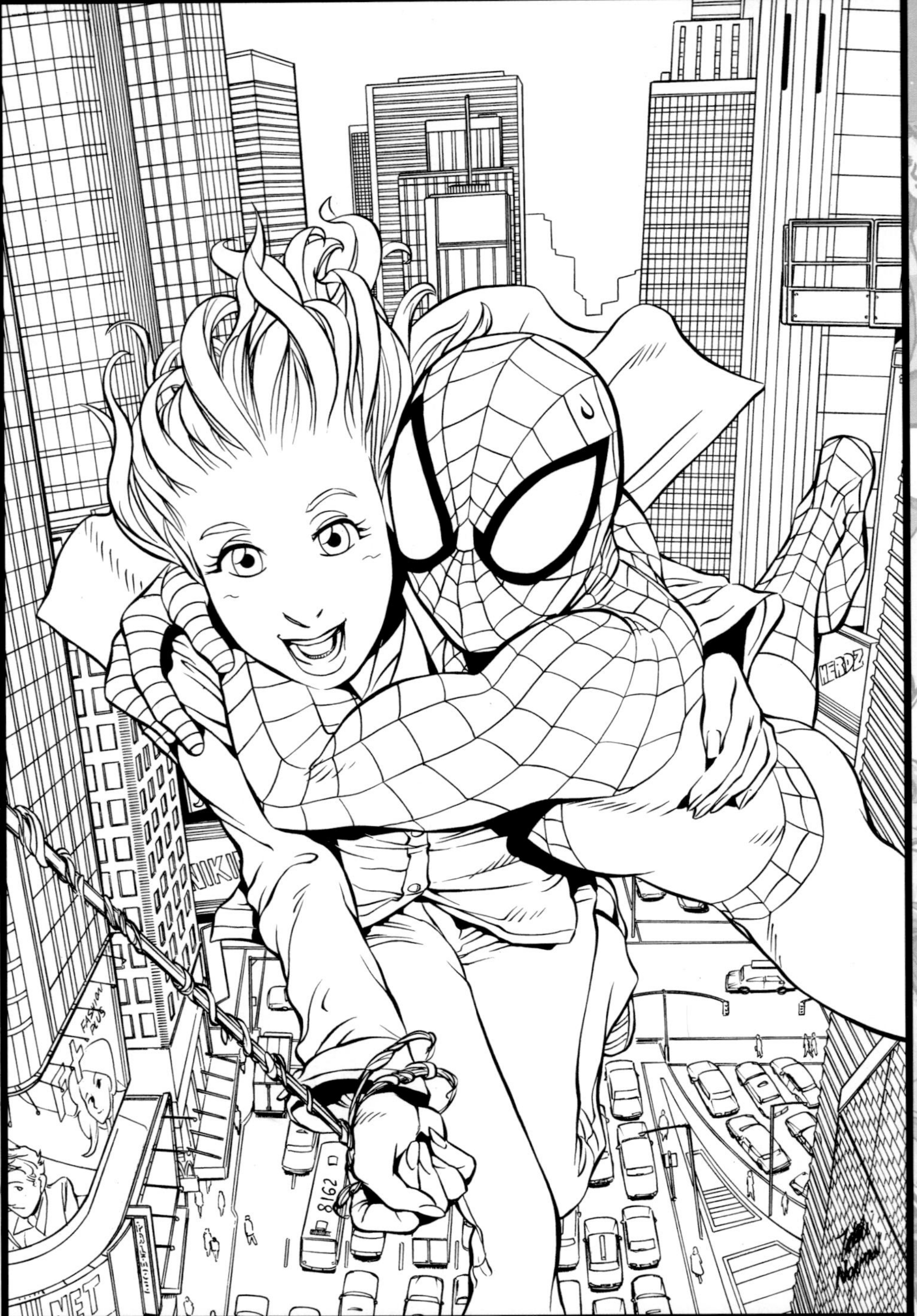
NERDZ
8162

SPIDER-MAN LOVES MARY JANE #1

COVER ART BY TAKESHI MIYAZAWA & NORMAN LEE